Dragon Village
OUROBOROS

RONESA AVEELA

BENDIDEIA PUBLISHING

Contents

Characters

Theo: Thirteen-year-old boy who has connections to Dragon Village.

Pavel: Theo's best friend who invents gadgets.

Diva: Samodiva girl who lives in Dragon Village. Diva's name means "wild." *Samodiva* means "Wild alone." From Bulgarian mythology, Samodivi were wild creatures who shied away from humans.

Baba Yaga: Witch from Slavic folklore who lives in a house with chicken feet.

Bendis: Thracian goddess of the moon, often said to be the mother of the Samodivi.

Boo: A magpie.

Bor Stobor: A Karakonjul. *Bor* means pine in Bulgarian, and *stobor* is a strong person (strong like a big pine wood).

Dracoville: A nickname Pavel gives Theo, combining his dragon and Samodiva heritages.

Firebird: In Slavic mythology, a bird that can be both a blessing and a curse. Its feathers glow brightly, and some say the bird can see the future.

Harpy: Half-woman, half-bird creature from Thrace and found in Greek mythology.

Jabalaka: The Keeper of Secrets. A man Lamia turned into a frog creature. *Jaba* is the Bulgarian word for "frog."

Jega: A Kuker (mummer) who wields fire. The word *jega* means "hot" in Bulgarian.

Karakonjul: Half-man, half-horse creature.

Kikimora: Creature who lives in the marsh, where she brews beer.

Knights of Darkness: Knights of Light who were corrupted by Zlo.

Knights of Light: Zmey's special guards who remained faithful.

Kosara: Guardian of the Znahar Tree.

Kotka: Baba Yaga's flying cat. *Kotka* is the Bulgarian word for "cat."

Kuker (plural, Kukeri): A man who wears animal skins and huge bells that scare evil spirits. The tradition dates back to Thracian times.

Lamia: Zmey's sister. Female dragon with three dog-like heads. She is cruel and brings hail to destroy crops, as well as stopping the flow of water.

Lesh: Vulture that once guarded one of Lamia's souls.

Lord Vodnik: Leader of the water creatures.

Lucky: One of Lord Vodnik's male water buffaloes.

Magda: Zunitza's sister.

Milka: The Kukeri's female water buffalo.

Mora (plural, Mori): A type of demon that causes nightmares.

Mraz: The oldest of the Kukeri brothers. The Bulgarian word is for "cold."

Mush: The Kukeri's male water buffalo. The Bulgarian word is for "nudge."

Nav (plural, Navi): A demon that looks like a bird with a distorted infant's head.

Nia: Theo's twin sister.

Radan: A warrior, Lord Zlo's second-in-command.

Rusalka (plural, Rusalki): Bulgarian word for water spirits, often called mermaids.

Samodiva (plural, Samodivi): Woodland nymph in Bulgarian lore. You may be more familiar with one of their other names: Veelas, like in the Harry Potter stories.

Sava: Diva's oldest sister.

Shar: Theo's deer companion. *Shar* means "colorful" in Bulgarian.

Sitara: Blacksmith. Former Vurkolak (werewolf) who once guarded one of Lamia's souls.

Sly: A Vodnik, friendly toward Theo.

Sur: Diva's deer companion. *Sur* means "gray" in Bulgarian.

Tangra: Thracian god of light and the sun.

Ula: Diva's sister.

Uroki: Evil spirit.

Vodnik (plural, Vodni): Slavic water creature that looks like an old man or a frog-like creature.

Vurkolak: Bulgarian word for "werewolf."

Water Bull: Demonic creature, part bull, part fish, part human, that lives in Rabisha Lake.

Whirl: Pavel's deer companion.

Youda (plural, Youdi): Evil Samodiva who lives in forests and mountains. She has the power of witchcraft.

Youda Stana: The leader of the Youdi.

Zima: A Kuker who has the power of freezing. The word *zima* means "winter" in Bulgarian.

Zlo: Lamia's lord and mentor. The word in Bulgarian means "bad" or "evil."

Zmey: Theo's birth father. Villages throughout Bulgaria have invisible patrons who protect their villages.

Zunitza: A Samodiva. Theo's birth mother. The word comes from *zuna*, the Bulgarian for "rainbow."

Glossary

Banitsa: A flaky food made from feta cheese, eggs, and more. A Bulgarian favorite.

Cherna Mountain: *Cherna* is the Bulgarian word for "black." This is where the dragon castle is found.

Cheshma: A fountain made from a spring.

Chutura: An old Bulgarian word for "mortar."

Cold Marsh: Home of the Vodni, Jabalaka, and Kikimora.

Devil's Throat: A cave in the western Rhodope Mountains in Bulgaria, said to be the entrance to Hades.

Eniovden: Midsummer's Day, celebrated on June 24.

Forest of Souls: The place where the souls of Dragon Village's ancestors reside in globes.

Forest of Whispering Bells: Forest where Baba Yaga lives. The bells jingle when someone approaches.

Kaval: Shepherd's pipe. A long, flute-like instrument that Samodivi like to dance to. They often make shepherds play the instrument until they drop dead from exhaustion.

Komuniga: Yellow sweet clover (*Melilotus officinalis*). Lethal to dragons.

Lamia's Bible: A book that contains secrets about those living in Dragon Village.

Magura Cave: A cave in northern Bulgaria where prehistoric paintings have been found. The cave is near Rabisha Lake.

Ouroboros: A snake or dragon swallowing its tail and forming a circle, symbolizing infinity.

Rabisha Lake: A freshwater lake in northern Bulgaria that legends say is the home of the Water Bull.

Rhyton: A conical-shaped drinking vessel.

Ribotron: Pavel's fish-catching invention. *Riba* is the Bulgarian word for "fish."

Selo: Fictitious place along the Black Sea. Bulgarian word for "village."

Smil: Magical flower harvested in Dragon Village.

Tililei Forest: Forest teeming with demons.

Vida: Village where Youdi and Sitara live.

Zandan: Prison in the dragon castle. Bulgarian word for "prison" or "dark place."

Zmeykovo: Bulgarian name for "Dragon Village." Mystical land where mythological creatures live. Said to be at the end of the world.

Znahar Tree: A fictitious World Tree connecting the three realms: heavens, earth, and underworld.

SAMODIVI LAKE
SAMODIVI FORTRESS
RODINA FOREST
CHERNA MOUNTAIN
RUSALKI BAY
MEGALITHS
FOREST OF SOULS
THE GATE
TEMPLE
ZNAHAR TREE
DEVIL'S THROAT
FOREST OF WHISPERING BELLS
COLD MARSH
BABA YAGA
MILL
DRAGON VILLAGE

Chapter 1
Sweet and Bitter Honey

JUNE 24, ENIOVDEN

THEO NEVER IMAGINED he'd spend his thirteenth birthday far from home, fighting demons in Dragon Village. Half-asleep, he lay on the cold, rotten floor of the deserted mill, with Pavel, Diva, and her sisters close by. They hadn't fought the fiends yet today, but without a doubt, the battles would continue. What did the demons care that it was his special day? Diva's, too, for she shared his birthday.

Constant attacks had forced them from the Kukeri sanctuary. Zima and Jega, the ancient brother warriors who lived there, had made the place as secure as they could with their magic. But after two solid days of enemy bombardment, Theo, Pavel, and Diva were forced to escape through an underground passage. Diva's sisters, Sava and Ula, retreated with the teens to show them the way through the maze. The Kukeri would join everyone as soon as they gathered supplies and maps of Dragon Village's underground world.

That was last night, and Zima and Jega still hadn't arrived.

Scratching sounded near the wall, and Theo opened his eyes. The sun peeked through cracks in the wooden slats near him, looking like laser beams in a sci-fi movie. The light scanned the room, as if searching for an enemy, but captured only swirling dust motes. Nothing had disturbed the flour they'd scattered beneath the gaping holes in the windows. They'd need to be boarded up before another night passed. Theo held his breath and searched the rest of the room with his eyes. All appeared safe. If an intruder was here, he hid in the dark corners.

The noise came again, this time closer to where Theo lay. Light thumping and a low growl followed.

Have the demons found us already?

He lay still, listening, tuning his dragon senses to his surroundings. His head pounded with the effort. He still had lots to learn about using his abilities, but his body felt different today, his pores tingling.

Something scampered over Theo's shoulder. With lightning speed, a rat disappeared into a canvas bag filled with moldy flour. If this had been a year ago, Theo's heart would have raced, and he would have screamed. But now, he was learning to expect the unexpected.

He tossed aside the rough sack he'd used as a blanket and pushed himself up to a sitting position. The floorboards creaked.

Next to him, Pavel stirred and stretched out his hand, which banged into a flour bag. A cloud of white powder flooded the floor, coating the glasses at his side. Yawning, he rubbed his eyes. "Time for breakfast, Mom?"

"I'm not your mother, and keep your voice down."

Theo crept toward a crack in the dilapidated wall and peered outside. Sunlight sparkled on the morning dew. Everything was a lush array of summer greens. It reminded him of the park in Selo where he played soccer with his classmates. The branches of a weeping willow near the creek swung to the ground, revealing the twitching tips of rabbit ears. The animals hopped around, eating grass within the shade of the tree's shelter. Birds sang and flew from branch to branch, while animals scurried among the undergrowth.

"What do you see? Demons? Zlo?" Pavel whispered. He grabbed the black bow and arrows Theo had let him use and scooted closer.

"Nothing, not even ravens." Everything appeared as it should be to Theo's enhanced dragon vision and hearing. He was worrying for nothing. Every noise made him jittery these days. But still, something felt a little off.

"That's weird," Pavel said. "They've been spying on you for the last week, ever since we got here. You don't think they've given up, do you?"

Theo snorted. "Zlo and Lamia threatened to eradicate me and everyone I love. So no, I don't think so."

"Don't worry. You escaped from them once. You can do it again."

"I doubt they'll be so careless to let that happen again."

Theo's newfound courage didn't extend to Zlo. Having faced the evil lord once, Theo trembled at Zlo's plan to take over Dragon

Village and the human world with the demons he'd released from the underworld.

Theo scanned the area once more for signs of Zlo's servants. Nothing appeared out of the ordinary. Holing up in the mill wasn't an ideal situation, but it suited their needs for the moment. The building was rundown, but occupied a remote location on the island. They could avoid detection and be safe here. If only temporarily.

A harsh drumming, as if someone was beating on a metal plate, came from near a window.

Pavel crouched even lower. "What's that?"

"Shh."

More noises followed from the loft: a rattle, pottery breaking.

Theo swiveled away from the crack so he could see what was happening.

Ula was securing a plank over a window opening. A stream of light danced across her brown hair, making the auburn strands sparkle. With her robe swaying around her each time she pounded a wooden peg into the board, she resembled an Amazon warrior training for battle.

"Great idea," Theo said. "I was just thinking we had to block the windows."

"Why am I the only one who's told to be quiet?" Pavel muttered and went back to sit on his blanket.

Ula stopped pounding and looked in their direction. Although her hand held a hammer steady, her quivering lips, normally upturned in a playful grin, betrayed her anxiety. "It's not much defense against demons, but it'll keep prying eyes out while we plan how to find and rescue Zmey."

"I hate that we're here wasting time fighting when we should be looking for my father." Theo kicked a flour bag. "He's been stuck in some dungeon for a whole year. Some help I've been."

"Don't berate yourself," Ula said. "You did the human world a favor by closing the portal Zlo tried to open."

"Yah, Theo," Pavel said. "That's a huge accomplishment."

Ula continued, "It's better for us to battle demons here than for them to have swarmed into Selo and other villages. Would you rather fight them, or have them attack your family?"

"You're right." Theo sighed. "I just hate the fact that Zmey's been suffering all this time. He's probably wondering if anyone's trying to find him."

"I'm sure I can come up with a way to rescue Zmey." Pavel rubbed his belly, got up, and peered into a clay bowl with scattered dried berries. "But it's too early to think about inventions, especially on an empty stomach."

Creaking came from above. Theo tensed. He'd forgotten about the noise in the loft. He hoped demons hadn't crawled in through holes in the roof. He crept closer to check, but sighed in relief when Sava lugged down a barrel. It would make a good table for them to strategize on. Offering her assistance would be useless. The stairs were too rickety for him to climb. As a Samodiva, Sava could glide over them with no trouble.

Ula pounded more planks over the window, casting the front of the room into a gloomy darkness. "There, done. Now on to the next window."

"Now it's too dark to look at maps when the Kukeri get here." Pavel's stomach grumbled again. "And too dark to know what I'm eating."

Theo sniffed. A sweet aroma drifted toward the mill. He peered out the dilapidated door. Diva must have ventured outside while he and Pavel had been peeking through the crack. Now, she ambled forward, carrying a basket topped with red berries.

She opened the door and strode inside, letting in a stream of light. "I see I'm just in time."

"You are. I'm starving." Pavel's stomach rumbled from across the room.

"Not quite what I meant about being just in time." Diva laughed and held the basket toward him. "You better eat something, or the demons will hear you."

"You don't have to tell me twice." Pavel hurried over to take the basket, and he stuffed berries into his mouth. "Mmm, good."

"I found candles in an abandoned hut, so we'll be able to see in here," Diva said. "Pavel, do you have any of your matches left?"

"Yes." His mouth filled with berries, he momentarily set the basket onto the barrel and dragged his backpack closer to the open door. He pulled out a box of wooden matches from a pocket and scratched one against the side, the flame bursting forth. "Here." He handed it to Diva before he picked up the berries again.

She lit a candle and set it onto the wooden barrel.

Theo wasn't hungry. His stomach was unsettled. He needed something to do while he waited for the Kukeri to arrive. He looked around the room. Sacks of old flour and seeds rats hadn't devoured lay propped up against the walls. He couldn't think of anything to do with them. In case of attack, he imagined he could hurl one against an intruder, slowing his enemy somewhat.

Maybe Sava needed help now. He found her speaking in a hushed tone with Pavel, who had finished the berries. Pavel gestured around the room, but stopped when Theo approached. Sava shrugged, but nodded. Theo caught a few words: "A good idea."

What was Pavel up to? Asking for more food? Or, now that he'd eaten, was he telling the Samodiva about an invention that would help rescue Theo's father? As much as Theo loved his friend, Zmey's safety was too important to take a chance on Pavel's ideas working. Theo wished the ancient, wise Mraz would join the group, but the eldest of the Kukeri brothers had gone into hiding to keep *Lamia's Bible* safe from Zlo. The dangerous book held the secrets of everyone in Dragon Village.

Theo turned away and paced the room. It seemed nobody needed him to do anything. A hero with no task.

"Theo," Sava called to him.

"Yes?" He stopped his endless steps.

"Don't worry. The Kukeri will be here soon enough."

"I know, but—"

"Why don't you and Diva survey the area? You should be able to sense anything unusual with your abilities and warn us of dangers."

"And while you're outside," Pavel said, "could you get more berries and maybe some honey?"

Theo rolled his eyes. Pavel and his stomach. "What's the matter? All your cookies gone? Or are you craving pancakes now?"

Pavel nodded. "I'd love pancakes, but we can't cook here. The smoke would give our location away. But I wouldn't mind a bowl of fresh berries with honey drizzled on them. Maybe you could find some fruit trees, too."

"I think that's a splendid idea," Sava said. "By the time you and Diva return, the Kukeri should have arrived."

"Diva was just out there. She would have told us if there were any dangers." Theo raked his fingers through his hair. He wanted to be busy, but not doing a mindless task. "I need to rescue my father. I don't want to look for berries, honey, or fruit."

"I do." Diva picked up the empty basket and grabbed her bow and quiver of arrows. "It's better than worrying. Besides, Samodivi love honey. Its sweetness is worth the risk of venturing outside. It shouldn't take us long. I came across wild bees when I was out earlier."

"Oh, all right." Theo retrieved his sword. "Are you coming, too, Pavel, since you want sweets so badly?"

"Uh, no." Pavel shuffled his feet and avoided looking at Theo. "I have stuff to do here. Maybe I'll see if I can catch some fish."

Theo raised his eyebrows and shook his head. Pavel rarely gave up a chance to be around Diva. Had his infatuation with their Samodiva friend worn off?

"Well, at least let me use your matches. We'll need fire to smoke the bees if we find honey."

Pavel handed the box to Theo, who put it into his pants pocket before stepping outside after Diva. He squinted, his eyes sensitive to the blinding light after the darkness inside the mill.

Small clouds, drifting like feathers, roofed the blue sky, and mild heat from the summer sun warmed Theo's face. A gentle breeze brought with it an assortment of smells: some sweet and fruity, while others were fragrant, woodsy, and minty.

It all reminded him of his home in Selo. Today was a special day when his mother and other women in the village gathered herbs. Magical herbs, they called them, because the ones picked in the morning had special healing powers.

Will Mom venture outside today?

He was sure his sister, Nia, would encourage their mother to participate in the day's activities, instead of staying locked inside the house, worrying about Theo. Worrying wouldn't bring him home any sooner. He was glad Nia was there to support their mother. At least this time, Mom knew where Theo was. When both he and Nia had disappeared last year, no one had a clue where they had gone. The sooner he accomplished this mission, the sooner he could return home.

Theo gripped his sword and crept around their immediate surroundings with Diva. A branch snapped in the forest. Theo slung his weapon around, but Diva made a sign with her hand to keep silent, and they put their backs together. Two rabbits hopped out into the clearing, looked at the intruders, and scurried back into the safety of the woods.

"All clear," Diva said, and they continued to the end of the path.

Theo stopped. With the instinct of a wild animal, he scanned their surroundings with his enhanced vision and hearing to make sure the immediate area was clear of dangers.

He encountered small animals scurrying through the underbrush. They acted skittish, running back and forth with no destination. He caught their words now and again: "Hurry" and "Keep up," plus mumbled or rushed words, too difficult to make out. His returning ability to understand animals made him smile.

He hoped he'd once again be able to know what his magpie friend, Boo, was saying.

Theo strained against his mind, probing deeper into the woods. The birds there were more silent. A bad omen, but his senses noted nothing evil or out of the ordinary. Even so, his gut told him to be careful.

Diva looked at him as if waiting for him to decide how to scout out the area. When they'd first met, she'd encouraged him to reason out problems, things she already had the answer to. Her silence now shouted at him that she was doing the same. At least today, he felt surer of his ability to make good decisions, to trust his instincts. Right now, they told him something was definitely wrong, even though he couldn't pinpoint the source.

"I'll circle around the right side of the mill, and you can take the left. We can meet over by the large, rotten tree." He pointed to one that he had used for archery practice when they'd been at the mill once before.

Diva nodded and darted uphill to complete her task.

Theo walked down the slope toward the water wheel. It creaked, shaking with the breeze, but refused to spin any longer. Green ivy wrapped around the paddles like a blanket. Nothing was amiss this close to the mill. He searched farther out, first with his mind. Picking up no bad vibes, he slunk through the forest. Every bird in the branches was a suspect, each animal scurrying along the ground, a potential threat. Zlo's servants who kept tabs on Theo could shape-shift. He didn't want to fall for that trick again. They'd already suffered enough when they'd rescued a puppy, which wasn't really a puppy.

No animal glared at Theo with glowing red eyes during his search. The demon Zlo's messengers hadn't infiltrated the area near the mill. For the moment, they were safe.

Now that he was outside doing something useful and danger wasn't imminent, Theo relaxed and rubbed his stiff neck. The pounding headache he'd woken to had lessened to a dull throb, but the tingling in his pores remained. Since Diva was thirteen today, too, perhaps she was feeling the same strange sensations.

He trudged back up the hill toward their designated meeting place. Diva wasn't waiting at the location, but he felt her presence nearby. He searched the trees and found her picking fruit.

"Diva?" he called.

"Be there in a minute." She crawled down a tree, the folds of her garment overflowing with fruit. "Well, that should be enough even for Pavel." Diva deposited the bounty into the basket and wiped off twigs and leaves from her clothing. "Ready to look for honey now?"

"Sure." Theo strode beside her as she made her way toward a cliff. "Diva, did you feel any different this morning? Tingly?"

"Some, but nothing I didn't expect." She continued walking without breaking her stride. "My sisters explained my body would be changing inside once I turned thirteen and gained my full powers."

"Oh, good, I guess. I wasn't sure exactly what was happening," Theo said. "It's not like how I felt when Lamia's spirit possessed me. That was excruciating." He thought back to how he'd been in so much pain he couldn't move at times. Although he didn't understand this new sensation, it energized him. "Do you feel like someone else is inside you?"

She shook her head. "No, just me. Do you feel that way?"

"Yes. It's like there's a soldier there, someone I can't control." Theo paused. "He's asleep, but I know I can harness his strength. I don't know how to wake him. Or if I want to. He feels dangerous."

"Hmm." Diva stopped and walked around Theo. "That must be part of your dragon powers. My sisters and I can aid you with some things, but you'll need Zmey to help you understand that better."

"I guess until then I'll have to wing it." Theo smiled at his unintended pun.

Diva laughed. "You'll figure it out."

Theo's mind wandered, but he kept a cautious eye on his surroundings as they ventured deeper into the forest. Gaining supernatural powers wasn't what he had thought becoming a teen would entail. He'd always imagined this stage of his life would mean taking one step closer to adulthood and independence. Not that he wanted to be free of his family or home. Until he'd discovered the mystical land of Dragon Village, the people and way of life in the village of Selo were all he'd known.

What he had wanted was adventure, the ability to soar through the sky. Of course, back then, he didn't know he was the offspring of a dragon father and Samodiva mother. Pavel called him Dracoville, and Diva had added "The Red Dragon" to the name. A new species. Not only that, but he was the "Unborn Hero," a child destined to save Dragon Village, a place he'd thought existed only in the stories his adoptive, human mother told him.

Something louder than a twig snapped deep in the forest. Had the demons, or worse, Lamia, now arrived? He listened more intently as he continued walking. Whatever the creature was, it wasn't a demon. It lumbered farther away.

Theo had saved Dragon Village once already, with the help of his friends, but now he worried. Zlo was too strong. *How will we stop the demons? And how many more times will I have to fight them before my second home is safe? I have powers now that I never did before. Sprouting wings, shifting into a dragon, and breathing fire are awesome, but I need to be able to understand how to control these dragon powers. Only my father can help me understand how to do that.*

The problem was that his father wasn't here to help. Theo would have to learn on his own.

"Theo." Diva's voice brought him back to their surroundings. "The honey is just ahead."

Bees buzzed high up in a rotten tree that had grown within a cleft in the side of a rock wall.

Theo craned his neck to look for the hollow. "The honey must be up there, but how are we going to get it? It's out of reach."

Diva looked up and down the tree. "I can climb that easily enough. But first, we'll have to calm the bees, so they don't sting us."

"Right, with smoke."

Theo recalled his school class visiting a beekeeper. The woman had stuffed pine needles inside a device she said was a smoker. Next, she puffed the smoke into the hive opening, saying it was like knocking on the door, letting the bees know she was coming in. That statement brought giggles from some of his classmates, but Theo watched the woman closely, desiring to learn the process. The smoke, she said, disrupted the bees' sense of smell, so they wouldn't become alarmed and communicate danger to the rest of the colony. A few puffs were all it took.

"Exactly," Diva said. "Will you collect a pile of pine needles?"

"Sure." Theo scooped up the items while Diva scoured the area, returning a moment later with a long, straight branch, and several ivy vines she'd twisted together.

"This should reach the hive." She coated the end of the branch with pine pitch, then rolled it in the needles. "Now can you light it?"

Theo blew on the torch.

Diva laughed. "Unless you want to shift into a dragon first, that's not going to work."

"I know." Theo grinned. "Just checking." He removed the matches from his pocket, struck one against the side of the box, and lit the torch.

White smoke billowed out.

Diva tied one end of the ivy rope around her waist and tossed the other over a tree branch. Pulling on the loose end, she scrambled up the cliff, keeping her feet pressed against the rocks. When she reached the hollow where the bees gathered, she called out, "Hold the torch up here and move it a little, so the smoke envelops the trunk."

Theo directed the smoke into the hollow opening. A bee buzzed around his ear, and Theo shooed it away with his free hand.

"Try to keep the smoke coming into the opening." Diva glanced down. "Just a little more."

"Sorry. A bee's annoying me." As Diva reached inside the tree, two more insects buzzed around Theo. "Hey, Diva, you better hurry. We have angry customers down here."

"Customers?"

"More bees." A loud buzzing came from behind him, and Theo turned to look. A fast-moving black cloud neared like an angry storm. "A swarm's coming. And they don't sound happy. Leave the honey and hurry."

"Your 'customers' must have sent a message to the others, saying the hive was on fire." Diva shimmied down the vine rope. In her hand, she held two pieces of honey comb. She tossed them into the basket along with the fruit. "Let's go. Follow me."

Theo took one last look at the growing black mass. He wanted to shift. *Even if I turned into a dragon now, though, it wouldn't save me. And it certainly wouldn't help Diva.* He sprinted after his friend, who was racing through the bushes.

The outline of the mill appeared ahead, but it was too far to reach before the bees surrounded them.

"Jump into the water," Diva shouted as she dropped the basket onto the bank and dove into a small pool, covered with green leaves.

Theo took a deep breath and leaped in, steps behind her. The torch fizzled as it touched the surface. Debris swirling in the disturbed water stung Theo's eyes. He crouched as low as he could in the shallow pool. Sharp pebbles dug into the bottom of his sneakers.

The muted buzzing of the enraged bees spun like a windstorm overhead for what seemed an eternity. Theo released his breath a little at a time. He pushed aside leaves that blocked out the sun. The swarm had thinned.

A little longer. I can hold my breath just a little longer.

Exhaling the last of his breath, Theo emerged from the water and panted on the grassy bank. Diva surfaced and sat next to him.

"Ow." Theo scratched his cheek and arms, where bees had left ugly, red welts.

Diva mixed dirt with water. "Here, let's put this on your stings." She dipped her fingers into the moist mixture and patted it onto his face first, then she applied globs over the redness on his arms.

"Thanks. That feels good."

"The best treatment is often the simplest," she said. "I've tended to many wounded animals with herbs, but clean water and dirt help every time when nothing else is available."

"Those bees were as threatening as Zlo's spies," Theo said. "I've never seen insects so angry. Even the smoke didn't calm them."

"It's possible they weren't regular bees."

Theo clenched his hands into fists, his fingernails biting into his palms. "You think they may have been demons? Our location has been compromised?"

Diva nodded. "I think so."

"But why didn't I sense the evil, the way I have before?" When one of Zlo's servants had masqueraded as a puppy, Theo had been on constant alert, always feeling as if someone was watching him. This time, however, when he and Diva patrolled the area, he hadn't detected immediate danger.

"Maybe insects can hide it better. Or maybe the demons are approaching, and that affected the bees' behavior," Diva said. "Either way, we have to warn everyone."

Theo shivered and flapped his shirt to dry it as he bounced from foot to foot. Not only had the coldness of the water seeped into his pores, but he was angered by the threat of advancing demons. "Let's hurry before anything else attacks us."

Ignoring her wet clothes, Diva twisted her curly hair, wringing out the water. She stood, picked up the basket, and hurried toward the dark silhouette of the dilapidated mill.

Everything was quiet as they approached, too quiet. The place appeared deserted. Theo strained to hear voices inside using his dragon abilities, but only the mill wheel creaked as it attempted to move.

He stopped and signed with his hand for Diva to slow down. She set the basket on the ground and nodded her agreement. Holding her now-nocked bow steady, she crouched as she continued with quiet steps toward the entrance. Theo held his sword ready for defense. Pebbles along the path clattered as they advanced. When they reached the mill, Theo peered into the darkened room through a gap in the door.

Silence.

Holding his breath, he pushed the creaking door open a crack.

Chapter 2
Surprise

DARKNESS ENVELOPED THE MILL, the candles no longer flickering. A muffled sound, like constrained breathing, came from behind the loft stairs. Theo tightened his grip on the cold handle of his sword as sweat dripped from his brow.

"Pavel? Sava? Ula?" he whispered. "We're back. Are you here?"

A rat scuttled out of the door, past his feet.

Theo focused on his enhanced vision to see through the blackness, but all he viewed were silhouettes of barrels. Where were his friends?

Diva hovered behind his shoulder. "I scouted the area and didn't find any unusual tracks. If they've been attacked, it had to come from the air."

They both scanned the sky and mill roof. Nothing hovered overhead.

"Let's go in," Theo said. "On the count of three. One. Two. Three."

He slammed the door open and rushed forward. A flash of light blinded him.

"Surprise." Figures jumped out from behind barrels.

Scattered around the room, candles flickered on, emitting an aroma of beeswax. Theo blinked and stared. A magic wand appeared to have transformed the mill. Fragrant garlands of wildflowers, twisted around ivy, hung from the wooden beams. Around the white, red, blue, yellow, and orange blossoms sparkled hundreds of fireflies. Violet-tipped butterflies, with iridescent, intricate-patterned wings, fluttered overhead, creating a rainbow effect.

Theo brought his gaze toward the center of the room where enticing aromas beckoned. Planks covered three wooden barrels to form a table. On top, colorful glazed pottery held fruit, berries, mushrooms, cooked fish, and … He sniffed. Yes, freshly baked bread. His stomach growled, and he covered it with his hand.

With smiling faces, his friends shouted in unison, "Happy birthday, Theo and Diva," and rushed toward them like a tidal wave.

Diva scooted closer and gave Theo's arm a squeeze. Jega reached them first and grasped both their hands with an iron grip. "Happy birthday. May the joy of this day remain forever in your life and future."

Zima dragged his brother out of the way and gave a hearty thump on Theo's back.

"Not so rough, boys," Sava scolded as she wrapped her arms around both Theo and Diva. "Look at you two. In just one year, you've grown so much. I hope you like your surprise."

Theo could only nod. Having the unexpected happen wasn't so bad—when it was a happy event.

"Me next." Ula stepped closer, holding a wreath of wild flowers. She had changed from her simple white robe into one with red embroidery along the neck and sleeves. "We know this is a bad time and place for celebrations, but we couldn't let the day go by without doing something special." She hugged Theo and Diva and placed the wreath on Diva's head.

Ula's warm gaze met Theo's. For a moment, sparks like a bouquet of fireworks flashed in her eyes. He imagined his Samodiva mother's eyes would have lit up like that, too. He wished Zunitza was here for the happy event, and his father.

He wanted to hide his emotions, but a tear trickled down his cheek. He sniffed, turned his head, and wiped away the moisture.

Nia would have loved to be here, experiencing the kindness of all their friends, especially Jega, whom she had a crush on. She would have eaten up all the attention. Now, his sister had to spend their shared birthday alone. Had Mom organized a surprise party for him and Nia, never expecting that her son would venture off a week before his birthday? He had ruined the day for both his sister and his mother.

This was his first birthday not spent at home with his family. He hadn't even considered celebrating the day here in Dragon Village. How could he, when he and his friends had to focus on escaping and hiding to save their lives?

Theo vowed to never spend another special occasion without his entire family with him. Somehow, he'd make it work.

Ula gave Theo a sad smile, as if understanding his sorrow amid his joy. "Every day is a gift, but birthdays are even more special," she said. "In normal times, we would have held rituals and a week of celebrations to cherish the day you both were born and became part of this beautiful world. That would have included visiting our beloved goddess, Bendis. The birds, animals, and all creatures in Zmeykovo would have been invited to such a celebration."

"Hey, don't forget about me." A beaming Pavel pushed his way closer and stood before the birthday pair. "Well, you finally caught up to me. Now you can both be cool teens, too."

Theo laughed and tapped Pavel's shoulder. "You're only two months older than me, but I've always considered you 'cool,' even before you were a teen. Who else among my friends has so many ideas for inventions? I'm glad you're my friend."

Diva smiled and gave Pavel a quick hug. "Is this party what you were talking with Sava about earlier this morning?"

Pavel's cheeks flushed, and he shuffled his feet. "Uh, yah. I couldn't let the day go by without doing something. Theo's my best buddy, and you're … Well, you should have fun, too." His stomach gurgled, and his cheeks became an even brighter red.

"And you're still hungry." Diva pulled him toward the makeshift table. "Oh, wait. I left the fruit and honey outside. Be right back." She returned a moment later and set the basket on the table. "Now, eat. You have plenty to choose from. Try a bit of honeycomb."

Theo joined them and broke off a piece of honeycomb before Pavel devoured it all. As he chewed it, a drop slid down his chin. He tore off a chunk of warm bread from the loaf and captured the escaped sweet. Looking toward the hearth, on which no fire or coals burned, he asked, "How did you guys manage to make bread?"

"Jega," Pavel mumbled, his cheeks stuffed like a chipmunk. "He used his fire power. Plus, a little Samodiva magic."

Each of the Kukeri brothers had a special skill. Theo didn't know what most of them wielded, since he'd never had the opportunity to spend a lot of time with the elder brothers. But Jega controlled fire, while Zima could manipulate ice. Their abilities had saved him and his friends on many occasions.

Diva's sisters came closer. Ula had her hand wrapped around an object, while Sava held her arm behind her back.

"A birthday isn't complete without presents. For you, dear baby sister, from both of us." Ula opened her fist and held out a small green-velvet box toward Diva.

"Thank you." Diva opened the gift. Inside lay a silver barrette in the shape of a falcon with its wings outstretched. A sparkling pink amethyst formed the bird's chest, and two black beads its eyes. Words had been etched into the wings.

"It's lovely, just like you." Pavel blushed. "What does it say?"

Diva pointed to one side. "This says, 'Fly high like a falcon,' and the other one says, 'Dream big.'" She set the box on the table, bowed to her sisters, and made a sign like a flying bird with her hands. "*Blagodaria*, thank you. It's amazing. I couldn't ask for a better present."

"Even though all Samodivi protect nature and animals, we each have a special ability, so that together we are stronger," Sava said.

Ula added, "May our gift bring you reason, and help in your responsibility for protecting our land and its creatures."

Sava nodded. "You're the protector and patron of birds, so the falcon represents your Samodiva powers, which you'll now have full control over. The barrette will let you hear what they say or think, and with it, you can soar as high as they can. If you need help, call on them, and they'll come. They'll be under your control as long as your intent is to do good. Mostly, you won't need to force your will on them. They'll freely do your bidding."

Theo felt lightheaded, imagining the possibilities. "Maybe you can control the Harpies or the nasty ravens Zlo keeps sending to spy on us."

"Unfortunately, not." Ula shook her head. "Neither of those is a true bird. The Harpies are demons, and the ravens are shape-shifters."

"Bummer." He snapped his fingers. "It's still an awesome gift."

"We didn't forget you, Theo." Sava brought her arm from behind her back and handed him a silk drawstring bag. "Guard it carefully. It'll protect you when you're in trouble."

A tingling warmth crept through Theo's limbs. The generosity of Diva's sisters overwhelmed him with a sense of belonging, like being made part of their family. He felt blessed to have three sets: Nia and his mom, Zmey and Zunitza, and now Diva and her sisters, plus the Kukeri. Diva had become like a sister to him. He stood silent for a moment, his mouth slightly open, drinking in the images of everyone surrounding him.

"Theo?" Sava shook the bag. "Do you want it?"

"Oh, sorry. Thank you. That's so thoughtful of you."

He took the gift, opened the bag, and pulled out a white scarf. Downy soft to the touch, the cloth felt like air in his hand. A light fragrance of honeysuckle clung to the ethereal fabric.

But it was a *woman's* scarf.

What was he supposed to do with that? Maybe he could give it to Nia as a belated birthday present when he returned to Selo.

Not to offend Sava, he wrapped the scarf around his neck. It covered him like a mist.

"Wow!" Pavel exclaimed with eyes bugged out.

"What?" Theo said.

"You're invisible. That's a magical scarf." Pavel slid his glasses up and down his nose. "I most definitely need to research the material and see how it works."

Theo stretched his hand out in front of him. He couldn't see his own flesh. This went way beyond expecting the unexpected. He kept moving his invisible hands in front of himself. He walked forward and backward, feeling the boards beneath his unseen feet.

"Hey, man." Pavel came closer, patting air where Theo had been. "You're scaring me. Say something."

Theo looked into Pavel's confused eyes. No one else appeared worried. Diva and her sisters were smiling. Jega was snorting with laughter, while Zima tapped his feet and stood with his arms crossed, annoyed with the world as usual. Theo smirked and grabbed Pavel's shoulder.

His friend jumped and screamed, "Demon attack."

Theo removed the scarf from around his neck and reappeared. "Sorry, that was me. I couldn't resist."

"I forgive you, but only because the scarf is so cool." Pavel came closer and touched the fabric. "And so soft."

"It's amazing." Theo smiled at Sava. "Thank you."

"It belonged to Zunitza."

Theo hugged the scarf to his chest and inhaled the honeysuckle scent once more. He had smelled that aroma the first time he'd seen his birth mother, the queen of Dragon Village, in the Forest of Souls. The fragrance had come from the amber globe her spirit dwelled in. This made the scarf all the more endearing to him. Wearing a woman's scarf wouldn't be so bad after all, especially since this one made him invisible.

"Thank you, again. It's priceless." He rubbed a corner against his cheek before he replaced the scarf in the silk bag and secured it in his backpack. The gift reminded him of his baby blanket, one he later found out his Samodiva mother had wrapped around him when she left him in Selo. "If someone had told me a year ago that I'd find such great friends, a new family, who'd give me a magical scarf for a birthday present, I would have laughed."

"I thought you were nuts when you told me you heard birds talking before we ever came to Dragon Village," Pavel replied. "If you'd talked about magic scarves, I would definitely have thought you'd lost your marbles."

"You're right," Theo said. "I could never have imagined all of this. But I've learned we all need to believe in our dreams, in magic, in the unbelievable."

"You've helped make that magic possible." Ula touched her forehead and bowed to Theo. "We're glad we've had the chance to get to know you, too."

One of the butterflies landed on the wreath on Diva's head. The insect fluttered its wings, creating shimmering light across her wild, white-blond curls. She reached to touch the creature, but it flew away.

"Why don't you put on your birthday gift?" Pavel said. "I think the barrette would look even lovelier on you than a butterfly."

"Do you, now?" She smiled and reached for the box on the table. Her smile disappeared. She moved around fruit inside the basket and then picked up one pottery dish after the other.

Pavel came closer. "What's the matter?"

"The barrette's not in the box. It must have fallen."

"Let me look." He got on his knees and searched in the space between each barrel. He stretched his hand in deeper but brought it out empty. "It's not there."

Diva looked among the food items on the wooden planks once more. "Not here, either. Where could it have gone?"

"Look what I found hiding here." Zima strode from a dark corner of the room. He dragged a cowering green creature, covered in a worn cloak, and shoved him toward Diva. "He has the barrette. Give it back."

The small figure raised his head, and the hood of his cloak fell back. Bulbous eyes, bulging from an old man's wrinkled face, appeared sorrowful.

"Sly." Diva crouched to the Vodnik's level. "Did you take my barrette?"

The creature nodded and mumbled, "Me love shiny. It beautiful."

"You know it's wrong to steal, don't you?"

He vigorously shook his head. "Me no steal. Me borrow."

"Then if you borrowed it, you'll give it back. It's a gift from my sisters, and they'd be disappointed if I lost it." She held out her hand toward the creature.

He hung his head and pressed his clenched fists to his chest. "Me hold a little longer? Sly love purple sparkles."

"Purple?" Diva looked at her sisters. "Maybe this isn't mine. The one you gave me was pink."

"Or it could be Sly doesn't know his colors," Theo said. "He had trouble with left and right before."

"No, it's yours." Ula kneeled by the Vodnik. "Sly, the stone changes colors if someone other than its owner takes it. It'll lose its power and turn black. Do you want that?"

Sly's bulbous eyes bulged even more. "Oh, no, no, no." He thrust his hand toward Diva and unclenched his webbed paw. The barrette was hooked over one sharp claw. "You have now. Me sorry."

"Thank you, Sly." Diva took her jewelry, and the stone returned to its pale pink color. She braided her hair and clasped the barrette over an unruly curl.

"You look like a goddess of nature," Pavel stuttered and walked closer.

"Goddess, goddess." Sly crept between Diva and Pavel. "Me have special gift for you, too." He reached under his tattered cloak and handed her a book with a scorched cover. "Me save it from Master's house."

She pressed the worn, dusty book close to her chest. "One of Jabalaka's books?"

"Yes, yes." Sly bounced on the tips of his webbed toes. "It have maps. Old, old Zmeykovo maps. It help you find Dragon King."

Without waiting for Sly to say more, Diva eased the cover open. Theo looked over her shoulder as she flipped through the pages. Scribbled notes lined the margins of many of the maps.

"There are places I've never heard of," Diva said as she perused a scorched page.

"Well, if you're all done with gift-giving, it's time to plan how to find Zmey." Zima cleared a spot on the food table. "I'm sure Jega and I brought all the maps of the underground we'll need to find where Zlo has hidden Zmey. We spent all last night searching for them, and fortunately ours aren't burned." He dumped rolls of parchment onto the table. "Let's start looking."

Diva approached with Sly's gift open. "I'm sure you have maps of every place in Zmeykovo, but Jabalaka's notes will probably help us solve the puzzle."

"That's true, brother." Jega stepped next to Diva. "The answer is probably in *Lamia's Bible*, since our father knew all secrets, but since Mraz is keeping the book safe, Jabalaka's notes could give us a clue."

Zima snorted. "Unless they say 'Zmey's held captive here,' which is unlikely since our father often wrote riddles, we still would have a lot of work ahead of us deciphering his notes."

"Hey, guys. We have another problem," Theo said.

He'd gotten so caught up in the birthday celebration that he'd forgotten to tell the others about his and Diva's encounter with the demonic bees. He detailed what happened and that they thought the demons were closing in on them, that the mill was no longer a safe haven.

Zima waved at the table. "Then we'll have to hurry and look through the maps."

"Here, let me sort them." Jega rushed to his brother's side, looked through the maps, and handed several to Sava and Ula. "These are near the Samodivi villages. They might spark an idea."

The women took the items to a corner of the room and unrolled them. Diva joined her sisters, looking through the book Sly had given her and reading notes when they found matching maps.

Theo peered at the remaining maps on the table. "I'd like to help."

"How?" Zima said without glancing up. "You don't even know our ancient written language."

"I do now. At least some." Theo briefly explained how he'd been able to read the words on his father's sword, or rather, as he'd learned, the sword that had been forged for Theo himself. "So, even though I'm not familiar with your underground tunnels, I think the sword woke more of my dragon or even Samodiva powers."

Zima groaned, shook his head, and covered his forehead with the back of his hand. "You think just by *looking* at a map you'll know where Zmey is?"

"Well, not just looking, but *sensing* something." It sounded crazy, even to him, but he had to try to help someway.

"I can't stop you," Zima said. "Just don't interrupt Jega and me." The Kuker bent over the parchments, tracing his fingers along various routes.

Jega looked at Theo and shrugged, mouthing the words, "Sorry about my cranky brother." He returned his attention to another map.

Pavel picked up one. "Even if I could read this, it would be impossible to find where the dungeon is. We'd have better luck asking Zlo to tell us."

"Leave these alone." Zima snatched away the map. "I'd be quite happy if you did leave and go visit Zlo. Maybe you can mess up his plans the way you've done with ours too many times."

Pavel backed away. "Just trying to help."

"Well, don't." Zima turned back to examining his map.

At times like this, Theo desperately missed Mraz. It was critical for the eldest Kuker brother to keep *Lamia's Bible* out of

Zlo's hands, but Mraz had been the only one Zima listened to. Theo wished one of the other nine Kukeri brothers was their leader, but they, along with many of the Samodivi, were looking for ways to seal off all portals to the human world. Constantly battling the demons loose in Dragon Village made that task almost impossible.

"I think we may have found something." Diva stood, book in hand, and approached Zima.

A howling wind pierced the air. The mill trembled, and the walls buckled as if being blown in from the outside. Crockery on the table clattered along the boards and crashed to the floor.

"Earthquake," Pavel yelled and scurried around the room before ducking behind a wooden crate in a corner.

Sava and Ula caught up the maps nearest them, clutching them to their chests, while Jega helped Zima stuff the ones they were looking at back into their satchels.

Diva ran to a gap in the window overlooking the stream and forest.

Theo peered out a crack by the mill door. Dark clouds covered the sky, but no rain fell. "It's just an approaching storm."

Diva turned around, her body rigid. "It's not a storm. It's Navi. The demons have arrived."

Chapter 3
Demon Bird Attack

WITH THUNDEROUS CRASHES, the demon Navi landed on the mill roof. The building shuddered and groaned under their weight. Fighting a losing battle, the floral vines that had twisted tight around the rafters trembled and loosened, swaying like jump ropes. Flower petals exploded off of the vines and littered the floor in a swirling mass, mixing with scattered food and broken pottery.

"Everyone, grab a weapon." Zima slung the satchel of maps over his shoulder. "Prepare for battle."

He and Jega rushed toward the doorway, decked themselves out with animal skins and frightening Kuker masks, and attached a belt of bells around their waists. Attired as warriors, they grabbed their spears and brandished them toward the boarded-up windows, which buckled as if a ramming rod pounded them.

"This is the weak spot," Zima shouted over the clanging of the copper bells and pounding against the mill. "My brother and I will massacre the demons when they break through. Everyone else, pick a spot."

Sava shouted as she gathered her bow and quiver, "Ula, guard the tunnel entrance. If the Navi break through and overpower us, we can escape on the route that leads to the gorge. Diva, come with me and secure the upper room."

Diva put the book from Sly into her leather pouch, and both she and Ula seized their bows and arrows and disappeared into their ordered territories. Sava glanced into the dark corners of the room before she, too, rushed to the loft.

Pavel stood in the middle of the room, his face pale, his mouth open, and his eyes wide.

Theo ran over and gently shook his friend. "Get my bow, then help me stack bags of flour against the door."

Pavel nodded and scrambled away as Theo ran toward his backpack, where he'd left his weapons. He slid the dagger into a belt loop and took up his sword.

After he and Pavel secured the door, Theo glimpsed the outside through the crack again. Now that the black clouds had neared, they resembled a swarm of buzzing hornets expelled from their nest. Only these hornets were bird-sized and had disfigured baby heads, covered with curly white hair that had a bluish tinge. Their light purple bodies were those of ravens, but looked like plucked chickens where they lacked feathers. Each creature had round, sad eyes protruding over a beak. Their wails tore at Theo's heart.

How can such pathetic beings be demons?

As if reading his mind, Jega said, "Don't let the Navi fool you. They cry to lure you toward them. They're vicious monsters who normally suck the blood out of women giving birth. Zlo must have ordered them to attack us instead."

Scratching came from the roof, and soot trickled onto the hearth.

"They're trying to get down the chimney. Fire will keep the monsters away." Pavel grabbed an axe and pulled a crate toward the fireplace. He chopped the boards off and hurled them into the hearth, along with kindling. Next, he lit a match and tossed it onto the dry wood.

More rustling came from the top of the fireplace.

"C'mon, burn." Pavel gave short, quick breaths on the sparks.

Jega left his place beside Zima and came closer. "Here, let me get it going."

Above them, a flutter of wings disturbed the fireplace chains. An ash-covered black creature swooped onto the hearth, filling the dark room with soot.

"I've got it." Zima thrust back his hand, ready to hurl his spear.

"No, don't kill him." Theo grasped the Kuker's forearm.

"We can't let these monsters live."

"It's not a monster. It's Boo. See his beak?"

The trembling creature with a yellow beak shook ashes from himself and hopped onto Theo's shoulder before flying to the floor.

"Boo, buddy, why are you here?"

Instead of the usual "Waak" Theo was used to hearing from the magpie, the bird spoke with a throaty voice, "Kosara sent me to help."

Theo took a step back and covered his mouth with his hand. "I … I can understand you again."

"What'd he say?" Pavel scooted closer. "All I hear is that obnoxious sound."

"Ko—"

Another black, soot-covered creature flew out through the fireplace. This one wailed like an infant and lunged at Jega. Hissing, the creature bit the Kuker's shoulder. Jega spun around as if performing a ritual dance and tugged at the hideous being.

"That one's not a friend. It's a monster." Zima lunged forward and pierced the creature through its purple feathery stomach.

Wailing, the demon hit the floor. Large eyes stared blankly above an open beak-like mouth full of sharp teeth.

Pavel leaned closer, shuddering. "That's a Nav? Baby or not, it looks like the little brother of the Devil."

Before anyone could answer, another screeching demon flew from the fireplace opening and dug its claws into Pavel's back.

"Help!" Pavel yanked on its wings, but the creature clamped onto his shoulder with its jagged teeth.

Theo drew his silver sword and, in one fell swoop, cut off the Nav's head. The creature shattered into wisps of black smoke.

Blood oozed from Pavel's shoulder. Clasping his hand over it, he ran to the hearth and looked up the chimney. "Quick, Jega, light the fire now. A bunch more are glued to the chimney ready to attack us."

Jega formed a ball of fire between his palms and hurled it onto the stacked wood. Flaming orange-red tongues erupted and crawled like snakes up the chimney. With screams and flapping wings, the demon offspring retreated.

A deep voice boomed outside, "Line up and prepare to attack the mill."

Theo ran toward a crack in the wall and peered out. A hairy, beast-like man with antlers stood with his back to the mill. Beyond him, men decked out with black metal armor and helmets stood directly behind the man, and more soldiers formed a line for as far as Theo could see. The flapping of wings and the smell of rotting carcasses suggested even more dangerous creatures had arrived to help Zlo's demons. He couldn't see his aunt, but he felt her presence.

Clenching his fists, he turned back to face his friends. "It's Radan. He's brought his Knights of Darkness, plus fifty or more soldiers and Harpies. And Lamia's here as well."

The mill trembled, the old beams cracked, and the remaining garlands of ivy plummeted to the floor. Disturbed from their resting places, the fireflies darted around, forming a chaotic trail of fire in the darkness. A thunderous rumbling grew louder, and the wooden door jumped on its hinges. Receiving a second blow from the outside, one of the boards shattered to reveal the soldiers in black armor through the gap.

Sava shouted from above, "They're breaking through the rafters, too."

"We have to get out of here." Shaking, Pavel collected his gear. "We'll never be able to defeat them all."

"I agree, we have to save ourselves." Theo shouted above the pounding, "Everyone, I have a plan. Listen up."

Sava and Diva peered over the loft landing, Ula approached but remained near the tunnel, and the Kukeri nodded their understanding, while they kept defensive positions by the boarded-up windows.

"Ula, please get Sly … Where is he?" Theo glanced around.

"I heard a splash in the river," Pavel said. "I think he escaped."

"Good, he's safe at least. So, Ula please get Pavel out of here through the tunnel and go to Kosara's. He'll be safe there."

"What about—?" Pavel started.

Theo held up his hand. "No time. Let me finish."

Pavel clamped his mouth shut, but fire burned in his eyes.

"Diva." Theo turned toward her. "I know you're a soldier, born to fight, but I need you to find a safe way out and summon Sur and the deer to help us."

She nodded.

Theo took a deep breath. "The Kukeri, Sava, and I will hold off Radan's troops for as long as we can, so the rest of you can get out. We'll meet you at Kosara's when we can. Everyone understand?"

Everyone except Pavel said, "Yes." He crossed his arms in front of his chest. "No, I'm not leaving without you. I'm terrified, but I'm not a baby. True friends don't desert friends in trouble."

"You're injured." Theo nodded toward Pavel's blood-soaked shirt. "You're not deserting me."

"I don't—"

"We don't have time to argue. Just go." Theo gave Pavel a gentle push toward Ula. "I need you to be safe. It would be madness for us all to stay here to be captured or killed."

Another hard blow against the door shattered more boards and toppled the flour bags stacked against it. A blanket of white scattered around the mill. The gaping hole revealed new arrivals: the half-horse, half-man Bor Stobor and numerous human-goat monstrosities. More banging came from a side wall.

"They must be on the mill wheel," Diva shouted.

The wall shuddered as the wheel freed itself from its ivy-covered bondage and began to turn. In moments, creaking and clopping from outside grew louder and faster, followed by grunts, giggles, and crackles. The sound grew to a crescendo as the speed increased.

Pavel pulled himself away from Ula's grip and looked out a crack. "Are those goat things *playing* on the wheel?"

The cracked, worn millstone inside creaked and spun, scattering sparks. As the tempo on the wheel outside increased, so did the stone's spinning. A piece split off and hurtled toward the wall.

"Watch out!" Theo rushed forward and shoved Pavel to the floor.

The broken missile missed them by inches and crashed into the wall.

Theo breathed heavily, his body still on top of Pavel's. "This is why I need you to leave. None of us can look out for you if we're fighting. Especially since you're hurt."

"Fine." Pavel shoved Theo away. "You don't need me. I'll go."

"It's not that …" Dizziness overwhelmed Theo, and he put his head between his knees.

"Theo?" Pavel sat beside him. "Are you okay? Did the stone hit you?"

"No, I'm fine. I just …"

Theo's head pounded. The soldier raging inside him clamored for release, but Theo fought to maintain control.

"Theo, what's wrong? Can you hear me?" Pavel's voice sounded distant.

"Something's … clawing inside me," Theo managed to say. "Trying … to get out."

A beak pecked at his hand, and a raucous voice said, "Theo, it's okay. Let him out."

"Boo?" Theo raised his head and looked at the magpie. "I. Can't. Lose. Control." He forced each word out, above the roar of the soldier in his mind, shouting at him. "Can't let him destroy everyone. Take over my mind."

"He won't. Only the enemy." The magpie hopped around. "I'm here to protect your body while your spirit fights. That's why Kosara sent me."

"My spirit?" The soldier inside was his spirit, wanting to wage war?

Boo bobbed his beak. "Yes, yes."

"Stop that awful noise, Boo," Pavel shouted. "We have to help Theo."

"Boo *is* here to help," Diva said. "To protect Theo."

Theo placed his hands on his throbbing temples. "You can understand him?"

"Yes, with the barrette my sisters gave me." Diva sat on Theo's other side. "Relax. Let your spirit guide you."

Less fearful that the soldier warring inside him would consume his essence and murder his friends, Theo closed his eyes, letting himself relax, despite the pounding on the doors and walls. He imagined his father, the majestic white dragon, before him and looked deep into Zmey's blue eyes. Theo pictured his mother, and Zunitza's encouraging smile urged him on. Dragon and Samodiva power flowed through him, filling his body with energy. A prickling sensation crawled over his shoulders and muscles and down into his very essence. He retreated into his mind, where he met a shadowy figure of his dragon form, raging and spitting fire.

"We must destroy them all," his dragon self roared. "We are powerful."

"How do we do that?" Theo asked.

"Step into me. Become one with me, and we'll soar to the heavens to do battle."

Theo hesitated. Is this how he wanted to fight? He could shift into a dragon himself. Why would he give control to his spirit?

"Yes, you are wise to ponder that." His dragon form puffed out smoke. "Don't worry. You have full control, and you have my added strength and wisdom of the ages. But … you must also consider the consequences. Any harm that comes to you in spirit form also happens to your physical body. Don't be reckless."

Theo reached out to his Samodiva friend with his mind. *"Diva, can you hear me?"*

"Yes. Hurry, the door's ready to give way."

"Is this wise to do, to fight in spirit form?"

"I think so. In our history, I've read it's the most successful way for dragons to defeat demons."

Theo nodded to his dragon spirit. "Let's fight then."

He stepped into the shadowy figure. The last thing he recalled before his physical body fell into a faint was Radan yelling to his soldiers, "Bring the king's son to me alive. Do with the others what you will."

Another brutal blow pounded against the mill, and the door split in two. Splintered wood and a cloud of flour scattered into the room, and daylight dispelled the darkness. Theo and his friends found themselves face-to-face with Radan's horde.

Everyone took action at once.

"Protect Theo," Zima screamed. The Kukeri brothers formed a barricade in front of the demolished door. Zima plunged his spear into the oncoming soldiers, while Jega heaved a ball of fire at them.

Sava shifted into a hawk and attacked the enemy, while Diva nocked an arrow in her bow, shooting one weapon after the other.

"I'm not leaving." Pavel fought against Ula and dragged Theo's prone body to a dark corner under the stairs, and the magpie followed. "Boo can't guard Theo alone."

"Waak, waak, waak." Theo knew that's what it sounded like to Pavel, but what Boo really said was, "I can. I can. I can."

Ula stepped in front of the bird and boys. "I'll stand guard over all of you, then." She turned to face the advancing mob of Navi and Harpies that had flown through the door above the spears and flames of the Kukeri.

Theo took in the scene for a moment as claws and arrows tore into the attacking creatures. Yellow slime oozed from dying Harpies, sizzling on everything it touched. Navi wailed their pitiful cries as they breathed their last.

The Kukeri brothers didn't fare as well. Their weapons and flames bounced harmlessly off of the knights' armor. His face distorted with rage, Zima hurled a sack of flour toward the advancing warriors. A rising white curtain covered them, and they waved their hands in front of them.

Jega grabbed the nearest soldier and bound him with vine ropes and secured an empty flour sack over the knight's head. He tossed the man toward Ula. "Guard him. A captive might come in handy in case we kill all these others."

More and more demons and soldiers flooded into the mill.

My friends are going to be overrun.

Theo's dragon spirit roared. "It's time for us to save them. We must defeat Lamia, and they'll retreat."

Strength filled Theo's spirit body, and his dragon form appeared in the midst of the chaos. He thrust out his wings. White powder from the spilled flour swirled around him like a windstorm. Knights stopped mid-thrust and stared, wide-eyed. Navi screeched and flew out the door, while Harpies settled near the wall and sniffed the air.

Radan ran to the hole in the doorway, blocking his fleeing soldiers, and shouted, "What's wrong with you fools? We're demons. We can defeat a dragon spirit. He's still just a boy. Attack, now."

Theo took a deep breath and hissed. Smoke erupted from his nostrils, and a scorching flame raced toward the exit. Radan raised a shield forged with the image of a three-headed dragon. The flames enveloped the leader of the knights, who pushed forward nonetheless.

"Go, Theo," Zima shouted. "We'll deal with these monsters."

He would go, all right, but he wasn't abandoning his friends the way Zima implied. Theo looked for Diva, and found her beside his human body. He sent a thought to her. *"I'll distract them so you can escape to get help."*

She gave a slight nod of understanding.

Theo folded his wings, lunged upward with his powerful legs, and slipped through the opening of the shattered door above his enemies. The air grabbed him and hurtled him like a magic carpet toward the roof. Navi and purple bats hissed as he flew in their midst. He shot fire at a flock of Harpies, who screeched, scattering before him, leaving behind an overwhelming scent of carrion. They weren't his ultimate goal.

Where is Lamia?

The shadow of gigantic wings blocked out the sunlight. "*I see you've learned a new trick, nephew. You can harness your inner spirit. Now, we can fight on equal terms.*" Her words reached out to his mind.

"*Lamia.*" Theo turned to meet his nemesis. "*We'll never be equals. I refuse to be like you. You're just the evil Zlo's puppet. You'll never have your own power.*"

"*You're right. We're not the same.*" The air whistled as the three-headed dragon beat her wings, keeping her position steady, out of reach of Theo's fire. "*You'll never learn to be my equal, because Zmey isn't alive to help you with your spiritual and physical growth. We got tired of your games and killed him.*"

Theo shot out flames in all directions. Harpies, Navi, and bats that had come closer scattered once more. "*You're a master of lies. I know my father is alive, and we'll find him—right after I crush you.*"

"*Stupid boy, don't you understand yet that it's pointless to battle me?*" Lamia's roar shook the trees. "*I'm invincible. The stronger I get, the weaker your father becomes. Soon he will be dead.*"

"*I don't believe you. Get ready to die.*"

"*I could kill you with one blow.*"

Theo gazed at the demons that had once more gathered and formed a circle a safe distance around him and Lamia. *"And yet you surround yourself with mindless creatures that you manipulate. Are you afraid to actually fight me one-on-one?"*

"They won't touch you. They know you're mine."

"Enough of this verbal battle," Theo said to Lamia, while at the same time sending a thought to Diva. *"Get ready to escape when I say, 'Now.' "* He stretched his wings to their full extent, flapped them with mighty thrusts, and raced toward his adversary. *"Now."*

With a piercing shriek, Lamia rushed at him, eyes on her three heads glowing a fiery red. From all three mouths, she blasted streams of fire in Theo's direction.

The scales on his skin bubbled and emitted a burning odor. He pushed the scalding pain aside and zoomed toward Lamia, swerving at the last moment in his attempt to bash her with his wing. Misjudging his position, like a fledgling eagle learning to fly, he lost his balance and tumbled in the sky. The audience of Harpies, Navi, and bats scattered.

Lamia lashed out her tail, striking Theo's wing with the sharp thorn on its tip. Pain pierced his body, paralyzing him. The demon dragon continued her assault by clamping her jaw onto his neck and squeezing until he couldn't breathe. When he went limp, she released her hold, and he gulped in air. His demonic aunt hadn't finished with her torture. She latched onto the sensitive tip of his tail and dragged him in circles. He roared in agony but could do nothing to protect himself.

She stopped, still clutching his bloodied tail. Her eyes, now dark orbs, stared at him, gloating.

Theo looked away from the penetrating gaze. Something was different about her. Before, only red scales had lined her underbelly, while the rest were golden. Now, two entwined dragons—one white and one golden—appeared like a tattoo above her heart. They differed from the symbol on his medallion. These dragons formed the infinity symbol, and each was eating the other's tail. Where had it come from?

Theo returned his gaze to his tormenter. Lamia still held his tail tight. A malicious grin spread across her face.

What pain does she intend to cause me next?

Out of the corner of his eye, he watched as a white falcon disappeared into the distance. Diva had escaped. The deer would rescue his friends. All hope wasn't lost.

Lamia raced downward, and the ground approached rapidly. Theo's dragon spirit had failed to save him.

He was going to die.

Chapter 4
The Messenger

JUNE 27

THE EARLY-MORNING DRIZZLE ceased as Theo sat beneath the massive branches of the ancient Znahar Tree, where he, Diva, and Pavel had escaped during the demon attack. A golden-orange glow from the protective dome the Thracian spirit god, Tangra, had created illuminated everything beneath it. The birds that tweeted and darted from branch to branch. The squirrels that scampered around the violet-hued trunk. And especially the golden apple that had blossomed after the Firebird's rebirth. Even the water droplets trickling from the silver, heart-shaped leaves held a glow before they collected in the golden water of a pool. From there, the moisture fed the tree's robust roots, which stretched throughout the land, nourishing all of Dragon Village.

But, the idyllic scene didn't calm Theo. Neither did the glorious, tender melody from the reborn Firebird as it sang from the crown of the sacred tree. Too many concerns troubled Theo's mind.

He missed his human family.

He was worried about his absent friends.

He didn't know how they were going to find Zmey.

But the most confusing thought was why Lamia hadn't killed him when she had the chance. As she'd dashed him to the ground, the last thing he recalled was her hissing into his ear, "Until we meet again, dear nephew." When he came to, he was here, beneath the Znahar Tree in the priestess Kosara's sacred grove, the only truly safe place in Dragon Village.

Earlier, Diva had told him the battle had raged on when Sur and his herd had arrived. Zima had ordered her and Pavel to get Theo to safety while the brothers and Samodivi sisters fought to keep the demons at bay. Theo chided himself for not being strong enough to remain conscious when he returned to his physical body, so he could help the others fight. Even Boo stayed to battle the demons. The magpie had come a long way from the baby bird frightened at his own reflection when he had arrived in Dragon Village in the chariot along with Theo the first time.

A sigh escaped Theo, and he put his head between his knees. Would he ever be worthy of the title of Prince of Dragon Village?

Munching on a red apple, Pavel plopped beside Theo. "Hey, gloomy Gus, cheer up."

"It's been *three* days, and we haven't heard anything from the Kukeri or Diva's sisters."

Theo ran his fingers over the neck wounds his physical body's had suffered when Lamia had attacked his dragon spirit. Bruises, burns, and cuts covered his skin, and it hurt to sit. Diva and Kosara had mended the worst of his and Pavel's wounds, but pain still exploded every time Theo moved.

"I don't want to sit here, being babied. I want to find our friends. Make sure they're okay." Theo groaned as he stood. He leaned against the tree to steady his wobbly legs and looked at the sky clearing of rain clouds. "I'm willing to fight more demons to get our friends back if I have to."

"I'm sure they'll join us soon." Pavel tossed his apple core to the birds pecking at bugs on the ground. Squawking, they flew off, only to return as soon as Pavel moved farther away.

Theo hobbled to the water's edge and startled a frog toasting under the sun on a blossoming water lily. The creature leaped into the pool from its perch and hid under a large green leaf, peeping at Theo with its wide-open, watery eyes. The disturbed pool caused a school of goldfish to scatter, sending the lilies into a flurried dance. Bereft of its hiding place, the frog disappeared beneath the surface.

So much like my life, Theo thought as he lowered himself to the ground. *One event disrupts what's happening, and everything ends up in chaos. I feel like such a failure.*

He'd gone over the battle with Lamia numerous times in his mind. What had gone wrong? He'd felt so powerful, invincible, certain he could stop the beast. His powers were growing, and he was controlling them better. He'd done what he could to beat her. And yet, she'd had no problem overpowering him.

How can my dragon spirit have failed me? He said he had the wisdom of ages.

Maybe the opposite was true. Theo had failed his dragon spirit by not trusting him and forgetting to focus on his inner power.

Was I too intent on making sure Diva escaped that I let down my guard?

That's when Lamia attacked and got the better of him.

I wish I could talk with Mom. She always lifted my spirit when I was down.

Theo leaned closer to the golden water and gazed into its mirrored surface. Kosara had once told him the pool revealed truths to those who respected it. Would it give him answers now? Mostly, he wanted to see his family.

He stretched his hands over the still water the way he had once before and whispered, "Please show me Selo and my family. I want to know how Nia and my mother are doing."

A sweet aroma of honeysuckle wafted over the water lilies and made him sneeze. The water rippled. He waited for the pool to bubble and a glow to appear beneath the surface. Before, when the pool had responded, the glow had become a spinning orb that pulsed through the colors of the rainbow in reverse. Theo sat still until the water settled. He sighed. All that the pool reflected this time was the glow of his red hair and his sad eyes. The oracle hadn't been willing to give him a sign. He turned his face away and wiped a tear from his cheek.

Mist formed around the trunk of the holy tree. From within it, emerged an ethereal figure of a woman with snow-white hair flowing over her shoulders. The black symbols of the sun and moon appeared to orbit her silver robe as she glided toward him.

Theo stood, straightened his pants and T-shirt, and bowed his head. "Kosara, I'm sorry for being selfish. I didn't mean to disturb the oracle's peace. I wanted to find out about my family."

"Theo, you didn't disturb the oracle, and you're not selfish. We're grateful you've come to our land."

Her sweet voice seeped into the air like the mist surrounding them, soaking into Theo's pores. He relaxed as invisible gentle hands seemed to lift heavy burdens from his shoulders.

"The oracle of the water requires all its strength to revive the soul of the Znahar Tree." Kosara circled the tree, her hands stretched out toward its bark. "Every day, its roots grow stronger, deeper, keeping our land from annihilation. Even the rebirth of our beloved Firebird has aided in the tree's nourishment."

"Unfortunately, the rest of Dragon Village is still suffering."

"Yes, suffering and renewal are the paths of life." Kosara smiled at him. "But I have faith you'll find a way to unravel their mysteries."

"But not here. Lamia and the demonic Zlo continue to burn and destroy everything. I need to be out *there*." He pointed beyond the perimeter of the protective golden dome to the scarred and burned land.

"I agree." With silent footsteps, Diva joined him with her bow slung over her shoulder and a quiver of arrows secured to her back. "Who knows how long before they discover a way to break through the dome's defenses. Lamia nearly destroyed Zmeykovo by herself. With Zlo guiding her, she may succeed this time."

From behind, Pavel wrapped an arm around each of his friends' shoulders. "We're leaving then?"

"Well, we can't wait here forever." Theo glanced at two birds, one black and one white, that fought over a twig.

Even in this holy place, all was not serene and calm. Animal nature didn't change, and he didn't believe Lamia would either.

Her hatred of her brother was too strong. It had to stem from something more than jealousy of Zmey's love for Zunitza. Something, at some point in her life, must have made her choose evil over good. He couldn't get out of his mind the picture of her peaceful countenance after he had killed her. She had reverted to what must have been her original nature.

Kosara bowed to Diva and Pavel, then faded from their view. Theo hoped she didn't think he was ungrateful for her hospitality of letting them stay here. They couldn't remain forever.

"Okay, but …" Pavel said.

Theo twisted his head to look at his friend. "But, what?"

"If we go out there," Pavel said as he waved his hand in a wide arc, "without any clue where to start looking for Zmey, we'll spend all of our time fighting demons. We at least need a destination."

"But we don't know where he's imprisoned." Theo tried to keep his face calm, but frustration filled his voice. Every time he encountered Lamia, her strength was greater than before. Without the maps and his missing friends' intricate knowledge of the world of tunnels, they had little hope of finding Zmey.

"I have an idea where he could be," Diva said.

"Where?" Theo asked while Pavel said, "Really?"

"I found something on a map, right before we were attacked."

Theo bit his lower lip and shook his head. "But Zima has all the maps. We're back to waiting for him and the others to return."

"I can show you on—" Diva started.

An ominous roar drowned out her words.

Pavel pointed toward the sky, beyond the halo surrounding the Znahar Tree. "Look. One of Sur's herd is coming. And something black's chasing it."

"Navi." Theo covered his ears and cringed from the screeching and crying of the infant-like demons, who were still at a distance. The noise pounded in his head. He focused on one, which tore feathers from its own body with its beak-like mouth. What kind of control had Lamia spelled the crazed demons with?

"Someone's on the deer," Diva yelled as the creature neared. "We need to let him in, save him and the deer."

Kosara reappeared and pulled a silver rod out of her robe. With one swipe through the air, she opened a hole in the halo enough for the deer to rush through. As soon as the animal entered, the hole closed like a magical portal. Moments later, Navi smashed into the dome. Their shrieks and pitiful wails clamored along with the scratching of their talons and snapping of their beaks at the impenetrable surface.

A young man in beige, shredded clothing limply hung from the neck of the deer. Blood flowed from a jagged gouge in his shoulder.

The deer, its tail clamped down and its wings still flapping, stomped its front legs and let out a screech that sounded like a cross between a fox's bark and a crow's caw. The fireball between its antlers sparked a deep purple.

"Quick." Theo rushed forward. "It's Jega. We have to help him."

"Stop, Theo." Diva, making shushing sounds, stealthily approached. Keeping her voice low and calm, she spoke to the terrified animal. "Don't worry. It's safe here. We won't hurt you."

As she crept closer, the deer threw its head up and stared at the swarm of creatures that continued to crash into the dome of light. It screamed once more, but maintained its stance, as if ready to fly off at a moment's notice if the demons broke through. The dome held firm, and the deer's spinning sphere turned from sparkling purple to a welcoming pink-violet color, and finally to amber, the color of calmness. Diva stroked the panting deer's side, and it folded its wings and ceased pawing the ground.

"Guys, it's okay now," Diva said. "Can you get Jega down while I keep the deer calm?"

Theo and Pavel approached. Theo straightened Jega's slumped head and slipped his hands beneath his friend's arm, while Pavel grabbed hold of the Kuker's ankle.

Pavel grunted. "Oomph, he's heavy. Can't budge him."

"Jega, can you hear me?" Theo tapped the older boy's pale, sickly face. "Can you move?"

The Kuker made no reply. Only his bleeding shoulder indicated he was still alive.

"Diva, can you get the deer to kneel so we can roll Jega off?"

She whispered into the jittery animal's ear, and it bent its front legs, with its back end sticking up. Jega slid forward.

Theo tightened his grip on Jega's arm. "Pavel, can you get on the other side? We'll roll him gently off from the front."

When Pavel was in position, Theo said, "Okay, carefully now."

Pavel lifted Jega's arm, while Theo pulled the Kuker down. Little by little, they moved his tall frame and laid him on the soft grass carpet.

A moan escaped Jega's lips.

"Here." Kosara came closer and held out a clean white towel toward Diva. "Let me tend to the deer, while you aid Jega."

Diva took the cloth, and Kosara led the deer toward the Znahar Tree. The priestess filled a clay bowl with water from the pool and crumpled dry leaves into it. As they soaked, she chanted, and the deer calmed enough for her to get it to drink the liquid. It ceased its jerking movements and began to eat grass near the tree.

Diva tore away material from Jega's jerkin and examined his wound. She opened her leather pouch and removed several colorful jars, selecting one with a small amount of yellow paste and another with a reddish decoction.

"I'm glad you're here." Pavel poked his head over her shoulder. "You always have so many herbs to heal the wounded, both us and animals."

"And they're running low." She sighed. "With so many attacks, I haven't had a chance to replenish my supplies. Can you bring water from the pool, so I can clean Jega's wound first?"

"Sure." Pavel took the bowl she held out to him, ran to the pool, and rushed back with water slopping over the edges.

"Thank you." She grasped the bowl, dipped the cloth into the golden-colored liquid, and gently patted away the crusted blood. Next, she dipped her fingers into the yellow mixture and applied it to the wounds.

Jega's body twitched, and he moaned.

"Theo, Pavel. I'll need both of you to help now. I have to get Jega to drink this potion." She uncorked the bottle with the red liquid. "He's likely to fight it, even unconscious as he is."

"Okay, what do you want us to do?" Theo asked.

"I want you to hold his head straight, and Pavel to keep Jega's arms down. Sit on him if you have to. I must get it all down him."

Theo held Jega's head as tight as possible, and scowling, Pavel scrutinized the Kuker.

"C'mon, sit on him or something, Pavel," Theo said. "I can't hold his head this tight for long."

"All right already." Pavel put Jega's hands together on the Kuker's stomach and plopped down on top of them. "Ouch. He's as solid as stone."

Diva squeezed open Jega's lips and poured in the red liquid. The vapor from the bottle reached Theo. His eyes watered, and he smacked his lips trying to get rid of the bitter taste it left in his mouth.

Jega's body tensed. Theo squeezed his friend's face tighter as the Kuker arched his back.

"Hurry!" Pavel yelled. "He's trying to push me off."

"Almost done." Diva shook the last of the drops down Jega's throat and rubbed his neck to make sure he swallowed the potion. "There, you can let go."

Pavel jumped off the still-unconscious Kuker, who writhed on the ground. Pavel, wrinkling his nose and wiping his glasses on his shirt, asked, "What was that stuff? It made Jega smell like a smoked ham." His stomach grumbled, and he laughed nervously.

Theo shook his head at his friend. "Do you think this is funny?"

"No, of course not. I can't help it if my stomach always thinks of food."

Theo turned to Diva. "Is Jega going to be okay?"

Just then, the Kuker coughed and sputtered, shaking his head. His face still pale, he opened his eyes. "Water," he croaked.

Diva removed an empty jar from her pouch. "Pavel, please get some fresh water." She turned back to Jega. "I'll bind your wounds now."

Pavel returned and handed Jega the water, which the Kuker sipped, while Diva bandaged the gashes on Jega's shoulder with clean strips of cloth. He winced but didn't cry out.

Theo asked, "What happened? Where is everyone else? We've been so worried."

"The Knights of Darkness … nesss … destroyed …" Jega coughed and wet his lips with his tongue. His eyes wide and unfocused, he jabbed his free hand into the air as if thrusting a spear at the enemy. "Destroyed everything."

"Shh, calm down." Diva spoke softly. "You're safe here among friends."

"Everything. Ruined. Destroyed." Jega collapsed and closed his eyes.

Theo whispered to Diva, "What do you think he means? What's destroyed?"

Diva shrugged and placed a folded bag under Jega's head. "He'll tell us later. He's lost a lot of blood. The potion will help him recover, but we must let him rest now."

Pavel slunk toward the edge of the dome where the wailing Navi scratched and pecked.

"Careful over there," Theo called out.

"I will be." Pavel stopped a few feet short of the glowing, transparent barrier. "I just want to look again. They resemble scorched chickens with a baby head sewn on, but I've never seen any infant with teeth that pointed."

Theo joined him. "They're like the devil's newborns."

The howling baby-birdlike creatures scrambled over each other, screeching at Theo. Claws, beaks, and feathers intermingled into a chaotic clutter.

Pavel jumped back, as if avoiding stepping on a hornets' nest. "Monkey poo, it looks like they want to tear you apart."

"Yah, it's me they're after." Theo sighed. "That's why I should look for my father on my own, to keep everyone else safe."

Pavel snorted. "You think we'd be safe? Just look at Jega. And remember, Radan said to take you alive, but he didn't care what they did to the rest of us. No, we *won't* be safer without you around."

"Stop trying to get rid of us." Diva walked up and nudged his shoulder with hers. "Or I'll have to make you drink a sleeping potion."

Theo laughed. "Not what you made Jega drink, please. You'd have to knock me out first … and I know you could do that."

"Easily."

"Hey, Diva," Pavel said. "The Navi are little vampires. Jega said they sucked blood from women giving birth. Are they really the Devil's spawn?"

"No." She shook her head. "They were once human infants, but I guess, in a way, you could say your Devil acquired their souls."

Pavel looked at her intently. "How?"

"You have a custom of baptizing babies to keep evil spirits away," she said. "If a child dies before that happens, or if he's stillborn, he'll become a Nav, one of the unclean."

"That's so sad." He stared again at the crazed creatures trying to rip a hole in the dome.

"It is," Theo added. "Too many wrongs in this world that we can't correct."

Was there a way to solve the Navi problem by fixing the demons themselves? This was another question he'd ask his father if, no *when*, they found Zmey. One more casualty of this chaotic world that Theo added to his list of those whose lives he wanted to improve. Demons or not, if they stayed in Dragon Village, then they would one day be his people to rule. For now, he'd have to avoid the creatures as best he could, and that started with finding a safe way out of the dome.

"Diva, how long will it take Jega to recover?" Theo asked. "Do you think we can find out what happened and begin searching for Zmey today?"

She shook her head. "He'll heal quickly, but he needs the night to regain his strength. Any plans will have to wait until tomorrow."

"Okay. It's best for us all to be safe for now." Theo closed his eyes and tried to push the anxiety from his mind. He couldn't drive his friends to exhaustion. He didn't even have a clue how to slip past the Navi, who surrounded the dome. Tomorrow would come soon enough. As his grandmother used to say, "The morning is wiser than the evening."

In the morning, Theo would ask Jega what had happened. After that, they could develop a plan for not only defeating the demons, but also for finding Zmey.

Chapter 5
The Gift

DAWN WAS STILL at least an hour from breaking, but Theo felt no wiser this morning than he had before he drifted off to sleep—what little rest he managed to achieve. Moments ago, the Navi had scattered. Perhaps Zlo or Lamia had called their minions back. Theo didn't care what the reason was. He was glad not to have to listen to their pitiful cries and maniacal laughter as they assaulted the dome with beaks and claws. And now, he and his friends didn't have to wonder how they would avoid the demons when it was time to leave the dome's protection. At least he hoped the demons wouldn't return before then.

He looked at Diva, lying next to him. Theo guessed that his Samodiva friend was already awake, even though her eyes remained closed. If she wasn't alert now, she would be at the first hint of danger.

Beside her, Jega rested. Theo watched his warrior friend a moment. The Kuker's cheeks had lost their pallor, and he had stopped moaning. Diva's potions, even though they sometimes tasted terrible, were miraculous cures. Theo was thankful his friend was well. He wanted to push the morning forward so he could question Jega about what had happened, and also to find out what Diva had discovered about Zmey's whereabouts.

On the other side of Theo, Pavel mumbled in his sleep under the Znahar Tree. Last night, he had bemoaned the fact there were no blankets. Kosara had told him, "You have no need for blankets here. Nature provides a cozy bed on her soft carpet of grass. And fireflies will be your night lamps, while frogs will serenade you with their evening songs." Pavel had shrugged, laid his head on his backpack, and was snoring within seconds.

Theo had enjoyed sleeping on the grass. He felt as if he were wrapped in a cotton blanket sprinkled with mist, which mixed with the aroma of lily of the valley. It reminded him of his home in Selo and hazy days along the Black Sea. He was torn between his two worlds. He missed his mother and sister and hoped they were okay, but he couldn't abandon his friends or father in Dragon Village either. Not that he had any way to return to Selo at the moment.

He shook off his homesickness and rested his hand on the Znahar Tree. Energy pulsed through its cracked bark, and water dripped down the trunk, collecting in a carved niche by the roots. Maybe the oracle had restored enough of the holy tree's strength overnight that it could show him a glimpse of his home now. Before he could move toward the water, the ethereal figure of Kosara emerged in a mist from the tree.

He stood and bowed his head. "Good morning, Kosara. Sorry, I didn't mean to disturb you."

"You didn't." A Mona Lisa smile crept over her flawless marble face. "I am at peace near our sacred tree. You wished to know something?"

"I was thinking about my family at home. And I'm scared for my father and friends here." Theo glanced at the serene faces of Pavel, Diva, and Jega. "Not only for them, but I'm afraid for myself, too. I feel so inadequate. How will we find Zmey? Without him, how can we save Dragon Village?"

"Believe in yourself, Theo," Kosara said. "Fear is not a weakness. It makes you strong, wise. Heart and mind work together."

Theo didn't feel strong. He hadn't even been able to work as one with his dragon spirit. If his battle was only against Lamia or Zlo, it might not have been so bad. He and his friends had beaten them once before. But now, with every move they made, they couldn't shake off the demons. Theo's gut told him it was more than Zlo's spies reporting their whereabouts back to him. It was as if Theo had a tracking device on him, or he glowed like a beacon, flashing to the enemy where he was. He looked toward the sky where the baby demons had been.

"You fear the return of the Navi?" Kosara's ethereal face remained calm, unpredictable.

He nodded.

"You are wise to do so. They don't give up prey so easily."

"I can sense them nearby." He scanned the forests, peering into branches, but saw nothing unusual.

Kosara glided like mist to the pool, kneeled, closed her eyes, and chanted, her arms extended over the water. She waved her hands in an upward motion. Silver particles glittered off of her fingertips and spread like dust over the water. Where the moisture touched the land, fragrant lily of the valley flowers sprouted and blossomed. Remaining granules came together to form white butterflies. They spread their wings and flew to the top of the Znahar Tree and formed an arch, which dissolved into droplets that sparkled like a rainbow.

"Zunitza, the sign of Zunitza," Theo exclaimed.

"Yes, the spirit of our queen, your beloved mother, is here to protect you." Kosara rose and approached Theo.

The rainbow droplets wavered and spiraled in slow motion around the Firebird. As the first drop touched the bird's outstretched wing, he emitted a long, low hum and shook his wings. A blinding flash lit the pre-dawn sky.

Theo squeezed shut his eyes and covered them with his hands. All around him noises exploded: birds singing, frogs croaking, insects humming and buzzing. And the most beautiful song he had ever heard poured from the tree's branches as the Firebird sang. The melody seeped into Theo's pores, replenishing his soul like water restoring a wilting flower. When the tune faded, he opened his eyes. Kosara stood before him, a glowing feather cradled inside a thin, dark-brown box about a foot long.

"The Firebird has granted you help in your mission." She held the box out toward Theo.

"A golden feather?" Pavel's face popped up over Theo's shoulder.

"You're awake?" Theo spoke the obvious.

"I thought the sun had risen." Pavel yawned and stretched, and then removed his glasses and rubbed his eyes.

"Thank you, Kosara." Theo took the box and gazed at the magnificent gift. Even the box itself was impressive. Leather-bound, it displayed the Firebird etched into its surface. The brass latch to close it resembled a snake eating its tail.

"Be warned, however," she said. "The feather can be a blessing and a curse. Its magic will aid you when you need it, but bearing it with you ensures your journey will be difficult and filled with loss."

"Difficult is a word I think we're all used to by now." Theo closed the box lid, and the light dimmed, replaced by the rosy hue of the rising sun. He placed the box within an internal pocket in his backpack.

Jega stirred, stretched, and opened his eyes. He flinched, bolted upright, and thrust his hand out as if jabbing his spear. Stopping, he stared at his empty hands.

"You're safe," Diva said softly at his side. "Stay calm."

He blinked and looked at her, then at Theo, Pavel, and finally Kosara. "Where am I?"

"A deer brought you to the Znahar Tree," Diva said. "You were injured badly. I tended to your wounds."

"The others?" Jega jumped up and jerked his head, scanning the area. "Zima? Sava and Ula? They're not here? Where are they?"

Theo cleared his throat. "We were hoping you could tell us what happened. What do you remember?"

Jega slumped back to the ground and placed his hands on the side of his head. "After we fought Lamia and her hoards, we took our prisoner to the castle. Zima wanted to interrogate him there to find out where Zmey is."

"Interrogate?" Pavel said.

Jega hung his head. "Zandan has devices that get people to talk."

Pavel's face paled. "The prison? You tortured him?"

"Not me. Zima." Jega wrung his hands. "I tried to convince my brother to try other methods … but you know him. Might over reason."

"And did you discover anything?" Diva asked.

Jega shook his head. "Not much. Not a location. I think all Zlo's servants are spelled not to reveal critical details."

"What did the soldier say?" Theo approached and sat next to the Kuker.

"He spoke of a dark place, which we already knew." Jega hesitated and shook his head as if to clear cobwebs from his mind. "And a lake."

"A lake?" Theo reached over for his backpack and rummaged for his map of Dragon Village. "That narrows the search down. There are only two, Samodivi Lake up here in the northwest corner and Cherna Lake at the foot of the mountain. I can't imagine they would hide Zmey in the Samodivi territory, do you?" He turned to Diva.

She shook her head. "No, but—"

"Then my father must be somewhere near the mountain lake." Theo jumped up and hugged her. "We'll find him yet."

"We will." She loosened his grip on her. "But not there."

"It has to be."

"No. Let me show you something in the book Sly gave me." She located her pouch and removed the tome. Her fingers lingered on its scorched cover before she eased it open to a page marked with a leaf. "Does this look familiar?"

Theo looked at the map. "Yes, it's the same as mine. Well, not exactly. It has words written all over it."

"And … it's not burned where yours is. Look here." She pointed to a place in the southeastern corner, a bit north of the mill.

"Another lake," Theo said. "But why do you think that's the place and not the one near the mountain?"

"Because of Jabalaka's notes." She lowered her eyes toward the page. "This one in particular mentions 'the deepest, darkest pit of despair.' Since we've been here, I've gone over the map, all the maps in the book, endless times. Jabalaka's note and now Jega's confirmation about a lake point to this—Rabisha Lake—being the place where Zlo imprisoned Zmey."

"I think you're right." Jega pushed himself up from the ground and paced by the tree. "Mraz told us ages ago about a cave hidden there. Magura Cave. I've never been, but I'm sure we have a book about it back at the sanctuary."

Pavel poked his head between Theo and Diva to look at the map. "Well, let's go look for it."

"I don't know if it's safe there," Jega said.

"It's not safe anywhere, except under the dome," Theo replied.

They'd never be rid of the demons until they rescued Zmey. Theo was certain his father would make everything better in Dragon Village, once he regained his freedom. He was strong, brave, a mighty leader. His people would rally behind him, instead of cowering in fear of Zlo and Lamia. Zmey would—

"Jega," Diva said as she closed her book, interrupting Theo's thoughts, "can you tell us what happened? How you got injured?"

The Kuker stopped pacing. "We were ambushed at Zandan. Soldiers and Youdi with their bloodthirsty wolves swarmed out of the tunnels into the torture room when Zima finished with our prisoner. We were in such tight quarters that it was nearly impossible to defend ourselves. A wolf attacked Zima. Another one must have rushed me when I became distracted. The rest is hazy. Somehow, I got on a deer. Ula told me to come here. Before I passed out, the deer flew over our sanctuary. Smoke was everywhere. The next thing I remember was waking up here."

"Do you know if Zima and my sisters managed to escape and where they would be now?" Diva asked.

"They have to have survived." Jega shook and wrapped his hands around his face. "We had agreed beforehand that if we became separated, we'd meet up in a hidden grove in an oak forest near the Kukeri sanctuary."

Kosara appeared from the tree like a mist. Theo hadn't even seen her disappear. He'd been too intent on Jega's story.

The priestess held a jug, which she filled with droplets of water from the Znahar Tree. She handed it to Jega. "Drink the tree's holy tears. They will give you strength and erase your pain."

"Thank you." Jega bowed low to Kosara. He took the jug and let the healing water flow down his throat.

"All of you need to refresh your bodies and minds before you begin your venture." Kosara picked up a basket of fruit and bread lying at the base of the tree.

Something else that wasn't there before, Theo thought.

She approached Jega first, and he selected a shiny red apple. His eyes rolled back as he took a bite. "Oh, what a marvelous flavor. So delicious, like ambrosia."

Theo glanced at the tree. The golden apple was the only fruit growing there. A humorous thought crossed his mind, and he stifled a laugh. Did Kosara have a factory inside the tree like the elves who made cookies?

Kosara approached him and smiled as if hearing his thoughts. "These apples are not from the Znahar Tree. That bears only the Golden Apple. These are a gift from our goddess, Bendis. She cannot return to Zmeykovo until the menace has been removed and order restored, but she is watching over all of us, helping in any way she can."

Theo selected a thick piece of bread slathered with honey. "Does the tree produce a Golden Apple every year?"

"No. Normally, it yields its produce once every thousand years." She pointed to the golden flower on the branch beneath the Firebird. "This year is an exception. The Firebird's rebirth ignited the fruit's growth. This marks a new cycle for life in Zmeykovo. Changes are coming."

"It's a good sign, though, right?" Theo asked. "It means there's hope for peace, doesn't it?"

"In truth, the Golden Apple causes discord and rioting. I have seen much conflict for possession of the tree's fruit in my many years of service protecting the tree." Kosara's voice deepened and sadness poured forth with each word. "It's like a magnet, not only for the gods, but also for demons and anyone craving power. The one who consumes the fruit becomes like the gods, perhaps even more formidable. I fear this is what Zlo's plan was when he captured and murdered our holy bird."

Electricity surged through Theo's body and his muscles tightened as his anger built. He reached out, placing his hand on the priestess' shoulder. "We'll stop him and Lamia. Once we rescue Zmey, my father will know what to do."

Kosara sighed. "At least we have time. The apple is not yet ripened." She stepped away and held the basket toward Diva.

The Samodiva took a piece of bread with honey and ran the tip of her tongue over the sweet treat. "Mmmm. The way to a girl's heart."

Pavel looked at her with bright eyes. Theo could see the wheels in his mind turning, inventing devices that mass-produced honey.

"Pavel?" Kosara held the basket out toward him.

"Huh?" He turned his gaze toward the priestess. "Oh, sorry. Thank you." He snatched bread in one hand and an apple in the other.

This time, Theo did laugh. It felt good to release his tension, if even for a moment. His friend's boundless appetite was annoying and amusing at the same time. Or maybe it was the restorative power of the bread Theo had bitten into that made him feel calm. Either way, he relaxed his tight muscles and savored his food.

Kosara set the basket down, and it dissolved into mist.

"Oh." Pavel moaned, gazing at the empty space.

"Don't worry," Kosara told him. "What you have will sustain you for the day."

Theo said under his breath, "You don't know Pavel if you think that."

Pavel stepped closer and elbowed Theo. Munching on an apple, Pavel said, "Thanks for nothing, pal."

"Always glad to put in a good word about you." Theo grinned.

Pavel grunted as he continued eating.

When they'd all finished their food, Kosara raised her hands to the sky and said, "Fare well on your mission, my friends, and stay brave. I will pray to Tangra for your protection. May our sun god provide you with his light and strength."

"We won't let you down." Diva bowed and then called the deer.

When they approached, Theo and Pavel assisted Jega onto the deer that had brought him to the Znahar Tree.

Pavel climbed onto Whirl and positioned himself as if ready to drive a fast car. "Do you want to race again?"

"Not today," Theo said. "Maybe we'll—"

"Boys, we don't have time for this now." Diva slung her bow and quiver over her shoulder before she mounted Sur, the leader of the deer.

Theo got on Shar, his own deer companion. In no shape to fly alone after being wounded, Theo had sped away on Sur with Diva keeping a tight grip on Theo. Shar had followed. Theo's bond with Shar was deeper than a simple "choosing" of companions. The deer had once been Theo's mother's companion.

Stroking the deer's neck, Theo said, "Let's go." He closed his eyes as he and his friends flew to the sky to search for their missing companions.

Chapter 6
Devastation

THE WIND BATTERED Theo's face as he gripped Shar's neck. The scent of smoke permeated the air, even at this height, and far below, black spots littered the ground—so many destroyed settlements in such a short distance from the Znahar Tree to the Kukeri sanctuary. If it was so bad here, what did the rest of Dragon Village look like? The hurt land called out to Theo for help.

As soon as we rescue my father, he thought to the countless beings living there, *I promise, everything will be better.*

Theo hoped he and his friends found his father soon so he could deliver on that promise.

"*Hold on, Theo,*" Shar thought to him. "*We're here.*"

It can't be, Theo thought.

The smell of death clung to the air. And so much thick, black smoke blanketed the Kukeri sanctuary that Theo strained to glimpse the megaliths but failed to find them, even with his enhanced dragon vision. He landed moments after Sur and Diva, with Jega's and Pavel's deer pounding the ground soon after.

Jega leaped off his animal and raced into the smoldering remains. The Kuker's wail reached Theo as the latter slid from Shar. "My home. It's destroyed. The megaliths have been smashed, and everything's been burned."

By the time Theo trudged through the ashes to where the circle of stones had once stood, Jega was dashing around from one activity to the next, one moment righting toppled pillars, then the next, hurling stones away from the entrance to the underground living quarters.

"Jega, stop." Theo approached his friend. "It's too extensive. We'll all help you rebuild your home after we've defeated Lamia and Zlo."

"That's right," Diva added. "And my sisters and I can restore all the vegetation and heal any creatures that survived."

Pavel circled the toppled stones. "When I was here the first time, I mapped out the positions and heights of the megaliths, so I could create a portal between your world and mine. If you remember, that's how Theo and I arrived here this time. It'll be easy enough to get them back into place. Well, I can't move them, but I saw how you and Zima rolled those boulders into the ravine, so it should be easy-peasy for all the Kukeri."

Jega slumped to the ground and put his hands over his face. "Why? Why did they do this? We weren't even here."

Diva crouched beside him and lowered his hands, waiting until he looked at her. "Do you think they were looking for the book you mentioned? The one about Magura Cave. To prevent us from finding it."

"I don't know." He groaned. "I can't think straight."

"How would they know what we'd discovered?" Pavel asked.

"Spies." Theo glanced toward the trees, but didn't sense the demons. "We can't forget that Zlo has them everywhere. You never know what creature could be his servant."

"Like my puppy." Pavel's shoulders slumped.

Theo gripped Pavel's forearm and recalled the puppy they'd found in their travels and taken with them, an animal that had turned out to be a shape-shifter who served Zlo. "Don't beat yourself up about that. It taught us a valuable lesson to be wary."

"Or maybe they're looking for Mraz," Diva said.

Jega jerked his head up. "My brother? Why him?"

"He has *Lamia's Bible* with him." She paused. "And—"

"Oh no." Theo squeezed his eyes shut for a moment. "Since Jabalaka's dead, that would mean Mraz would have to take over writing in the book. Jabalaka always knew what was happening. So, it's natural that Mraz would now, too."

"Wait, no, you're wrong, *Dracoville*." Pavel shook his head so violently Theo thought it was going to twist off.

"Why are you calling me Dracoville?" Pavel had nicknamed Theo that when he was trying to come up with a name that included Theo's dragon and Samodiva heritage.

"I like the name," Diva said. "Dracoville, the Red Dragon. You'll grow to like it."

Theo snorted. The name was cool, and before, it had sounded fun. Now, Pavel's tone made it sound like a curse. "So why am I wrong, Pavel?"

"You said Jabalaka's human—er, Kuker—form had been restored when you found him in the fortress, right?"

Theo nodded.

"Then that has to mean the curse was broken," Pavel continued, "and he wouldn't have to record any more secrets in the book. So, his eldest son, Mraz, wouldn't have to either."

"Maybe." Theo didn't understand how magic and curses worked. "What if it took more than Lamia's death to reverse the curse? Especially now that she's alive again."

Pavel spread his feet wide and crossed his arms tight against his chest. "No. I'm sure I'm right about this."

"What suddenly makes you an expert in magic?" Theo leaned closer. "You're the one who always only believed in science."

"I—" Pavel started, a scowl on his face.

"Guys." Diva stepped between them. "We don't know the answer. And, to be honest, it's not worth arguing about. We need to find the book Jega told us about. If it's still here. Then we can figure out how to proceed with the rescue." She looked from one to the other. "Or did you both forget that's what we're trying to do?"

Theo hung his head. "You're right. I'm so worried about my father that my nerves are on edge. Sorry for arguing with you, Pavel."

"It's okay." Pavel looked away from Theo. "Let's just go and find that book, all right?"

"Jega," Diva said softly as she laid a hand on his shoulder, "do you want to look for the book now?"

Jega looked at her through misty eyes. "What?"

"The book," she repeated. "The book that mentions Magura Cave. You said Mraz told you about it. Can you get it for us?"

"No. Everything's destroyed." He pointed at the entrance to the underground dwelling. "I can't get in."

"But I can," Diva said. "Remember how I got out of a cave-in before?"

"Oh no." Theo groaned. "Sitara."

He remembered that event. He, Diva, Pavel, Jega, and Zima had been searching for Lamia's final hidden soul so they could destroy it. They had to travel through a forest teeming with demons, and ended up at an entrance to Devil's Throat, a creepy passage to a place that reminded him of Hades. Down there, they found Sitara, a Vurkolak. The goddess Bendis had banished the man-wolf creature for the crime of trying to swallow the sun and moon. Lamia had somehow discovered him and hidden one of her souls for the creature to guard.

In the process of retrieving the soul, Theo had stabbed the beast. This had not only broken Sitara's curse, but it also had triggered an avalanche. Theo had begged Diva to help Sitara escape, but later regretted that request when she hadn't made it out before the rocks blocked the entrance. He feared she had died, crushed by boulders.

But she hadn't. Diva had managed to hide Sitara in a tunnel. She then transformed herself into a mouse and crawled to safety.

"Sitara," Theo repeated. "Did anyone go back and rescue him?"

Diva shook her head. "Not that I recall. At least not the Samodivi. With so much chaos here, no one's had the chance."

Theo kneeled beside Jega. "What about the Kukeri? Did they ever go back?"

"No, sorry," Jega replied. "Zima said it was too dangerous to have Sitara loose. He'd have to be caged again, in the castle prison, even if we had rescued him."

"But he'd be alive," Theo shouted. "He could have died of hunger and thirst down there."

"I think I agree with Diva and Jega," Pavel said. "Sitara managed to survive by eating bats and insects before. I'm sure he found food, especially since he was no longer chained."

"What's wrong with all of you?" Theo tore at his hair. "It's inhuman to treat someone like that."

"But, Theo," Diva said as she reached out and grasped his forearms. "We're not human. Our ways of justice and life are not like what you've grown up with. The law of nature rules here."

Theo stood slack-jawed. His conscience wouldn't allow him to live that way. He'd always been taught that life was precious. Something to be protected. But in nature, life and death were part of a cycle, neither good nor bad, just something that kept order and balance. Lamia and Zlo were a threat to that balance. And so was Sitara, apparently.

Theo closed his eyes and let out a deep breath. *Will I ever be able to rule this world? Will its inhabitants allow me to if I want to "humanize" Dragon Village?*

The need to help everyone in distress overwhelmed him, but he now didn't know if that would be possible—or even sensible. "Humanity" could be even crueler than nature.

Theo opened his eyes. "I-I think I understand. It's a lot to consider. Let's find the book and locate everyone else so we can figure out how to rescue Zmey."

Diva looked at him askew.

Theo could only imagine she was trying to figure out human emotions. When she'd first met him, her eyes had sparkled at the thought of meeting a human. She'd told him that she'd always wanted to meet one, to learn about the human world, which she'd only read about in books before. But how could books ever adequately explain human nature, especially to someone whose life was so different?

When he shrugged at her unspoken questions, she turned her eyes away and focused on their Kuker friend. "Jega, can you tell me where to find the book? And what it looks like?"

Jega stayed where he was and gazed at Diva with bleary eyes. "It's in one of the bedrooms, Zima's, I think. The cover has images of the solar and lunar calendars."

"Thanks." She walked to the entrance blocked by one of the fallen megaliths and got on her knees searching for an opening.

Theo joined her and tossed aside rocks and broken clay pots that had sunk into the thick ashes. "It doesn't look promising. Nothing's small enough for a mouse to get through."

"Hey, guys, over here," Pavel shouted.

They rose and shuffled their way through the rubble to where Pavel scraped aside debris to reveal a flat rock. He kicked away a pile of stones to uncover a small entrance.

"Can you squeeze through that?" Pavel asked.

"I think so."

Theo peered at it. "It looks kind of small."

"I'm sure I can get through," Diva said. "It's large enough for me to hand you a book through it, anyway. I can shift into a mouse to go in and out myself if I have to."

"Okay, might as well give it a try." Theo waved her forward.

Diva set her pouch onto the ground and put one leg into the hole, then the other. She sat on the flat rock and shimmied through the opening. Moments later, her curly head popped out of the hole. "It's so dark in there. Even too dark for me."

"I've got something you can use." Pavel searched through his backpack and pulled out a flashlight. He clicked the button to turn it on. "Here, this will help."

Diva wiggled her fingers next to her head and took the offered item. "Thanks."

She ducked back into the opening. The light flickered on and off.

Pavel stuck his head near the hole. "You better hurry. It looks like the battery's low."

"Battery?" Diva asked from the darkness.

"It's inside the flashlight. It makes the light shine."

"Oh, I thought the button you pressed did that. I've been pushing it to see how your magic works."

Theo and Pavel both laughed, and Pavel said, "It's not magic. Press the button once, and the light comes on. Press it again to make it shut off."

A click sounded from within the hole, and light illuminated Diva's face. "I'll be back as soon as I find the book."

Pavel moved away from Theo and sat on an ash-covered piece of a broken megalith.

Theo came closer. "Are you still angry with me? I said I was sorry for arguing with you."

"No, I'm fine." Pavel shrugged.

"You don't sound fine." Theo sat next to him. "Talk to me. What's bothering you? Are you still upset about the puppy?"

Theo and Pavel's friendship had been strained when they'd fought about the puppy, that ended up not being a puppy. But Theo thought they'd resolved that issue.

"No, it's not about the puppy." Pavel turned his head and stared at Theo with a blank look until Theo started squirming. Finally, Pavel spoke again. "I guess I'm tired of being the one who's always wrong. It seems like since you've become a hero, everyone idolizes you and treats me like nothing."

"I don't." Theo stopped.

He thought about what Pavel had said. Zima treated Theo with as much respect as he did anyone, but the Kuker always put down Pavel. Diva deferred a lot of decisions to Theo. Her sisters often looked at Pavel as if he were crazy. Jega seemed to be the only one who treated Pavel as clever.

Theo could understand Pavel's insecurities. In the human world, Pavel had been the golden boy, the one whom everyone went to with questions or problems. He had innumerable friends. Theo counted himself blessed that Pavel said Theo was his best friend.

On the other hand, Theo was the one whom other people put down, humiliated for his strange passions, like flying. No one wanted to know what Theo thought, no one except Pavel and Theo's mom, of course.

Now, here in Dragon Village, everything was reversed. So, yes, he sympathized with Pavel. But, they had so much at stake now that Theo didn't feel any of them could cater to Pavel's insecurities. Somehow, though, Theo would have to try. Pavel's friendship was too important to him to lose.

Theo started again, "I don't mean to come across that way. I meant it before when I said I wanted you to help me make decisions when it came time for me to rule Dragon Village."

"Maybe you could start now, instead of waiting that long." Pavel pursed his lips. "And maybe you could stop making everyone else think you're always right and I'm always wrong."

"That wasn't my intention. I—"

Coughing came from the hole Diva had entered, and Theo and Pavel got up and looked down as she reached out and laid the flashlight onto her pouch. A few books followed before she herself emerged.

She handed Pavel back his flashlight and picked up the books, hugging them to her chest. "The book we're looking for was there, plus some others I didn't want to leave behind."

Theo smiled. Diva loved books. He was certain she scoured the Kukeri living space to find as many as she could. After the devastating fire at Jabalaka's hiding place that destroyed so many that chronicled their history, she wouldn't leave unprotected any book she discovered. She wouldn't allow Lamia or Zlo to destroy any more of the knowledge of ages, the detailed history of Dragon Village and its inhabitants.

Diva placed the books into her pouch. "I want to cover the hole so no animal crawls inside."

"Why bother?" Jega trudged over, pulling a wobbly cart with a rope. Two buffaloes lowed mournfully as they ambled next to the cart. On the bed, two black hens squawked inside a wooden crate, while a rooster crowed in a second one.

"You're bringing chickens?" Pavel asked.

"What? Why are you looking at me like that?" Jega said. "Chickens are important. They'll give us eggs for breakfast and lunch. Who doesn't like eggs?"

"I'm all for eggs," Pavel said. "I just didn't expect you to have chickens. The Kukeri are so … warlike, not farmers."

Jega shrugged. "Well, even warriors need to eat."

Theo peered into the cart. The bed held ash-covered, broken weapons, an assortment of large copper bells, and frightening Kuker masks.

"Everything's ruined," Jega said. "This is all I could salvage."

"They didn't touch anything inside," Diva said as she replaced stones over the entrance.

A bit of light shone in Jega's eyes. "Nothing's destroyed?"

"No, everything seemed fine. I think since a megalith blocked the entrance, the demons weren't able to find a way in, so they kept their destruction to the outside."

"What a relief." Jega wiped a hand across his dusty forehead. "I'm—" He stopped and pointed toward Diva's belt. "Did you find that inside?"

She removed a palm-sized rag doll and handed it to him. "Yes, I found this in Zima's room on top of the book you sent me to find."

"Zima has a doll?" Pavel raised his eyebrows.

Jega snatched it away from Diva and glared at Pavel. "Yes, and don't make an issue of it. It's his favorite reminder of our mother."

Pavel backed away, putting his hands out in front of him. "I wasn't going to. I still love my baby blanket. I don't go anywhere without it."

"Don't tell me it's in your backpack," Theo said. "You complained to Kosara that she didn't have any blankets. Why didn't you use that one?"

Pavel shrugged and walked away. "Is there anything else anyone needs, or are we ready to go find the others?"

Jega shook his head. "There's nothing left. Let's go."

In silence, they walked away from the sanctuary. Jega rubbed the white star on the cow's forehead while he pulled the wagon, leading everyone to the shelter where Zima, Ula, and Sava hid. He kicked aside rocks and other debris left from the demons' assault. As they progressed beyond the smoky air, the bull wandered off of the path to munch on a clump of grass, while the cow stayed close by the Kuker's side.

Pavel ran up to Jega. "Do you want me to try to coax him back?"

With a shake of his head, Jega said, "No, Mush will be fine. He'll be along shortly. He doesn't usually stray far from Milka, his mate. But thanks for asking."

"Okay. Mind if I walk here with you?"

"That's fine, but I don't feel like talking right now."

"I understand," Pavel said. "I'll be quiet."

From behind the wagon, Theo's stomach clenched. Pavel didn't want to be near him. Once more, he was going to have to try to win back his best friend's trust. Would this back-and-forth emotional ride ever end?

A dark cloud passed overhead, and he shivered, feeling a presence more menacing than a storm. He glanced upward. A giant white creature filled the sky.

"It's Lesh," he screamed. *But that's impossible. I killed that vulture.*

Pavel echoed his thoughts. "Can't be. She's dead. It must be her mate. We have to hide."

Diva stood like a warrior, holding her bow steady. "Don't panic."

The vulture swooped down and grabbed Mush with its talons, carrying the lowing bull away high into the sky, until it became a dot.

A moan came from Jega. "Mush, Mush, not my Mush."

Theo stared at Diva with his eyes wide. "Why didn't you shoot the vulture?"

"It wasn't attacking us. It was here for a bigger prize. I don't kill creatures hunting for their food."

"But, that's not natural." Theo paced. "Don't you find it odd the vulture took a *living* creature? There must be plenty of dead animals in all this chaos that it could feast on."

"Lamia must have commanded it," Pavel said from behind them. "The bull must have been a key to us rescuing Zmey."

"How ...?" Theo stopped. It made sense. Lamia always seemed one step ahead of them. "You know, I think you're probably right. We have to hurry and get to the others so we can figure out why."

Chapter 7
Water Bull

JUNE 29

EARLY THE NEXT DAY, Theo scanned the densely packed oak forest. The leaves barely quivered in the gentle breeze, and only a few birds had begun their practice notes before the full symphony began in earnest. Others preferred to peck at bugs skittering along old, cracked bark. If he hadn't known Dragon Village was under Lamia's attack, it would have been a normal, serene morning.

Their hideaway wasn't secured by magic, but his senses told him they were safe—at least for the moment. He collected twigs to revive the coals in the fire outside the shack where they'd found Zima and Diva's sisters. The structure was less of a hut and more of a jumble of sticks woven together like a basket, with mud and grass plastered on the roof and sides. It did, however, provide shelter for Zima while he recovered from his injuries. The Kuker had been in no shape to review the book they'd retrieved from his room, but Sava had said he was recovering quickly, and they could talk with him this morning.

Boo hopped onto Theo's lap. "Seeds? Seeds for me?"

"Sorry, buddy. I didn't realize I'd be here so long. I didn't bring enough."

"Okay, okay. I'll find bugs." With that, the magpie pecked at overturned soil.

The clanking of bells startled Boo, and he flew into the sky, looking one way then the other, as if being aerial security had been his plan all along. Theo looked toward where the noise came from. Jega was by the cart, cleaning ash from his ceremonial bells.

Possibly woken by the noise, the rooster flapped its reddish-gold and black wings wide. Its red comb jiggled when the bird crowed as if proud of the sound of its voice.

Pavel jumped up from the spot where he'd been sleeping and plugged his ears. "Oh, man. He's as loud as a bugle."

Theo laughed. "Our alarm clock's not as pleasant to listen to as the Firebird, but the rooster's voice can wake an entire village."

"He woke my stomach, too." Pavel rubbed his belly. "I'm starving. I'd love some bacon and eggs."

Theo stirred the coals. "No bacon but see if the chickens have laid any eggs."

Pavel shuffled toward the wagon and stuck his hand into the crate with the chickens. Squawking and the flapping of wings followed.

"Ow!" He wrenched out his hand and sucked on it. "One pecked me. And all for nothing. No eggs."

"They won't be laying yet." Jega approached and made shushing noises. He let the chickens out, and they scrambled to the ground where they pecked at bugs. "They're too traumatized. Give them a couple of days. I have some fresh buffalo milk, though." He handed a jug to Pavel.

Pavel took a few gulps. "Now if you could find some feta cheese, we could make a warm, tasty banitsa."

"I don't have cheese, but I found these." Diva strode from the woods, cradling several large white eggs in her arms.

"My hero." Pavel rushed over and scooped up a couple to free one of Diva's hands.

She laid her load by the fire and used a stick to remove several coals. She nestled the eggs within the embers, letting them cook until the shells became charred.

Theo curled his upper lip. His stomach churned as he recalled stumbling across a burned, half-eaten creature a Harpy had left inside a fort where he had taken shelter the first time he arrived in Dragon Village.

"Don't look so disgusted." Diva snorted as she handed him a stick and another to Pavel. "Use this to spear the egg."

Pavel didn't hesitate. He poked his stick into one, pulled the crusty object from the coals, and used a knife to chip away the blackened outside. The scent of baked eggs drifted out with the steam, reminding Theo of times his mother made omelets.

"Mmmm. You gotta try one, Theo," Pavel said with his mouth full.

Theo set the stick aside and impaled an egg on his lightning-bolt knife. "Do you have ostriches here? This looks the same size as the ones I've seen in books."

"Stritches? What are they?" Diva pulled an egg apart, releasing more of the delicious aroma.

"Not stritch. Os-trich," Pavel interrupted. "It's a large bird that can't fly."

Diva shrugged. "These aren't bird eggs. They're from a lizard."

Pavel spat out the bite he'd been chewing. "A lizard? We're eating baby lizards?"

"No, just the eggs," she replied. "These weren't fertilized."

"How do you know?" Pavel choked out his words.

"I'm a Samodiva."

Theo smiled. That statement said it all. Diva, a child of nature, understood nature. She didn't need any more of an explanation.

"You should be happy I found a nest," she said. "You need to eat something before we get going. We have a long journey still."

Pavel looked longingly at his half-eaten egg, shrugged, and took another bite.

Theo's stomach grumbled. He could do this. He flicked off the burned outer edge and took a small bite. His taste buds tingled. He closed his eyes, savoring the flavor, before he took a larger bite. He finished his egg and reached for another one, but stopped when Pavel raised his hand to his mouth and made coughing noises.

"Pavel?" Theo dropped his knife by the coals and thumped his friend's back. "Did it go down the wrong way?"

"No," Pavel said. "Poisoned."

Theo frantically rubbed his hands together. He couldn't lose his best friend. "Diva, can you help him?" Even though Theo had eaten an egg, too, he worried more for his friend. Diva had already taught Theo how to force poison out of his system.

"Impossible." Diva stared at Pavel. "Some lizards here are venomous, but their eggs aren't. He must have swallowed too big a chunk. Give him a good whack on the back to dislodge it."

Pavel continued to cough and started making gagging noises. Shaking and moaning, he fell onto the ground.

"We have to give him a potion," Theo shouted as he grabbed Diva's pouch and dumped the contents onto the ground. "Find something, please."

She picked up a vial and handed it to Theo. "This won't hurt him if he isn't really poisoned, but it will counteract poison if he is. But, if he's choking, he's not going to be able to swallow it."

"Thanks." Theo sat on the ground next to Pavel. "Here, open your mouth, and I'll pour it in."

Pavel stopped moaning and started laughing. He sat up and said, "Fooled ya."

Theo gaped at him for a moment. "What the heck was that?"

"Just a joke." Pavel shrugged.

"It wasn't funny." Theo grabbed Pavel by the shirt and pulled him up when he stood. "I'll give you a whack on the back all right."

"Ha, not today." Pavel pulled away and ran into the bushes, with Theo running after him.

A little farther down the path, the ground shook, and branches on a bush flattened as a creature thundered closer.

"Run!" Pavel turned around, bumping into Theo on his way back.

Theo waited until a scaly green head protruded from the bushes. Curved horns at each side of the creature's snout pointed at him like bayonets. A foul-smelling mucus fell in globs from its jaw as it tossed its head.

Theo reached for his knife, but grasped nothing. He'd left it lying by the coals when Pavel had started choking.

"Yup, time to run." He rushed back to the campsite.

Diva had already nocked an arrow in her bow. She took aim. "The mother lizard must have followed my scent."

Pavel backed away. "That's the biggest lizard I've ever seen. It's as large as a horse."

Crouched low, the creature thudded forward out of the cover of the bushes, leaving a trail of overturned dirt like skid marks in its wake. It rose to its full height on four legs, towering over them by a foot. A growl rumbled deep in its throat as it scratched at the ground. Hissing, the lizard latched its yellow eyes onto Diva.

Theo grabbed one of the cooked eggs and threw it into the bushes beyond the lizard. When the creature swung around to race after the egg, its long, spiked tail whipped Theo's legs.

"Ow!" He pulled up his pants leg and rubbed his shin, but it hadn't cut through the skin.

"Stay here. I'll make sure it doesn't come back." Jega rushed over, now clad in his frightening Kuker mask and his waist burdened with a belt of large clanging bells.

"What's all this racket?" Zima, wrapped in a blanket, coughed as he staggered from the makeshift hut. A white cloth, spotted with blood, encircled his head like a turban, and red welts on his face stood out against the unusual pallor.

"Just our normal, everyday excitement," Theo mumbled.

Diva looked over her shoulder. "Welcome back to the land of the living, Zima. Your brother's off chasing a lizard."

Zima shook his head. "Leave it up to Jega to interrupt an amazing dream."

"Were you playing with your doll in it?" Pavel snickered but backed away when Zima inched his head around to glare at him.

Without a word, Zima reached into a bag he had looped through his belt and removed the doll Diva had found in the Kukeri living quarters. Turning the doll's sightless face toward Pavel, Zima chanted, "Kikimora doll, kikimora doll, remember that face. Remember that boy. Haunt his dreams. Give him no peace."

Pavel's face blanched, and he stumbled as he scuttled away.

Zima let out a screech and wiggled the doll toward Pavel.

"Ahhhh!" Pavel screamed and ran into the forest.

"That was mean, even for you, Zima," Theo said.

The Kuker shrugged. "This doll is not something either Jega or I *play* with." He glanced around. "And where are your sisters, Diva? I expected them to be hovering around me constantly the way they have been."

"They left early this morning to patrol the forest. They decided it was safe to leave you here with the rest of us to watch over you."

"Like I need it." Zima dropped to the ground next to Diva and speared an egg. "Mmm. Haven't had one of these in a long time."

Theo looked toward the woods, then back at Zima. "You didn't really curse Pavel, did you?"

"No, Kukeri drive away evil spirits. We don't call them forth." He paused and, with a pained expression, looked up at Theo. "But it *is* something humans do. You don't know how many times my brothers and I have had to drive away evil from houses where *real* kikimora dolls have been hidden—by humans against other humans. Our job is to protect, not to harm."

"But … you would have let Pavel get lost in the mountains when his puppy ran away. He could have been hurt."

"No," Zima said. "He was safer there, away from the battle. Jega and I would have been able to track him later."

"I still don't understand." Theo sat next to Zima. "You act like you hate him, yet you say you'd protect him because he's human."

Zima grunted. "Kukeri have always protected humans with our dances—but from a distance. I've never had to be in such close contact with one before. Now I understand why. I find them rather annoying creatures—especially if they're all like your friend."

"We're not. They're not. Pavel's one of the good ones, one of the best. He cares about people and is a protector himself. That's why …" Theo took a deep breath, wondering how Zima would take his next statement. "I wish the two of you could get along. You really have a lot in common."

Zima's mouth dropped open, but then he laughed. "For a minute there, I thought you were serious."

"I—"

Zima held up his hand to stop Theo. "You don't have to worry. Even though I can't understand why my race protects humans, I always will. That's part of who I am, what I'm here to do."

"But—"

"Have you both had enough to eat?" Diva shook her head at Theo.

He guessed she wanted him to let the topic go. Theo cast a quick glance at Zima. Was the ice king's cold heart melting? Or was this another thing about Dragon Village that revolved around the natural order of the world? Jega seemed to have a heart. But, if put into a situation that called for disrupting nature, would he, too, behave like Zima? Theo heaved a sigh. Would he ever truly understand the inhabitants of this land?

When Theo didn't say anything more, Diva added, "I hear Jega returning. We should really talk about Magura Cave now that Zima's available."

Zima and Jega settled under the shadow of an oak. Theo and Pavel stood behind Jega, while Diva leaned over Zima's shoulder as he turned pages in the book.

Pavel kept throwing frightened glances at Zima.

Theo nudged Pavel. "Don't worry. He's not looking for a spell to cast on you."

Pavel shivered but didn't respond.

Theo hadn't had a chance to tell his friend that it was all a joke, that Zima hadn't cursed Pavel. *Besides, when Pavel finds out, I'm sure he'll think it's funny. He's always enjoyed a practical joke, like the one he played on me.*

The Kukeri were still poring over the book when Sava and Ula returned from their forest patrol hours later.

"How are you feeling?" Sava asked Zima.

"Better, despite you two suffocating me with your potions."

"Speaking of which," Ula said as she walked toward the hut, "you need another dose. You're still quite pale."

She returned a moment later carrying a silver rhyton shaped like a water buffalo's head. "Here, this is the last one."

Zima got up and took the drinking vessel and smelled its contents. He held the rhyton back toward Ula. "It's wine. You know I prefer your cures mixed with water."

"The wine will make you stronger. It's mixed with honey."

Zima continued to hold it out to her, so she added, "I can give you herbs with water, but you'll have to take several more doses."

"What a whiner," Pavel mumbled so only Theo heard, or at least Theo hoped Zima didn't. "No wonder he has such a bad temper. He won't take stuff that'll make him feel better."

Whether he heard or not, Zima brought the rhyton to his lips and gulped the liquid, and then laid the vessel on the ground. "Can we now continue looking for information about Magura Cave?"

"By all means. Sava and I will patrol the forests while you look." Ula grinned at Theo. "Our friend here always brings trouble with him wherever he goes, so it's best to keep watch."

Theo laughed but knew it was true. Even with his powers getting stronger, he still didn't know how to control them so much of the time. At least he had his friends to help him out of terrible situations.

When the Samodivi sisters left, Jega pointed to a page in the book. "I found the information we needed while Ula and Zima were 'discussing' drinking water over wine."

"Great. We can finally save Zmey," Pavel said. "Then we can go home."

"Not quite yet. None of you are going to like what we found," Diva added.

"What *now*?" Theo looked at the page. He was able to pick out a few words, but his grasp of the ancient language came and went. His father's sword had awakened that ability. Actually, it was Theo's sword all along, given to Zmey to guard until Theo needed it, but he still thought of it as Zmey's.

"The good news is that we don't have to worry too much about demons or Zlo's servants," Diva said.

"So, what's the bad news?" Theo asked.

As Diva nodded to Jega to turn the page, Pavel inched closer and peered at the book. "Raunchy dunghill, what *is* that thing?"

Diva looked up, her eyes wide. "The Water Bull."

Pavel furiously shook his head. "That doesn't look like any bull I've ever seen, not even in the craziest movie I've watched. Like the one Theo and I saw last summer, after we got back home from here. Remember that one, Theo?"

Theo nodded while Pavel rambled on about more scary movies. He understood why his friend didn't want to focus on the image in the book. Pavel was right. It didn't resemble any bull he'd ever seen. But then, what creature in Dragon Village had an equivalent counterpart in Selo? None.

The creature in the picture resembled a black, hairless Minotaur, with a bull's head and human torso, but the resemblance ended there. Rippling muscles, covered with silver scales, stretched all along his body. A dolphin fin jutted off the beast's head, along with four horns, each one erect and pointing straight ahead. Even more disturbing was the fact that eyes peered from the front of his ugly head, while a second pair appeared on the back. The creature had long-spiked, hoofed feet in front, but lizard feet in back, and a Rusalka fish tail swishing beyond that. It was like a video gamer went crazy coming up with a new, hideous creature.

When Theo looked up from the image, Pavel was still babbling about movie monsters.

Theo tapped his friend on the shoulder. "Hey, I think everyone gets it."

"Thank you," Diva said when Pavel stopped talking. "I don't know what a movie is, and now I'm sure I don't want to."

"We have more important things to talk about than fake human movie beasts." Zima sat next to his brother and took back the book and looked at the passages Jega indicated.

It surprised Theo that Zima wasn't sneering or hadn't said "human" in his usual derogatory way. Maybe he was getting used to Pavel, that is, humans. More likely, though, he was too concerned with how to deal with the Water Bull that he forewent taunting Pavel. Theo hoped it was at least a little of the first reason.

"What does the book say about the beast?" Theo asked.

"The bull guards Rabisha Lake. And as far as I can tell, the quickest way to get to Magura Cave is through Dubrava Forest on the other side of the lake."

"Theo and I have hiking boots," Pavel said. "A forest shouldn't be a problem."

Zima shook his head. "It won't be that easy. Dangerous cliffs surround the forest. It's safer to use tunnels, but they're endless, and we don't have time to search them all."

"Then we can build a raft and float across the lake," Theo said.

"That's a problem, too," Zima said. "The power of the bull comes from the water. He'll know you're invading his territory the moment you approach, and he'll attack."

Theo threw up his hands. Why was Zima making him play twenty questions? "How can we get to the cave, then?"

"We'll have to entice the Water Bull to come out onto land. When he does, he'll lose his magical power, and we'll have a chance to defeat him."

"Okay." Theo nodded. "Then I can shift into a dragon and fight him."

"Not unless you have golden horns."

Jega joined the conversation. "Even that wouldn't work. The book says we need a 'great golden bull' to defeat him. Animal must defeat animal."

Zima turned to his brother. "Where are we going to get such a creature?"

"We can't, but I have an idea how to fight him." Sadness etched Jega's words, and his voice cracked when he replied, "We can improvise."

"How?"

Jega picked up the rhyton and ran his fingers along the bull's horns.

"Oh, I see," Zima said. "We have to use Milka?"

"Yes." Jega dropped the rhyton, stood, and approached the water buffalo, caressing her back.

"You can't." Pavel rushed over and wrapped his arms around Milka's neck, protecting her the way he did his deer, Whirl. "How can she save us from the Water Bull? We're doomed. Females aren't aggressive. She'll never survive that creature's attack. What else can we do?"

"It's the only way." Jega sighed. "Do you think I *want* to endanger her? I can't see that we have any other choice. The vulture seized Mush. He would have been better. He is … was aggressive, more powerful, and his horns were longer."

"Then Lamia really must have sent the vulture to take him," Theo said. "She had to know he was a key to rescuing Zmey."

Jega and Zima both nodded.

"I agree." Diva went to Pavel's side. "Don't worry about Milka. We'll all be there, fighting alongside her. And even though

Theo can't defeat the Water Bull, he can still help Milka by attacking the creature."

"But, she's just a girl."

Diva huffed. "Don't underestimate girl power. Females of many species can accomplish much more than males can." She stroked the white star on the cow's forehead. "Everything will be fine, Milka."

The cow licked Diva's free hand and bellowed as if in acceptance of her fate.

"Okay, so if we're agreed that we use Milka," Theo said, "then what's next? How do we make her into a 'great golden bull'?"

Zima looked down at the book. "We have to do several things. Cover her horns with gold. Make silver horseshoes with endurable, sharp spikes. And decorate her body with impenetrable brass shields. The book says gold is the only thing that can harm the Water Bull. So, we'll have to melt down metals first and shape the objects we need."

"We'll also have to make the Water Bull angry in order to entice him out of the lake," Jega added. "I think the best way to do that is to include bells on her disguise. The loud noise will get his attention."

"Bells are the easy part." Diva smirked. "Jega has an endless supply."

Zima added, "Which have gotten us into plenty of trouble before. But I think that's a good idea."

"Okay, so to confirm." Theo counted on his fingers. "Cow, check. Bells, check. Metals. We'll have to get what we need from the castle. Does anyone know where Zmey keeps his treasures?"

"My sisters do," Diva said. "I'm sure we can send them to get what we need."

"Great. So, metals, check," Theo said. "Then all we need is some way to make them into the objects Milka needs. How do we do that?"

Everyone went silent. Even the cow stopped lowing. Zima and Jega gave each other a questioning look, before they turned to Diva. She, in turn, shrugged and nodded.

"What?" Theo asked. "Did I say something wrong?"

"No. It's the right question." Zima stood, stretching his legs, while he clutched the book to his chest. "We need a blacksmith."

Pavel left Milka's side and came closer to Theo. "Well, you must have one here in Dragon Village. Don't you?"

"We do." Jega joined his brother standing. "Only one."

Theo's mind raced. *What's going on? Why do they continue making me ask questions? What horrible thing is going to happen now?* Out loud, he said, "Who? Let's go find him to see if he'll help us."

With a quick glance again at Jega, Zima said, "Sitara."

Chapter 8
Unsettling Sight

THEO'S DRAGON SPIRIT RAGED, wanting to be set free and roar with anger as much as Theo did. He understood—sort of—their reasoning for keeping Sitara a prisoner in Devil's Throat. If the man was still dangerous—although Theo doubted that was true—they couldn't afford to have another evil being roaming Dragon Village.

But I broke the curse, didn't I? He remembered the scene vividly.

Theo had pointed the lightning-bolt dagger at Sitara, because he had trapped Diva. A laser beam from the tip pierced the creature's stomach, causing him to convulse. The blood that gushed out turned into a hissing yellow steam, which surrounded the Vurkolak. When the mist cleared, Sitara had transformed into a young, blond-haired man, no longer a savage, howling beast.

He can't still be evil.

Even if Sitara was, Zima's declaration that Sitara was a blacksmith also overjoyed Theo. They would *have* to rescue the former Vurkolak. Sitara had become a priority because they needed the man's help. Even though Tililei Forest, where Devil's Throat lay, terrified Theo, he was going to make sure they went back. He wasn't giving the others a choice.

Straightening his posture and standing with his feet wide apart, he said, "So, when are we going to rescue Sitara?" He wanted to say so much more, but he left it at that for now, afraid that if he let his anger out, his dragon spirit would take over.

"We'll leave in the morning," Zima said in a matter-of-fact tone as he looked again at the book. "Jega and I need to go back to the Kukeri sanctuary and get gear and supplies first."

Theo's fortitude vanished. He wasn't good at trying to be authoritative or demanding. Zima had already resolved to retrieve Sitara from the cave-in. Was the Kuker remorseful, thinking they should have made an effort to free Sitara earlier?

No, I doubt it. I'd expect that emotion from Jega, but not Zima. With Zima, life is all about being practical or brute force.

Jega touched Theo's shoulder, making him jump. He hadn't seen the Kuker move. "Theo, you could help us by taking care of Milka while we're gone. I don't want to bring her back home in case the vulture returns for another meal."

"Sure, I can do that. Pavel will probably cater to her, too." Theo looked at his friend, who nodded.

Pavel seemed to be fonder of animals than people these days, and Theo wanted to include his friend whenever possible. He'd shut Pavel out too often lately, wanting to protect his friend.

I need to trust that Pavel can take care of himself. He never babied me before I found my superpowers. Pavel has his own superpower: his inventiveness.

"Thank you," Jega replied. "Would you take her down to the cheshma to get a drink while Zima and I are gone?"

"Sure thing."

Jega walked over to the cow and gave her a pat. "We'll be back soon."

"Okay, brother," Zima said as he closed the book and took hold of the cart, "let's get going."

The cart rumbled back the way they had come only yesterday. After the Kukeri brothers had disappeared into the trees, Theo approached the cow.

"C'mon, girl. Let's go get a drink."

Milka looked up from eating grass and stared at Theo with her large brown eyes, but she didn't move.

"Do you need my help, Theo?" Pavel offered.

"Su—" Theo stopped from saying he'd like to have his friend keep him company.

He'd just said Pavel would help, but right now Theo wanted a few moments away from everyone so he could think about what he was going to say to Sitara when they finally rescued him. Would the man be grateful that someone finally came? Or would he be angry that he had been left there for so long? And most importantly, would he blame Theo, since Sitara had asked for Theo's help?

"Maybe," Theo said as he looked from Pavel to Diva, "you could stay and help Diva get food for Milka for when we return from the stream."

A quick flash of emotion blinked in Pavel's eyes. Was it anger or joy? Theo thought his friend would enjoy staying with Diva. He'd always liked to be alone with her before.

"Right." Pavel turned and walked away.

"Hey, I—"

"He'll be okay. You both need a little time from each other right now." Diva handed Theo a vine rope. "But you'll need this to lead Milka. Tug gently, and she'll follow."

"Thanks." Theo wrapped the vine loosely around the cow's neck and tied off the end. He pulled his end and took a step forward. "Here we go."

The cow lowed and moved with him.

"It worked." He patted the star on Milka's forehead. "Good girl."

"Of course, it did. Did you doubt me?"

"No, not you. Just me as a leader."

"You'll do fine. You know how Zima can get."

Theo raised his eyebrows. Diva had an uncanny way of knowing just what was bothering him. He didn't want to be a leader. Or did he? He'd always been the one in the background, but now he felt he had to make the decisions. Maybe it was his powerful dragon spirit that spurred him on. Or maybe he knew that one day he would have to rule Dragon Village. He hoped that day was far in the future.

All he knew right now was that he wanted desperately to win Zima's favor. That particular Kuker brother was always so determined that his way was the best alternative. Perhaps it was. Even Mraz had left Zima in charge when the eldest Kuker had to go into hiding. But Zima could be so infuriating. If anyone's ideas aligned with his, then everything went smoothly. But if someone disagreed—as Pavel often did—or had a different approach to a situation—as Jega did from time to time—then that person would face Zima's wrath and scorn.

Maybe it's not even Zima's favor *I want.*

So much anger bottled up inside the Kuker couldn't be good for him. Theo wanted to help Zima experience a better, happier life. Wouldn't Zima have more joy if he allowed others a place within his heart and encouraged them to participate in decision making?

Theo couldn't help wondering if Zima would mess up one of these days. Would his insistence on "his" way get them into even more trouble than they'd already been? Not that Theo's actions hadn't already done exactly that. His dragon spirit stirred within him to be wary of letting Zima always take the lead. The Kuker had plenty of knowledge and determination, but his lack of compassion could doom them all.

Diva nudged Theo, bringing him back to the present. "Aren't you going to take Milka to get water?"

He focused back on his friend. "Yes, sorry. My mind wandered."

"Don't worry. Let life unfold as it will. You were born for this. I have faith in you."

"And I have faith that you'll keep Pavel out of trouble while I'm gone."

She laughed. "I'll do that."

Theo pulled on the vine rope again, and the cow moved along with him. "Uh, Diva, where's the cheshma?"

She pointed toward a gap in the trees. "Follow that path down the hill. Could you fill these with fresh water while you're there?" She handed him two clay jugs.

"Sure thing." He took them and continued toward the forest. "See you in a bit."

He stayed on the path for a short time until he came to a sharp curve, which led downward. At the base, an old oak towered over lichen- and moss-covered boulders stacked to form a small hill. On the other side, water gurgled. Theo walked along flat, step-like stones to reach the cheshma. Clear water flooded out of a stone spout and flowed into a pool like a dam, which overflowed and meandered away from the site in a winding stream. The spout had been carved to resemble the gaping mouth of a giant lizard's head. Its bulging eyes glared at Theo as if angry like the live one whose eggs they had eaten.

"At least this one can't chase us, right, girl?" Theo patted Milka. "Go ahead and drink from the pool while I fill the jugs."

As the water sloshed into the first container, Boo swooped down from the sky and landed on the lizard's head. He hopped around, twisting his tail left and right.

"Hey, Boo. I thought you were patrolling with Sava and Ula."

The magpie started speaking with a high-pitched voice, but his words all ran together.

Theo laughed. "I'm excited to see you, too, but slow down, so I can understand what you're saying."

"He's probably telling you about our cheshma," a woman's voice behind Theo said.

Boo squawked and zipped off back into the sky, stirring up dust on top of the spout. At the same time, Theo whipped around. What kind of monster had terrified Boo?

Not a monster. A hunched-backed old woman leaning on a twisted branch like a cane. In her free hand, she held a jug. She wore an immaculate white robe, tied with a belt, its buckle hidden behind her cane hand. What showed of her wavy, well-groomed, gray hair beneath her headscarf tumbled down to her shoulders.

Theo stepped back. His friends had told him this was a secluded area. "Who are you? What are you doing here?"

"Just an old woman who's thirsty, too." She held out her container toward him. "Would you fill mine as well?"

He hesitated. The woman seemed normal, not an evil threat. He probed deeper with his senses, but even though his dragon spirit stirred, it remained calm.

Milka looked up and lowed. Smiling, the woman approached. When she reached the cow, the woman touched the animal's horn. The cow quieted and lowered her head to continue drinking from the pooled water. Then she wandered away to munch on grass farther down the creek.

"Water?" The woman held out the jug she carried and gently shook it. "This cheshma is protected by Zmey. You don't have to worry. Our king would want those using it to show respect and generosity."

Theo did one more search with his senses and, not uncovering any problems, grasped the vessel she held out. He filled it and stretched his hand toward her, offering her a sip of fresh water.

Laughing, the woman grabbed the container so hard water sloshed over the edges. She threw the jug onto the ground, where it exploded into a myriad of pieces. The water fizzled and hissed as it struck the air. Lines on the old woman's face smoothed out as her skin tightened; her saggy, hunched body firmed and straightened. Her headscarf became a royal tiara, set upon golden hair streaked with black, and the stick she held turned into a golden staff topped by a dragon skull with shining ruby eyes. Worse of all, Theo's heart thudded as black-tinged red and golden scales erupted all over the woman's lower body and her legs merged into a long, slithering tail. And those eyes—those dark reptilian eyes—he'd never forget how they terrified him.

"You're so gullible, dear nephew." Lamia hissed the words at him.

Theo reached for his lightning-bolt dagger, but once more grasped at nothing. It still lay by the coals from when they'd been eating lizard eggs. *How could I be so stupid to not bring a weapon with me?*

"Now, don't be so hasty to fight me." She pointed the staff at him, piercing him with a jolt of electricity, immobilizing him.

"Why come here to kill me now, when no one can see your glory?" Theo struggled to move his arms. "You had the perfect opportunity to kill me before, but you didn't."

"Now, now," Lamia said as she circled him, "I didn't come here to kill you. I need your help."

"Why would I ever help you, you treacherous monster?" he shouted.

Anger bubbled inside him, a raging fire cascading through his veins. His arms broke free of their paralysis. He stretched them wide, calling on his dragon spirit. Feathers sprouted beneath his arms and transformed into powerful red wings. He flapped them and tried to move his legs, but they remained frozen to the ground.

Lamia threw back her head and laughed. She ran her hand along the points of her tiara. "So pathetic looking. You look like a chick that's afraid to leap from its nest because it will fall rather than fly. I don't know why I bother with you."

"Then leave me alone. Get out of Dragon Village, and take Zlo with you."

"Ah, Zlo, my master." She drew closer and ran her long nails down his cheek. "That's why I'm here. I need your help with him."

Theo sneered as he pulled away. "Why would I help you and your master?"

"You misunderstand." She leaned closer and whispered, "You're the only one who can … help me defeat Zlo."

"What kind of trick is this?" Theo flapped his wings and struggled once more to move his legs.

"Oh, please stop squirming. You remind me of a worm drowning in a puddle." She slithered away. "I told you before we could rule together. You could achieve what Zmey never did because he was weak. We'd be brilliant as a team. Now Zlo …" She paused. "He's a master of destruction. All he wants is power—"

"From what I've seen, that's all you want, too."

"No." She whirled around, her eyes black and glaring. "I want to restore Zmeykovo. This is my home. I have fond childhood memories. And this is where I fell … Well, enough of that. Will you help me or not?"

"Never. You say my father is weak, but you're wrong. His love for my mother made him strong and loyal. His people love him."

Lamia smirked. "Do they? Any kind of power breeds contempt and jealousy in those who don't hold it. Your father has worse enemies than either me or Zlo. Beware the power of love."

"I don't believe you."

"Oh, but you will when it happens to you, when *your* friends turn against you."

"They won't." He hissed and beat his wings, trying to hit her.

Lamia slithered closer, wrapping her tail around his legs, her voice taunting as she spoke. "What will you do when your human friend abandons you?"

"Pavel won't." Theo's insides churned. Already Pavel was becoming more distant. Was Lamia somehow responsible? She couldn't be. She was just projecting her own failures with Zmey onto Theo.

"What will you do when your Samodiva friend decides she wants to rule Zmeykovo?"

"She won't." Theo snorted. Now Lamia was being ridiculous. "Why would Diva want to do that?"

"Secrets, my dear. Secrets."

Lamia rubbed her belt buckle. Theo had seen that image before, when his dragon spirit battled with his aunt at the mill. Two entwined dragons eating each other's tail. Then, it had been a tattoo on her chest. What did it mean?

She laughed as she caught what he was looking at. Uncoiling her tail from around him, she said, "Yes, Zmeykovo is filled with secrets, like the ones this buckle holds. Jabalaka wasn't the only person who held the knowledge of deep, dark secrets. Even he didn't know the secret that will tear you and your Samodiva friend apart."

"You lie," Theo screamed. "You want to confuse me. You're trying to stir up trouble."

"No, I'm trying to make you see reason. I didn't believe it either when … a friend warned me about Zmey's intentions. Think about what I've said. You don't have to make up your mind now, but I assure you that you'll come to my way of thinking before this is all over."

Lamia tapped her staff on the ground. Black smoke darkened the sky, and thunder boomed. When the smoke cleared, his aunt had disappeared. Theo's wings retracted, and he lurched forward from his struggles. He slid to the ground and held his head between his hands.

She's lying. I know she's lying.

His medallion burned his chest. Theo pulled it out. "Mom, can you hear me? Lamia's lying, isn't she? Dad never betrayed her. Everyone loves him."

No voice replied. No words confirmed his beliefs. Theo hung his head and cried.

Chapter 9
Truths Revealed

JUNE 30

THE NEXT MORNING, Theo wandered around the campsite while Pavel slept. The Kukeri hadn't returned, and Diva had slipped out before the sun rose, so she could scout the area leading to Devil's Throat. Her sisters had made only a brief stop the day before to inform the group about the strange rumbling they'd heard. During the discussion, Theo remained silent; thoughts about what Lamia had said churned in his mind. He didn't want to believe his father had ever betrayed Lamia, but something in his gut told him everything was not as he believed.

How can I talk about this with my friends?

Would they understand his turmoil? Would they even know the events of the past? Diva likely wouldn't, but her sisters and the Kukeri might have heard stories about the dragon siblings.

Do I really want to find out if it's true?

Theo paced until he was by Milka's side. "Ready for another trip to the cheshma? You must be thirsty this morning."

The cow lifted her head from eating grass, lowed as if understanding, and followed Theo without prompting.

At the water site, all remained quiet. Theo searched for evidence of his aunt's presence from the day before, but nothing remained except his disquiet spirit. When Milka finished drinking, he led the cow back to the campground, where he found Pavel slumped at the base of the oak tree. His friend's face was pale and his eyes bloodshot.

Theo joined him. "You look awful. With all your moaning last night, I bet you slept as badly as I did. Did the lizard egg make you sick after all?"

Pavel shook his head. "No, it wasn't the food. I dreamed that Kikimora kept dragging me into the swamp. Over and over again, she dug her sharp claws into me, telling me how tender she was making me, so she could make a Pavel-and-chicken soup."

"I don't think she'd really do that." Theo recalled the scrawny, untidy being they'd met in their travels. She had chickens running around her home in the swamp, and with her chicken feet and bill-like face, she herself resembled the birds. Although she had befriended Theo, he really wasn't certain Kikimora wouldn't try to harm Pavel. Theo was sure she had been the one who had dragged Pavel off the path as they approached her home.

"She would, too." Pavel threw Theo a sour look. "This is Zima's fault for cursing me. I've never had such a terrible time sleeping."

Theo slapped his forehead. "Sorry, I completely forgot to tell you. I was so upset about Sitara." And other matters he didn't want to talk about.

"Tell me what?"

"That Zima didn't really curse you. It was a joke. A sick one, but still a joke." Theo laughed, hoping it would ease the tension, but Pavel's face remained stern. "It's funny, right? You've always enjoyed practical jokes, even if they're pulled on you."

Pavel grunted. "It's *not* funny. Zima doesn't joke. I've never even seen him smile."

"He's not as bad as we think. He just needs to learn how to lighten up." Theo told Pavel about his conversation with the Kuker. How the Kukeri normally only dealt with humans from the distance. How the brothers had to resolve curses that humans cast on each other.

"Zima may fool you," Pavel argued, "but I still believe he cursed me. We have to do something to reverse it, or I'll go insane."

"I don't think—"

"What are you two making so much noise about this time?" Diva strode into the clearing, her arms loaded with fruit and mushrooms.

"I know what to do." Pavel jumped up. "I'm going to ask Diva for one of her potions. I'm sure at least *she'll* believe me."

Pavel sped off toward Diva. His hands gestured wildly, and his lips moved at a frantic pace. From time to time, he placed the back of his hand against his forehead. Theo wanted to laugh at the dramatics of the gestures. It would have been something he could tease Pavel about if they already didn't have issues between them.

Theo couldn't hear Diva's response, but she shook her head slightly, as if trying to dissuade Pavel. She was probably telling him the same thing Theo already had.

Sighing, Theo got up, discouraged that his earlier conversation about the curse hadn't gone as expected. He joined his friends and ticked off one more item to add to his list of things that seemed to be alienating him from Pavel.

"I'd really like to give you chamomile," Diva said as she looked through her pouch, "but I don't have any at the moment. You'll have to settle for tea made with lavender."

"Anything," Pavel said. "Just as long as it cures this curse."

"I've already told you it won't cure a curse." Diva pulled a vial with dried leaves in it. "It'll calm you down and help you sleep. You can take some more tonight."

Pavel stared at her with a puppy-dog look. "But you *can* find something that will cure me, can't you?"

"Getting rid of curses takes special herbs and a complex ritual, much like what Kikimora did to cure Theo. She could help."

"No," Pavel screamed. "I'm never going back there. I'd rather beg Baba Yaga if everything else fails."

"It may come to that, but let's hope not." Diva heated water on the coals and dropped the dried herbs into it to seep. "That treacherous old witch might still be stuck in the fortress torture room. Even if she's not, who knows if she'll be willing to help us since we left her there."

AFTER THEY'D EATEN and Pavel had drunk his lavender tea, the trio waited for the Kukeri's return. Birds of prey and a magpie flew above them from time to time, and Diva waved. Her sisters and

Boo continued to make sure the area was secure. Theo wondered how it could be with all the noises they'd been making while they were here. He shivered. Lamia already knew where they were, so what did noise matter? He'd thought about it while they all sat in silence. There had to be more to what Lamia had said than she let on. He wished he knew what game she was playing. First, she didn't kill him when she had the chance, and now she was trying to win him over to her side again. Or so she said. Maybe now was a good time to talk with Diva about his encounter with his aunt.

"Diva," he said, "remember how we all heard that thunder?"

"It was only yesterday. Why would I have forgotten already?"

"That's not what I meant. It's just a way of bringing up the subject again."

"I don't care about thunder." Pavel got up. "I'm going to sit in the dark shack for a while. I have a terrible headache."

"Hope you get better soon," Theo said, but Pavel didn't reply.

After Pavel stepped inside, Diva asked, "What about the thunder did you want to talk about?"

"I know what caused it." Theo waited for Diva to ask what it was, but she just looked at him expectantly. "It was Lamia."

Still, Diva said nothing.

Theo felt as if he were in an interrogation room, where the cops said nothing, letting the suspect ramble on, eventually confessing his crime. But Theo hadn't committed a crime. Well, not a criminal one. The only thing he could be accused of was not trusting everyone with his concerns. They were his friends, after all, and they would understand and help him through his doubts.

Taking a deep breath to calm himself, Theo spilled his guts. He poured forth everything Lamia had said and everything she had implied. Not stopping there, he told Diva all his doubts and fears not only about his father, but what she and the others would think about him.

Silence reigned. Theo took a stick and poked at the dying embers. He waited. This time, he'd force Diva to be the one to speak.

Finally, she did.

"So, that's why we heard thunder. Thanks for clearing up that mystery." She rose and wiped dirt off of her clothing. "We should pack, so we're ready to leave when the Kukeri return."

"Wait." Theo jumped up and blocked her way. "That's all you're going to say about it? You're not going to tell me what a bad friend I am for not telling you sooner? You're not going to tell me Lamia was lying? You're not going to tell me there's nothing to worry about?"

She tilted her head to the side, a questioning look on her face. "What more do I need to say? I thought you just wanted to ease your mind."

"Tell me what you think, please." He folded his hands together like praying.

"First, you've already tortured yourself enough about thinking you're a bad friend. I can't believe that anything Lamia knows would end our friendship. Okay?"

"Yes, I think so." It was difficult to get rid of the gnawing doubt eating away at his gut.

"Second, we both know that beast Lamia never tells the truth, or she distorts the truth until it becomes a lie. Right?"

Theo gave a little nod.

"Then why worry yourself sick believing a tiny bit about what she said?" Diva asked. "You're going to drive yourself crazy the way Pavel is doing, and then I'll have to keep an eye out for both of you."

"You're right, of course. I just—"

"I know I am. Let's get our stuff together, so we can go save Sitara. I'll wake Pavel." Diva stepped around Theo and went into the makeshift hut.

A rumble grew along the path where the Kukeri had left. The brothers were returning with gear to help them remove the debris from the cave-in. Theo felt as if a wall had grown up between him and Diva. Her words didn't reassure him; they lacked the warmth and compassion he was used to hearing from her when he was troubled.

Has she gotten tired of solving my problems?

Or had something in the words Lamia spoke resonated with Diva? She could be keeping a secret from Theo, one that now made sense to her.

What they all needed was time to relax and sort out their emotions. So much had happened in so little time, and they were most certainly going to encounter more problems.

Am I going to lose all my friends before this quest to save my father is over?

Chapter 10
A Tale of Terror

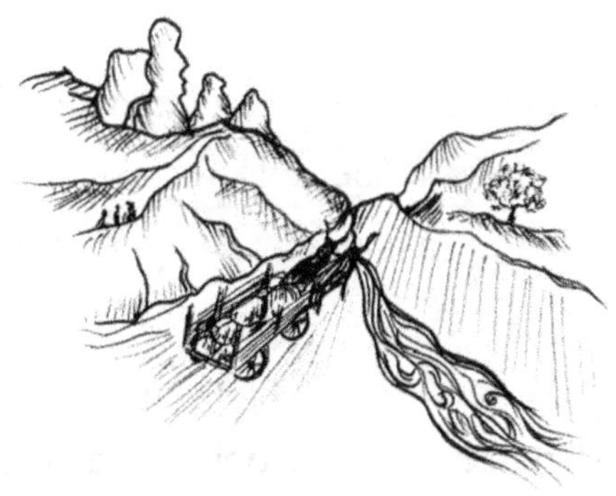

THE CART, LADEN WITH WEAPONS, ropes, tools, barrels, and more, rumbled into the clearing, with Jega pulling it by the handles. He set it down near the cow. Not a drop of sweat dripped down his face.

"How's my girl doing?" He stroked Milka's side and gently tugged the rope.

She lowed and positioned herself in front of the cart, allowing Jega to hitch her.

"What'd you do? Clear out your home?" Theo asked.

Jega laughed. "No, mostly essentials for rescuing Sitara."

"Where's Zima?"

"He's coming." Sadness crossed Jega's eyes. "He's still not healthy."

Soon, Zima staggered down the path. When he reached them, he coughed and leaned against the cart. "Is everyone ready to leave?"

Diva returned with Pavel. "Yes."

Jega turned to his brother. "Zima, you're weak and need to rest. Do you want to ride?"

Zima nodded and climbed onto the bench and covered his shoulders with a blanket.

Pavel gazed at the full cart and glared at Zima. Under his breath, he said, "I'd love to be able to take a nap in the back. I'm still exhausted from last night. But no one cares about my health."

"Didn't the herbal tea that Diva gave you help?" Theo asked. "I'm sure she could make more as soon as we stop."

Pavel shrugged. "I don't feel quite as jumpy, but I'm still tired."

"I'm sure you'll get your 'cozy bed' back when we stop for the night." Theo remembered how they'd found Pavel asleep in the cart once before.

"I suppose." Pavel's shoulders slumped.

Theo wanted to bring back the happy, joking friend he knew. He hated seeing him so depressed. Maybe he could make Pavel laugh. "If you like the cart so much, maybe Jega will let you take it back to Selo with you."

A small snort escaped Pavel. "Yah, maybe."

As Jega topped the cart with the crates for the hens and rooster, he gave Pavel a sideways glance. "Under normal circumstances, I wouldn't hesitate to make a spot for you to climb into the cart. For now, we have to be careful not to overload it. It's meant for two buffaloes to pull, but we have only Milka. She can get overtired and sick if we add a lot of extra weight for her to pull."

Pavel lowered his head. "Sorry for being so whiny."

"No, I understand." Jega laid a hand on Pavel's shoulder. "It's just that for Zima to willingly admit he's ill is a big deal. That tells me he needs to ride."

"Let's be on our way if everything's loaded." Zima snapped the harness ropes and Milka lumbered toward the path.

Theo stopped Pavel before he could follow. "Pavel, I do believe you about the curse, you know. We'll find a way to get rid of it."

"I'd like to burn that doll." Pavel clenched his fists.

"I think we'll be able to fix the problem without doing that."

Theo could only imagine worse problems if anyone dared touch the doll that had belonged to Zima's mother. He understood the pain of losing something that reminded him of someone he loved. It had been difficult to give up a kaval his Samodiva mother had once possessed. At least now Theo had her scarf. He touched his backpack, where he'd placed the gift.

"Hey, you two," Diva called out. "You'd better hurry or you won't know where we're going."

Theo glanced her way. The cart had already disappeared, and Diva stood at a bend in the path.

"C'mon, pal." Theo tugged on Pavel's sleeve. "We can find out more about the Water Bull from Diva while we're walking. That should keep your inquisitive mind awake."

They ran to catch up. Before they had a chance to speak, Diva said, "Stay with me and keep your eyes and ears open. I didn't detect Navi or Zlo's other demons when I checked out the way earlier this morning, but we *are* heading toward Tililei Forest."

"The forest of demons." Theo's heart raced at the memory. "How could I ever forget that adventure." The demons there preyed upon his mind, trying to lure him off the safety of the path, so they could physically harm him. The demons had tormented Theo, making him believe his sister, Nia, was lost in the forest and dying.

Pavel asked, "Boo and your sisters will warn us, won't they, if any monsters approach?"

"Boo will, but my sisters had to go check on the progress the other Samodivi are making keeping the portals to the human world closed." Choking back the tears, she continued, "And battling the demons destroying my world. My sisters have made shelters to treat wounded animals and people, but the devastation is across Zmeykovo. There's only so much Sava, Ula, and the other Samodivi can do to keep everyone safe."

"We'll make this right," Theo said.

He and Pavel walked slowly on either side of Diva southward toward Devil's Throat, which lay in the heart of Tililei Forest. The cart rumbled onward, with the steady thudding of Milka's feet.

Finally, Theo couldn't bear his friends' silence. "Diva, can you tell us more about the Water Bull?"

"What would you like to know?"

"Anything," Theo replied. "All we know is what he looks like and the best chance we have to defeat him is with a 'golden bull.' But first, we have to entice him out of the water to drain his magical powers."

"Yah," Pavel said, "that's not a lot to go on."

"He's a beast that not only terrorizes people, but also cattle," Diva said. "He's been known to mate with female buffaloes, but the calves are born weak and deformed. They never live for more than a day because they can't survive on land or in the water."

Pavel gasped. "He won't try to mate with Milka, will he?"

"I doubt it." Diva shook her head. "He normally kills livestock that grazes near the lake. So, if he thinks she's a bull, he'll want to fight her, not love her."

"Thank goodness." Pavel wiped away pretend sweat from his brow. "Not that I want her to fight either."

"Anything else?" Theo asked.

Diva nodded. "He also causes pestilence among cattle. And when he thrashes in the water, he creates flooding that destroys crops."

"Where did a creature like that come from?" Pavel asked.

Diva stroked her chin. "Let me tell you the legend I've heard about him. Ages ago, before Bendis claimed this land for all mystical creatures," she began, "the son of a powerful Zmey—"

"Another Zmey, not my father, right?" Theo asked.

Diva nudged Theo in the ribs. "No, not your father, but try to be quiet so I can tell you."

"I apologize. I won't interrupt again."

Diva looked at Pavel next.

He held his hands up as if surrendering. "I didn't say a thing and didn't plan to."

Diva began again. "Dragons have existed for thousands upon thousands of years, long before humans came into the world. The first Zmey born in this land was the son of a powerful dragon. Now, the father wasn't an ordinary dragon."

Diva paused and glanced from Theo to Pavel. She lowered her voice as she continued saying, "No, this dragon came from a different galaxy."

"An alien?" Theo and Pavel both said at the same time.

Diva scowled. "I'll never finish if you keep interrupting."

"Sorry, sorry," Theo said. "But you have to admit we couldn't have expected that."

"Not at all." Pavel shook his head vigorously.

"Well," Diva continued, "about three million years ago, the father appeared like a blazing star, shooting across the sky. He crashed into the ground, creating a bottomless pit. Thunder and lightning covered the land for many days. As the rains came, they filled the crater with water, which is our Rabisha Lake."

"If it's bottomless, how could it be filled?" Pavel asked.

Diva's scathing look made him press his lips tight together. "It's a legend. It's what people believed at the time." She took a deep breath. "To finish the story, no one knows the nature of the son's conception, but as you've seen, he has the appearance of a bull, a man, and a giant fish."

"He's certainly one ugly fellow." Pavel shivered.

"Even so, he demanded sacrifices of young, beautiful women."

Theo stuttered. "And p-p-people gave them to him?"

It shouldn't surprise him. People in his culture, and others around the world that they'd studied in school, did things that today people thought were inhuman. *Perhaps in the future, people will look at what our society believes and consider us primitive and barbaric as well*, he thought.

"Unfortunately, yes," Diva said. "The beast terrified the people with its mighty roar, and it devoured their animals that came too close to the shore. Finally, the people discovered that the beast appeared to be appeased after he'd seized a young woman. From that point on, they offered an annual sacrifice to the Water

Bull. They'd form a procession and sing and dance their way to the lake, where they'd put the girl onto a boat filled with other gifts for the beast. They set it adrift and left her to her fate."

Pavel took off his glasses and wiped them on his shirt. "Maybe she managed to escape. If she had a boyfriend, I'm sure he'd come back to rescue her. I know I wouldn't let someone I cared about be used as a sacrifice."

Diva smiled at him. "I believe you would create some gadget to save your girlfriend."

"What?" Pavel jumped back, his face turning red. "No, I didn't say I had a girlfriend. I just meant anyone special to me. My family, friends, you guys."

Theo suppressed a grin and refrained from commenting. Awkwardness replaced Pavel's gloominess. The crush he had on Diva was still evident.

"Anyway," Diva continued, "the legend says that one day the most beautiful girl ever born was sent off to the Water Bull. She was so gorgeous he fell in love with her and asked his sister—"

"He had a sister?" Pavel asked. "I hope she wasn't as ugly as he was."

Diva shrugged. "No one ever said. But the story goes that his sister was a sorceress, and she made the sacrificial girl immortal, so she could live with the Water Bull forever underwater."

"I wonder if we have to worry about him, then," Theo said. "If he's content now, he might let us get through to the cave."

"I doubt it," Diva said. "Remember, this is just the legend. The real monster still terrorizes people. He's not a kind-hearted lover who will listen to your pleas to save your father. He's a monster that eats cattle and tears apart people."

"That must be why Zlo put my father there, to make sure he would never be able to escape."

Pavel replaced his glasses. "Maybe we don't really even have to worry about him at all."

"Why do you think that?" Theo asked. "From what Diva and the Kukeri told us already, he's not kind."

"No, what I'm saying is maybe he doesn't really exist." Pavel's eyes took on a faraway look. "Maybe *all* of it is a legend."

Theo slapped his hand on his head. "Oh, no. Now we're in trouble."

"What's going on?" Diva waved her hands in front of Pavel's face, but he didn't respond. "What's wrong with him, Theo?"

"Nothing really. He gets this way when he's going to start rambling about something intellectual, which may or may not be completely true. He goes on like a boring textbook."

Diva raised her eyebrows. "You find books boring?"

"No, no no. Just some we have to read for school are dry and unimaginative."

Pavel started his spiel, interrupting them. "Legends are often based on reality, but skewed, since the people telling the tales were trying to explain some unusual phenomenon. In particular, folklore adapts facts about nature."

"Is there any way to stop him?" Diva asked.

Theo shook his head. "We just have to let him get it all out."

"People take those facts," Pavel continued, "and apply them to what they do know, creating a new phenomenon that explains the inexplicable."

"Should I play along?" Diva asked. "And ask questions the way the two of you do when I'm telling you a story?"

"Why not?" Theo shrugged. "I think he can hear, but he only processes what he wants."

"Pavel," Diva asked, "so what is this new phenomenon, I think that's what you said? How does it relate to the Water Bull not being real?"

Pavel's glazed eyes opened wide, and he grinned. "Great question. I was just getting to that."

"Unlikely." Theo snorted. "He usually goes on and on before he makes his point."

"Shh." Diva poked Theo. "I want to hear what he has to say."

"I'll go point by point." Pavel held up his index finger. "First, you mentioned the birth of deformed calves. This all has to do with fertility. Rural people were obsessed with the topic, not only with their livestock, but also with people. Births, marriage, death, all had an underlying focus on preserving the community. Traditions—"

"Water Bull," Theo said just short of shouting, "Focus on the Water Bull, please."

"Uh, yah." Pavel scratched his head. "Well, people depended on their livelihood from their produce and animals. So, when their animals became sick, that would mean death to the people. It went against the accepted norm, I guess."

"You guess?" Diva said.

"Well, anyway," Pavel responded as he held up a second finger, "along the same lines, farmers had to blame natural disasters on something, so they invented beasts like the Water Bull. Diseases ravaging your cattle? Must be a demonic creature. Flooding? That creature has to be angry, and you better do something to appease it. From that, they created new rituals and traditions to—"

"Pavel." Theo tapped his friend on the shoulder. "Focus. Water Bull only. Or we'll be listening all day."

"Okay, okay." The sightless gaze of Pavel's eyes dimmed. "Where was I?"

"Your next point, if you have one," Diva responded.

"Let's see. Point three … has to do with the Water Bull killing livestock near the lake."

"Go on," Theo said. "What does that mean, in simple terms?"

"That was a way to prohibit people from grazing their animals near the water," Pavel said. "Water was sacred then. Still is essential today. But back then, people worshiped water and the creatures they thought lived in it. They'd have to offer even more sacrifices to the monsters because they offended them. This offense would be another reason for cattle pestilence. The creature got angry and made the livestock diseased if he didn't outright kill them."

"That's all quite interesting," Diva said. "Do you have any more points?"

"Uh, no. I guess I'm done." Pavel's eyes returned to normal.

"That's good." Diva pointed to a grove ahead of them, where the Kukeri brothers sat on the ground, while Milka grazed. "Because we've reached the edge of Tililei Forest. It's best to be quiet now and not think about anything that's bothering you."

How's that going to be possible? Theo thought. *I have so many problems to think about. I can concentrate the way Diva taught me, to block out the voices, but what about Pavel?*

He took a quick look at his friend. Pavel's face had paled, and his lips trembled.

How is Pavel going to put aside the fear of his curse? And who knows what else is going on in his mind.

Out loud, Theo said, "Diva, do you think you could make more of your Samodiva tea? I could use something to ease my nerves."

Chapter 11
Return to Devil's Throat

A HOWLING SCREECH from Tililei Forest shattered the silence. In the cart bed, the chickens squawked and ran into each other in their crate, and the rooster crowed. The cow raised her head and pointed her ears toward the direction of the sound, her tail rapidly swishing. Jega got up and ran his hands down Milka's side, shushing the agitated cow.

Theo's gut clenched as he swallowed the "It's unusually quiet" remark he'd been about to make. All the soothing effects of Diva's tea had been wasted.

Better to be tense and on alert than super-relaxed when we pass through the demon forest, I guess.

On the ground next to him, Pavel, his head bowed, squirmed and fidgeted with his backpack. A small moan escaped his lips.

"It'll be okay, Pavel," Theo said. "Take a deep breath and think about all our fun adventures in Selo. Remember when you made me wings, and I crashed to the ground? Thinking back, it's rather funny I thought I could actually fly that way, right?"

Pavel shrugged. "Just another of my failures."

"No, it wasn't. You said I was in the air longer than my last attempt."

"And you know that's not true. I can't do anything right."

Theo grasped Pavel's shoulders and turned his friend to face him. "You *can* do things right. You got us here, didn't you? How many other people that you know could have done that? *None.*"

"Maybe …"

"No maybe about it, Pavel. You have a special talent. Never forget that."

Diva stepped over to them. "Guys, we should get going. It's already midday, and we don't know how long it'll take to find Sitara."

Theo and Pavel grabbed their gear. Pavel's head hung low, and he shuffled along beside Theo and Diva.

"Pavel, please snap out of it," Theo begged. "You've been in the forest before. You know how the demons made me believe things that weren't real, things that bothered me. You need to clear your mind and think of something pleasant. Please try."

"I am," Pavel mumbled.

"Maybe he should stay here," Zima offered, this time without sounding sarcastic and throwing his taunting "human" into the conversation. "It'll be safer."

Pavel jerked his head up. "No, I'm going with the rest of you."

"I agree with Pavel," Diva said. "It's no safer for him to stay here by himself than it is for him to enter the forest." She turned toward Pavel and whispered something into his ear.

Pavel's face turned bright red, and he burst out laughing.

Good for Diva, Theo thought. *She has a special way with Pavel, to get him to relax without using tea.*

"You can do this, Pavel." Diva smiled. "Just think about what I told you."

He nodded and stood with his head held high.

"Are we all set?" Zima asked.

Diva nodded. "Ready to go."

Theo added, "Make sure we all stay as close together as possible and keep our eyes and ears open for trouble."

"Don't forget, I can hear a ladybug's breath and see grass growing," Diva said in all seriousness.

Beside her, Pavel snickered.

I can, too, Theo thought, *thanks to my dragon superpowers.* But he didn't need to mention that. Doing so felt like it would be rubbing something else into Pavel's nose, and Theo didn't want to make his friend feel any more inferior than he already did.

Zima climbed into the cart seat while Jega hitched Milka. With Jega's gentle coaxing, the cow lumbered toward Tililei Forest. Theo, Pavel, and Diva followed. Keeping Pavel sandwiched between him and Diva, Theo looked at his friend. Sweat coated Pavel's forehead, and his body trembled. On the other side, Diva kept such a tight grip on Pavel's wrist that his skin turned as pale as hers.

Good. I'm glad she'll make sure he doesn't bolt into the forest. The way I did. Theo remembered the danger he'd put everyone in when he'd left the path, following the distressed voice of his sister—which ended up being a demon misguiding him.

Theo took one last look around the sunny grove where they'd rested. Northward, black smoke poured from Cherna Mountain, while south of that, smoldering pillars dotted the area that must be around the Cold Marsh. Besides those, no other signs of devastation were visible from the edge of the forest.

Darkness—and dread—overtook Theo the moment he stepped in among the trees. The evil presence of the waiting demons pressed down on him. Lurking. Waiting. Glowing red eyes and panting came from all directions, but no demons approached or whispered to him this time. Regardless, he placed his hand on the hilt of his sword.

This way through the woods lacked a clear path like the one they had followed the first time they ventured within. The cart clunked and rattled as Milka pulled it over roots and rocks, juggling the weapons and tools inside the bed. All the while, Jega hummed and coaxed the animal forward. The chickens and rooster had become surprisingly quiet.

"Jega, do you know how to get to Devil's Throat?" Theo said as loudly as he dared, hoping not to attract more demons. "The last time, the light from my dagger showed us the way."

"And protected us from the demons coming onto the path," Pavel muttered.

"Yes, I know the way. A Kuker never forgets." Jega stopped, bringing Milka to a halt. "I can do something about protection— and light."

"What do you have in mind?" Theo asked. "You're not going to look for a branch to use as a torch, are you?"

"No, something even better."

Jega flexed his fingers and rubbed his palms together. He raised his hands above his head, his thumbs touching. With a quick circular motion, he parted his hands and brought them back together. Instantly, a ring of fire surrounded them.

Screeches and hisses erupted from within the darkness beyond the circle. Grotesque shadows danced in the glow of the light. Theo could only imagine what the physical beings they belonged to looked like. He hoped never again to venture out there to find out.

"There," Jega said, "that ought to keep the demons at bay."

Theo stared at the dancing flames. Jega's ability to create fire never ceased to amaze him. He could understand Pavel's insecurities. Theo himself felt insignificant in comparison to Jega. To Zima, too, for that matter, with his ability to control ice. What was shifting into a dragon compared to that?

"Um," Pavel said, "we're stuck. We'll get burned if we move."

"No, you won't. Watch." Jega patted Milka on the side. "Let's go, girl."

The cow, surprisingly unaffected by the nearness of the flames, plodded onward. As she moved, the fire kept the same distance in front of her.

Theo looked behind him, expecting the fire to be creeping forward. It remained in position, not moving until he, Pavel, and Diva took a step forward.

"How cool is that?" Pavel exclaimed. "It's a fire Slinky."

Theo closed his eyes and said a silent "thank you" to anyone who'd listen. If Pavel remained preoccupied with the fire, likely trying to figure out its mechanics, then he'd be safe traveling through the forest. He wouldn't be focusing his thoughts on his troubles.

A tap on Theo's arm made him open his eyes. Diva gave him a quick nod and gestured toward Pavel. Theo took it to mean she also believed their friend would be okay. As proof, she removed her hand from around his wrist. Even if Pavel did become frightened and bolt, the protective fire shield would keep him within their grasp. Perhaps that had been Jega's intent all along.

"Let's get going to catch up with the Kukeri." Diva took a step forward. "We don't need to see how far this circle will stretch."

Pavel remained, mesmerized by the flames.

Theo nudged him. "Coming?"

"Huh?" Pavel blinked. "Oh, yah. Let's go."

All the way there, Pavel kept testing the bounds of the fire. No matter how quickly or slowly he approached the flames, they remained the same distance away. He even tried walking toward it backward. When he looked over his shoulder, he pursed his lips. The distance hadn't changed.

Before long, they reached the pile of boulders covering the entrance to Devil's Throat. Theo sighed in relief. Not only because Jega had found the place, but because they'd made it without the demons attacking him and his friends mentally or physically.

Theo scratched his head. *I wonder if Jega's flame deterred the fiends' thoughts as well.*

Jega raised his hands as before, and the fire blinked out. "Who's ready to start tossing rocks?"

"Huh?" Pavel said. "I thought you and Zima would do your one-two fire-and-ice routine, where you froze the boulders, then heated them so they exploded."

"Just kidding." Jega laughed. "Zima's too weak. That's why we brought tools that will haul the rocks away this time."

Pavel wiped his hand across his brow. "Whew, glad to hear that."

"So, let's get to it." Theo poked his head into the cart bed. "What do we start with?"

"Hey, guys," Diva shouted from the side of the rock pile, "maybe you won't even have to do that. There's already a hole. Looks like the rocks settled enough to let us in here."

Theo dropped the shovel-like tool he'd picked up and ran over. Jega and Pavel followed, while Zima remained on the cart seat, his head between his hands.

"Is he going to be okay?" Theo asked.

Jega nodded. "He was hasty to dismiss Ula's potions. I think he only needs one more to recover quicker."

"Serves him right," Pavel muttered, then pointed to the hole. "It needs to be a little larger for us to fit."

"You're coming in with us?" Theo asked.

Pavel snorted. "Of course. Did you think I'd stay out here and babysit the sick boy? Jega can do that."

"That was my plan," Jega said. "Not that Zima needs someone here, but it's better to have two of us out to ward off any danger."

After the four of them cleared away stones, Pavel removed a flashlight from his backpack. "I'll stay in the middle to light the way, so no one stumbles." He swung around, pointing the light at Diva.

"Unless I'm blind by the time we get there." She shoved his hand away. "Please get that thing out of my face."

"Oh, sorry." Pavel lowered the flashlight and stepped back.

"Worry about yourself seeing, not me." Diva swept back her curls. "I can see at night and hear sounds from miles away. Don't forget that I'm a Samodiva. I see great distances, fly high in the sky, and … can hear your thoughts. So be careful."

Pavel's face flushed.

Diva laughed. "Just kidding about hearing your thoughts."

Pavel let out his breath in a whoosh. "Thank goodness. I know you both have great eyesight and don't need my flashlight. I'm thinking of a way to invent new glasses with miniature LED lights powered by the sun so I can see as well as you do."

"Great idea," Theo said. "For now, at least you have the flashlight." He entered the darkness, followed by Pavel, then Diva.

Even though the frightful gaping maw, resembling a throat with jagged stone fangs lining its mouth, no longer existed at the entrance, and screeches and growling ceased to filter up from the depths of the tunnel, the passage downward felt even more sinister to Theo than before. It wasn't surprising the place was named after the Devil. It felt as if he was entering the throat of a monster, whose shadows crushed the breath out of him.

It must be because my new dragon abilities make me overly sensitive to my surroundings. I can feel evil.

Behind Theo, Pavel was talking to Diva about the rock formations that had survived. The words bounced off the walls and beat against Theo's head.

"Can you speak softer? It's giving me a headache." Theo rubbed his temple. "But more importantly, the echoing might irritate Sitara. We want him to come with us peacefully, and if he's annoyed, he might attack us instead."

"It'll be for his own good to come with us," Pavel shot back in a quieter voice. "Why wouldn't he?"

"You never saw him." Theo cringed remembering Sitara's beast form: fangs, fur, glowing eyes, and all. "Don't forget we're talking about a man who was a monster, maybe still is. The dagger changed him back to human form, but from what everyone's been saying, he's probably still a monster."

"Do you really believe that?" Pavel asked. "You're the one who was so upset Sitara was left here."

Theo stopped and turned around. "I don't know what to think. But the sooner we reach him, the sooner we'll find out."

"And don't forget," Diva added, "he's been locked in the darkness for years. Even if he's still in human form, he would have lost his human side a long time ago."

"Hopefully at least a small bit of his humanity remains, so he can be rehabilitated," Theo said.

"If he's not a beast, though, I think we can persuade him to come when we explain what we need," Pavel said.

"I don't know." Theo shook his head. "We … I left him here. Will he listen to anything I have to say? Whatever form he's in, it's not going to be easy, but we have to let him know we're coming in peace to help him. And that means being quiet."

"We won't know until we find him," Pavel whispered. "When we do, if he's not going to come peacefully, we'll think of a clever way to get him out of here. He might be stronger than us, but we're much smarter."

"At least you are." Theo didn't feel clever. His stomach churned not knowing what state they'd find Sitara in, or if he was even alive.

"We'll find out soon enough," Diva said. "The passage I left him in isn't too far away. Let's get going."

They walked down until she told them to stop.

"How do you know this is the right tunnel?" Pavel asked.

She gave him *that* look, one Theo had seen many times. Not from Diva, but from his mother. A look that told him the answer should be obvious, when to him it wasn't. Parents never saw things the same way their children did.

Without saying another word, Diva zipped down the tunnel.

Theo and Pavel waited. And waited. And waited.

"Diva?" Pavel finally said into the tunnel. "Where are you?"

It felt like hours later before she returned. Alone.

"Is he … is Sitara … dead?" Theo's voice quavered.

"No." Diva shook her head. "He's not there."

"He has to be here somewhere," Theo said. "That hole wasn't big enough for him to have crawled out. Let's look down these other passages."

They each disappeared into a tunnel. As Theo traveled down his, the air became thinner and hotter. The passage seemed to go on forever. Finally, he gave up.

There's no way Sitara can be in here. It's impossible to exist this deep for long.

He returned to find Diva and Pavel had returned. Without Sitara.

"Nothing." Theo laid his head against the rock wall. "What do we do now?"

"Maybe we should give up," Pavel said. "Find another blacksmith. Someone—"

"Shh." Theo held up a hand to Pavel.

A slight vibration tickled Theo's skin that lay against the stone. It stopped, then a moment later happened again. Theo tapped into his dragon senses, searching farther down into the pit. A sound. Like the jingle of chains.

He removed his head from the stone. "Someone's down there, in the pit of Hell. It must be Sitara."

Without waiting for his friends to reply, Theo tore away down the rock pile with a speed he didn't realize he had. Pebbles crashed against the walls, and a cloud of dust rose around him. In what now sounded like miles behind Theo, Pavel coughed and spluttered.

Sorry, friend. I have to see if that's Sitara down there. If it were the former Vurkolak, Theo didn't want his friend too close, in case everyone was right, and Sitara was still dangerous. *I can protect myself now, and so can Diva, but Pavel wouldn't stand a chance.*

Theo stopped at the bottom, in front of the sulfur pit that separated him from the small cave where they'd found Sitara chained to the wall. Before, only a thin ledge had enabled him and Diva to cross the pit. Now, so many rocks had fallen into the pit that an easier path lay in front of him. He looked back. Diva and Pavel were getting closer.

I have to go across now before they get here.

Again, the jingle came from the darkness in the direction of the cave.

Theo leaped across in as few steps as possible, not sure if the boulders would crumble into what was left of the sulfur pit. He stopped at the entrance to the womb of the cave. Red spots dotted the walls, like glowing moss in the darkness. It appeared Sitara still had a craving for red bats.

Across the pit, Pavel's voice reached Theo. "I feel like I'm inside the stomach of a giant lizard, trapped forever. It smells—"

Diva shushed him.

"Thank you, Diva," Theo said under his breath.

A low growl replaced the jingling from the cave.

"Sitara?" Theo said as calmly as he could.

His heart raced. The man *had* turned into a beast again. Everyone was right, and Theo had been wrong. His friends had made the right decision to leave Sitara in the cave. Well, Theo wasn't going to leave the man-beast here again. They'd find a way to cure him. Not because they needed Sitara as a blacksmith, but because the man didn't deserve to be left here any longer. He was just another of Dragon Village's residents who had a troubled past. If Theo was going to be ruler one day, he had to make decisions to help his people.

He crept closer. "Sitara, we've come to help you. I'm sorry you've been down here so long, but we're going to get you out now. I'm not going to hurt you."

The growling grew deeper. Rocks clattered as the beast drew closer. Seconds ticked by with no movement or sound from within the cave.

"Sitara?" Theo said again.

The word barely escaped his lips when the lurking beast leaped out of the darkness, straight for Theo's throat.

Chapter 12
Surprise at the Old Mill

THEO TUCKED AND ROLLED faster than he'd ever moved before, avoiding the beast's fangs by a hair's breadth. The creature's foul breath soiled the air, adding an extra layer to the already unbearable odor of the sulfur pit and decaying carcasses.

Crouched like a beast himself, facing his enemy, Theo said, "Sitara, please, I'm not here to hurt you."

His attacker spun around. Glaring yellow eyes stared Theo down.

Yellow? That beast wasn't Sitara. His eyes were gray.

Theo took in the entire creature. A rangy, snarling, hungry-looking wolf, not a wolf-man blocked the only exit from the cave.

How am I going to escape?

The cave was too small for him to shift into a dragon. And he didn't dare call out to Diva for help. The wolf might go after her and Pavel.

What else can I do?

He thought about his abilities and remembered he'd used his powers to burn through a cloth covering his eyes when he'd been captured.

Can I do something like that again? How did I do it before?

It had been advice from his mother, something to help him shift. Love. That was one thing. And … righteous anger. That was the other. Right now, fear overpowered his ability to feel love. And, it was one matter to battle an evil monster, but the creature in front of him was an ordinary animal. Theo didn't feel anger of any kind toward it. The wolf was merely acting according to its nature, and right now it must be extremely hungry by the looks of it. Theo didn't want to harm the creature, but he also didn't plan to be its next meal.

My powers have grown. I should be able to command them at will now, without any emotional trigger.

He concentrated on his eyes. *Burn like fire the way you did before.* Heat enveloped them.

Opposite Theo, snarling turned to whimpering. The wolf flattened its ears and tucked its tail between its legs. It lay pressed to the ground, making its body as small as possible.

"Good boy," Theo said as he crept around the cowering animal while keeping as near to the wall as possible.

The animal trembled as Theo approached. "It's okay. No one's going to hurt you."

Step by slow, agonizing step, Theo made his way out of the cave opening. He backed away, keeping his eyes on the animal until he could no longer see it. Not once did it change its position. When Theo reached the sulfur pit, he scanned the other side. Diva and Pavel were seated on a boulder, their heads together in muted conversation.

"Thank goodness, you're both okay." Theo ran across the piled-up rocks.

His friends looked his way, and Pavel screamed.

Theo whirled around. Had the wolf followed him? In his haste, he slipped on the stones and fell to his hands and knees, scraping them. He scrambled up, ready to fight the beast, but nothing was there.

"What was that all about?" He held out his bloodied hands toward Pavel.

Pavel continued screaming, his words unintelligible. He struggled against Diva's tight grasp. She managed to get him quiet by the time Theo crossed the sulfur pit and joined them.

"What's the matter with you?" Theo looked into his friend's terrified eyes.

"V-v-v" was all that came out.

Theo turned toward Diva. "What's going on? What happened to him?"

"Your eyes." Diva gestured with her own, while keeping her hands secured around Pavel.

"My eyes?"

"They're glowing," she said. "Pavel thought Sitara bit you and turned you into a Vurkolak."

"Oh, sorry, sorry." Theo closed his eyes and focused on changing them back to normal. Coolness replaced the heat, and he opened his eyes. "How are they now?"

Diva nodded, and Pavel fell into unconsciousness. She released her tight grip, and he sagged against her. "He's been jittery ever since we came down here. All day, really. Zima's curse is doing a lot of damage. Pavel can't rest."

Unsure whether Pavel could hear them or not, Theo whispered, "Do you really think it's a curse? Or is he imagining it? Zima said he didn't curse Pavel."

"Whether he intended to or not, I believe Zima is responsible," Diva said. "I thought you believed Pavel."

"I do. It's just … I don't know."

"Trust your friend," Diva said. "We've talked when you're not around. You don't know how much pain you cause him by not believing him."

Theo sighed. "I don't mean to. Everything here is so crazy and magical. I'm not sure what to believe anymore. I try to be a good leader, but it seems like I make everything worse."

"A leader has to trust his friends."

"I know. I'll try harder."

Pavel stirred, moaning and thrashing.

Diva tapped him on his cheek. "Pavel, wake up. Let's get you into the fresh air."

Pavel screamed and bolted up, staring straight ahead of him.

"Hey, hey," Theo said in a low voice. "It's okay."

Pavel's eyes focused, and he rubbed his temples. He jerked away from Theo, then let out a long breath. "Wow, I must have been dreaming. I'm glad you didn't change into a monster."

"What *did* happen, Theo?" Diva asked. "Did you find Sitara?"

"No." Theo choked back a sob. "There's only a wolf."

"A wolfy wolf?" Pavel asked. "Not a Vurkolak wolf?"

"Yes. And I-I think it killed Sitara."

Pavel tapped Theo on the shoulder. "Man, that rots. But, don't worry. We'll find someone else to make what we need. We'll get your father rescued somehow."

An ached throbbed behind Theo's eyes. Of course, he worried about how they'd rescue his father, but that wasn't what was causing him so much pain at the moment. He'd failed Sitara. He should have insisted they get the man out a year ago. But how could he do that? His sister's life was in danger. Why did choosing one person over the other have to be so difficult? Why did saving one person mean disaster for another?

"Let's go back and let the Kukeri know what's going on." Theo turned away and climbed up the rock slide.

He toned down his dragon senses so he could block out the whispered conversation between Pavel and Diva. Still, words, spoken a little too loudly, reached him: mistrust, mistakes, anger, changing.

Did my father have these kinds of problems when he was learning how to be a leader? What did Theo even really know about his father? He'd met the man for such a short time. Zmey had sent Theo, Nia, Pavel, and Vela—a girl Lamia had stolen from Selo—back home so the dragon king could restore his kingdom. Zmey could have let Theo stay. Nia would have told their mother he was okay and would return home when he could.

Everything would be so different now if Zmey had let Theo remain. He'd have learned about his abilities, his family history, Dragon Village, and how to be a leader. He clenched his fists and pounded them together.

I will learn. I have to learn. Too much is at stake for me to keep making mistakes.

A trickle of light let him know the exit was nearby. He crawled out of the hole and wiped dirt off of his clothing.

Zima and Jega sat at the base of a massive tree. Both looked up.

"No luck, I take it." Jega stood, helping Zima to do likewise. "Your face says it all."

"Sitara's gone." Theo explained everything to the Kukeri.

Diva and Pavel crept out of the hole and joined the group.

"Someone must have taken over Sitara's shop," Pavel said. "Let's go find out."

"But Sitara was the best," Jega replied. "I don't know if anyone else can replace him."

Diva added, "In all the time Sitara was imprisoned, another blacksmith could have become a master."

Zima cleared his throat. "The only way you'll know is if you go to Vida Village to find out."

"Not there." Theo moaned. That was where the witches who'd captured Diva lived. "Another place doesn't have a blacksmith?"

Zima, Jega, and Diva all shook their heads.

"I guess we have no choice," Theo said. "Let's hope we don't run into the Youdi."

"The three of you will have to go there alone," Jega said. "It's too long of a walk for Milka, especially lugging the cart. Zima and I will bring her back to our sanctuary and salvage what we can there."

Zima added, "And your sisters will eventually return there to update us on anything new that's happening in Zmeykovo. When I'm better, we'll come and find you."

Pavel nudged Diva. "Does that mean we'll get to ride our deer now?"

"As soon as we're out of Tililei Forest, I'll call them."

"Perhaps we could rest for the night first. Make plans." Theo rubbed the back of his neck. "I think we've all had a tiring day."

"Come back to the sanctuary with us," Jega said. "As Diva said earlier, the inside hasn't been touched."

Pavel cast a glance at Zima, then quickly spoke. "Let's go to the old mill instead."

"Is it safe?" Theo asked. "Is the building even standing after the demons attacked us there?"

"Yes, to both," Jega said. "Speaking of them, as pleasant as it has been that they haven't attacked us again, I'm worried that they're up to something worse."

"Maybe they haven't figured out where we are," Pavel added.

Diva poked Theo in the side. "Tell them."

Theo stared at Diva. "What?"

"About Lamia."

"Oh." He cleared his throat. "I should have said something earlier, but Lamia confused me." He told them how she'd found him by the cheshma and about his conversation with her.

"Don't concern yourself about her words." Zima shook his head. "Never trust her. She'll twist the truth around until it's the opposite of what it really means."

"Just like politicians," Pavel mumbled.

"We'll think about what it all means and discuss it with Sava and Ula." Jega moved toward the cart. "But now, we should all get going. We don't want to be in the forest when it gets dark."

Jega performed his ritual, creating a ring of fire around everyone, and they made their way out of the forest. At the glade, they parted ways, with the Kukeri traveling north.

"It's not far to the mill," Diva said. "By the time the deer get here, we could have walked there. Let's call them in the morning instead if that's okay."

"Sure," Theo said.

Pavel replied, "I'm okay with that, but I miss Whirl."

Theo missed Shar, his flying deer companion, too. At times, it felt like the animal was the only being in Dragon Village who understood him and didn't judge him. Their connection enabled the deer to perceive Theo's thoughts, but he hadn't been able to accomplish reading Shar's yet. All Theo could do was mentally talk with the deer. Diva often told him those things took time. She and her deer companion, Sur, could maintain a connection even from a distance.

When will I achieve that link?

More thoughts about his crumbling relationships raced through Theo's mind as he walked south in silence toward their destination. In a short time, the roof of the old building poked through the trees.

"Thank goodness." Pavel rubbed his thighs. "I'm so exhausted. I'm going to go to sleep early."

"Have something to eat first," Diva said. "I'll look for fruit while I forage. That'll give you an energy boost."

"Not hungry. See you later." Pavel jogged toward the mill.

Pavel not hungry? Matters were worse than Theo imagined. But more dangerous things could be in store for Pavel. Theo turned to Diva. "Shouldn't we check out the mill first? What if demons are waiting there for us to return?"

"No, let him be. He already feels you smother him."

"I'm just—"

Diva held her hand up to stop him. "I know. You want to protect him, but you need to give him more credit. He's human, yes, but he's not incompetent."

"I never said he was."

"No, but your actions indicate that."

Theo thought about what Diva said as they continued to the mill. *Is she right?* He'd have to encourage Pavel to be more active in their quest, without putting him into danger.

When Theo and Diva entered the mill, they found Pavel curled up by the wall on a grain sack, his backpack and Theo's bow and arrows by his side. Pavel twitched and moaned in his sleep, calling out Milka's name.

"I wish we could find a bull," Theo said. "Pavel's so attached to Milka. I wish she didn't have to fight the Water Bull, but what choice do we have?"

"I'm worried about her, too." Diva set her bow and arrow by the door and went over to Pavel. "But I'm more worried about Pavel."

Theo placed his weapons and backpack next to Diva's possessions and followed her. He whispered, "Can you help him while he's sleeping?"

"I'll try." She kneeled next to Pavel and removed an ointment from her pouch. "This has lavender in it. The tea helped him a little, so I'll rub this on his temples. It won't cure him, but it should let him sleep more soundly."

"Thank you."

A skittering sound on the other side of the mill caught his attention. He crept closer. A board creaked, and a splash in the river followed. Theo peeked out a knothole. The water rippled, but no Navi or other demons lurked nearby. He concentrated on his dragon senses, listening for the flutter of wings, but only the normal woodland sounds reached him.

It must have been a rat.

He returned to his friends. Pavel now lay still, his breathing more evenly.

"I'll go get things for him to eat when he wakes," Diva said. "I won't be gone long."

Theo nodded and sat near Pavel, waiting for her return. He closed his eyes. *Just for a moment, so tired.* The next thing he recalled was the deep lowing of a water buffalo.

The Kukeri must have returned. I hope everything's okay.

He stretched and yawned, and glanced at Pavel. Thankfully, his friend still slept without moaning, although he did fidget.

Outside, Diva said, "Sly."

What's the Vodnik doing here?

Theo got up and went outside to investigate. There, Sly led a massive brownish-gold water buffalo with long, curved horns.

"Sly," he called out, "what are you doing here?"

The Vodnik looked up to the mill, and a big grin spread across his face. Theo smiled back, even though Sly's glowing green eyes made him look creepy.

"My King, my King, me have gift for you."

"I've told you before, I'm not your king." Sly had started calling Theo that after he'd shifted into a dragon to save Diva. Now, Theo had a difficult time getting the Vodnik to stop saying that. Theo wasn't the king. His father was.

Diva was grinning, too.

What's going on? What is Sly's gift? Surely not the water buffalo?

Diva nodded as if reading his mind.

"Sly, you're giving us a bull?" Theo asked.

"No give. Lend." Sly leaned against the beast and sighed. "No ask Father. Just take. You use Lucky to fight Water Bull. Keep Milka safe."

Sly tended his father's livestock: cattle, horses, sheep, pigs. That was one place the youngest Vodnik felt most secure. Sly had once told Theo the animals were kind to him, unlike the Vodnik's father. Theo could certainly understand that. He himself felt less anxious in the presence of animals, especially Shar.

"How did you know we needed him?" Theo asked.

"Me hear you and Samodiva talk. Need bull. Me bring one."

"You were the one who was in the mill?"

"Yes, yes." Sly bounced on his webbed feet. "Me scared to leave when attacked. Me hide in barrel."

"Thank you, Sly," Theo said. "We'll accept your gift."

Sly stopped bouncing and gazed at Theo with a mournful look. "You take care of him? No let him die? Or get hurt real bad?"

"I will. We all will." He looked at Diva, who nodded.

Theo could imagine Lord Vodnik's rage if he found out, especially if one of his livestock died at their hands. The leader of the water creatures was brutal and had done horrible things to his wife—one of them—and their child. And to his own animals. It was acceptable for him to ride his horses to death, but Theo shuddered to think what Lord Vodnik would do to Sly if Lucky were harmed or killed.

"We'll definitely keep him safe," Theo said. "We don't want your father to harm you."

"No, no." Sly shook his head so hard Theo thought it would twist off. "Me worry about Lucky. He my friend. I ask him to help. Tell him danger. He say yes. Want to help. Fight bad bull."

Diva touched Sly's shoulder. "We'll protect your friend. All of us. We need him to lure the Water Bull out and attack, but we'll be fighting, too, confusing the monster."

"Thank you, thank you, lovely Samodiva."

"He'll be our warrior, our hero. He'll be doing us a great service," Theo said. "His name is Lucky, after all. He'll be our Lucky Charm."

"Yes, Lucky is a suitable name," Diva said. "And he's an important part of our mission."

"Oh." Theo paced. "Now we have to go back to the Kukeri's sanctuary to bring them Lucky, instead of looking for a blacksmith. And we'll have to walk. Because our deer can't carry him. Not even Sur. We're going to lose another day."

"No, no," Sly said. "Me can bring my friend. You find blacksmith."

"Are you sure?" Diva asked. "Won't anyone notice you're gone?"

The Vodnik's shoulders slumped. "Father no care. Friends no tell. Me can go."

Theo lifted the Vodnik's head to look in his eyes. "Thank you. We're your friends, too, and we won't tell."

"Me go now." Sly took hold of the rope and hopped away.

For the first time, Theo felt hope that everything would turn out right. Things were starting to move in a positive direction. They'd find a blacksmith, and he'd help them make golden horns and armor for Lucky. The bull would defeat the Water Bull. They'd find Zmey. Then everything would be under control. No more mistakes.

Nothing else could possibly go wrong.

Chapter 13
Pleading with the Blacksmith

JULY 1

THE DEER LANDED in a meadow outside of Vida Village, and Theo, Pavel, and Diva slid off. While Theo stroked Shar's neck, he stared at the gray, stone-walled fortress where the Youdi had held Diva captive.

"*Relax*," his deer companion thought. "*You don't have to enter that evil place again.*"

"*I know. It just brings back bad memories.*" Fighting. Death. Destruction.

"*And some good ones,*" Shar said.

Theo laid his head against his deer companion's side. Yes, they'd been able to rescue Diva. That was the best memory of all.

"Are we ready to go?" Diva strode toward him. "What's the plan?"

Despite his unease, Theo suppressed a laugh at Diva's disguised appearance. Her grin told him she was doing the same about his. Not only were all three of them wearing worn clothing Pavel had found at the mill, but Diva's white-blond curls were hidden beneath a head scarf. But that wasn't the humorous part. Theo and Diva no longer had pale skin—a giveaway to their Samodiva bloodlines. In order to make them fit in with other villagers, Pavel had coated their exposed skin with a concoction of hand lotion and ground chocolate—the unsweetened kind. They had tried a regular chocolate bar, but that had made their skin sticky. The final result with the sugarless chocolate had transformed Theo's and Diva's skin so they now sported a bit of a tan.

"We could sneak around the buildings," Theo said. "One of us can go first to make sure the coast is clear."

"That will be rather suspicious if anyone sees us," Pavel said. "Then our disguises will have been for nothing."

"You're right," Theo said. "Do you have a better idea?"

"Yes." Light shone in Pavel's bloodshot eyes.

He'd slept peacefully next to Theo for most of the night. But toward morning, Pavel had woken them with his screaming when the effects of Diva's lavender had worn off. Even now, puffy, dark circles made Pavel look haggard.

"Great," Theo said. "I'm all ears."

"We just walk in as if we belong there. Hide in plain sight."

"I like your idea better than mine. All agreed?" Theo glanced at Diva.

"It makes sense. Let's test it out," she said.

They ambled toward the village, relying on Diva to lead them to the smithy. Theo glanced around. No buildings had been destroyed, and the air was clear of suffocating smoke and ashes, unlike the devastation the rest of Dragon Village had suffered. Yet, something felt wrong here. Theo's dragon senses tingled with evil presences.

Pavel cast a quick look at Diva, who nodded, then he nudged Theo. "Hey, chill out. You're going to get us caught if you keep acting like a tourist looking at skyscrapers in New York."

"Sorry," Theo replied. "I think someone's waiting for us here."

"And they'll have no problem finding us if you don't cut it out."

The rest of the way, Theo kept his face looking straight ahead, despite the churning in his stomach.

Where are they?

People passed by or ducked into shops without looking at him or his friends. Laughter filled the air, and scolding from parents, as well. Girls sang, and boys kicked stones. Cats and dogs scampered through alleys. Nothing out of the ordinary.

I know someone's here.

Still, he kept walking, observing everything around him.

There. That person changed direction after seeing us.

He looked behind him. *And that person's been following us.*

Sweat trickled down Theo's face, and his heart raced.

I have to stop this. No one's come rushing at us, shouting.

"We're here." Diva stopped in front of an open ornate wooden door leading into a stone building.

"Amazing." The door's beauty overwhelmed Theo. "This is a master's work."

He ran his fingers over the brass knocker. Smooth and cool, no nicks anywhere. The artisan had fashioned panels displaying intricate depictions of flowers, birds, and twisting vines into the decorative copper plate behind the knocker. Even the wooden panels in the door contained the craftsman's inlaid metal designs.

"Sitara did this," Diva said. "This is why we wanted his help."

"I hope whoever took over the smithy is as talented," Pavel said.

"Don't stand there talking up a storm," the smithy shouted at them, without turning around. "If you're not here for my services, then be on your way."

The trio entered. Theo tugged at his shirt and took short breaths in the stifling hot room. "It's no wonder Sitara could survive in Devil's Throat," he whispered. "If he was used to this kind of raging heat, he'd be able to endure the temperature in the cave."

He looked around the room. Next to the blacksmith, a sandy-haired boy shoveled charcoal into the forge, then fanned the flames with a bellows. Sparks flew around him, some landing on his arms, but the lad didn't flinch. Nearby, tools of the trade lined the walls and lay scattered along tables and benches.

"This hammer head looks sort of like a fish." Pavel picked up the tool, but it crashed to the floor.

"Don't touch anything." The blacksmith whirled around, frowning at Pavel.

"Sitara." Theo gasped.

The blacksmith turned his gaze from Pavel to Theo. His frown turned into a grimace as he bared his teeth. "You."

"You're alive."

Sitara stomped forward, his eyes as hard as the metals he worked with. "No thanks to you. Have you returned to do more damage?"

"Damage?" Theo's mind raced. What had he done? He'd turned Sitara from a Vurkolak to his human form. "But … but I cured you."

"Cured me." Sitara's shout turned into a beastly roar. "You call what you did a cure?"

"Master," his apprentice said as he ran up to Sitara, "do you want me to go for help?"

"No," Sitara shouted. "Leave me."

As the boy ran from the smithy, Sitara grabbed Theo by the T-shirt and dragged him toward the back of the room. "I'll show you what you did to me."

"Leave him alone." Pavel rushed forward, pounding on Sitara's back.

Diva nocked an arrow. "Let him go, or I'll shoot."

Sitara dropped Theo to the floor and whipped around. "What do any of you know? Why are you here anyway?"

Theo rose, dusted himself off, and joined Diva and Pavel, a safe distance from Sitara. "We need your help to save Dragon Village. To rescue my father."

"The Water Bull guards Zmey's prison." Diva put her weapon away. "We've come to ask you to equip our water buffalo with golden horns and make him a warrior to battle the beast."

"Golden horns." Sitara snorted. "You'll need more than that to defeat the monster. Gold may make your bull appear royal, but iron is the only thing that can harm the Water Bull. What gave you the crazy idea you could beat him with golden horns?"

"A book the Kukeri have," she replied.

Sitara shook his head. "Fairy tales. Nothing but fairy tales. To defeat evil, you need iron."

"But gold shines and can draw the attention of the monster," Pavel added.

"Use gold to make your buffalo pretty if you want, but the tip of the horns must be iron." Sitara seized a hammer and banged golden and iron objects lying on a table. The blow crushed the gold, while the iron clanged, but stayed firm. "See. Iron for protection, not gold."

"Wow, I wouldn't want to make him angry at me," Pavel whispered to Diva.

"You'll also need armor on the bull's body," Sitara said as he paced the room. "From what I've heard of the Water Bull, he's fierce and relentless in his battles." Sitara stopped pacing and stared each of them in the face for a full minute, first Theo, then Diva, then Pavel. "But why should I help any of you?"

"Don't you care what's happening to Dragon Village?" Theo asked. "All the destruction."

Sitara spread his arms wide. "Look around you. What destruction do you see in my shop? Or outside? I'm prospering. My village is prospering."

"Don't you care about everyone else?" Theo asked.

"Why?" Sitara grabbed a hammer and squeezed it until his knuckles turned white. "What have any of them done for me?"

"What about my father, your king?" Theo's voice came out hoarse with emotion. "Don't you have any loyalty to him?"

"No," Sitara shouted and hurled the hammer against the wall, splintering the rocks. "How has he helped me? Or even our land's precious deities? Bendis imprisoned me—unjustly. And Tangra? I never saw his light nor felt his spiritual presence. Why should I care about any of them?"

"What happened?" Theo asked. "Why were you imprisoned?"

Theo had heard one side of the story, the one that detailed how Sitara had died in the wilderness and turned into a beast after forty days. Diva had told Theo that madness consumed Sitara, and he tried to swallow the sun and moon. That was when Bendis had banished him to Devil's Throat. What more did Sitara have to say about that?

"You want to hear *my* tale of woe?" Sitara snorted. "All right. I'm sure I already know the version you were told. It's the one *everyone* repeats. And, yes, it's true. But there's more to the story. I was cursed, and my family was murdered—by that slimy water creature who dares call himself a 'Lord.' It wasn't bad enough he killed my children and kidnapped my wife, but then he had a child with her and killed them both—brutally."

"That … that was *your* wife?" Theo recalled the horrifying story Sly had told him about Lord Vodnik assaulting his wife and child.

"So, you've heard that story, have you?" Sitara slumped to the floor, his head between his hands. "And *I'm* the one banished for my actions, while that monster lives free to do as he pleases."

"How horrible," Theo said. Pavel's pained stare and Diva's deep sigh told Theo the story had touched them as well.

"I went mad," Sitara continued. "I sought out the murderer, wanting to rip him to shreds. He captured me, cursed me, and left me bound in the wilderness to die. You know the rest. Bendis chained me and hid me away—out of sight, out of mind—so the rest of Zmeykovo would be safe."

Theo searched for something comforting to say. But what words ever truly eased another's grief? He spoke the only ones that came to mind, although they were meaningless, empty. "I …

I'm sorry you had to suffer that. I wish I could help."

Sitara shot up off of the floor. "You can't. No one can. What can you do to bring my family back? Nothing. Instead of helping, you now want *me* to help *you*. Again, I ask you, why should I?"

"If we rescue Zmey, he can bring you justice."

"Why would he now?" Sitara spat out the words. "He didn't before. Magical creatures are a priority over the humans who live here. If we serve a purpose, we can stay. If we don't, we're cast out. Back home, everyone believes we've gone mad, and oftentimes, they're right."

Theo looked at Pavel. His friend's face had paled. Theo shook his head as he squeezed Pavel's shoulder, willing Pavel to be assured that Theo would never do that. Even so, Pavel trembled.

"Only the Youdi have cared about me," Sitara continued.

Diva broke her silence. "The Youdi? Those selfish, evil witches."

"Yes, those 'selfish, evil witches' were the ones who restored my shop and health," Sitara replied.

"If they helped you, they must have wanted something in return," Diva added.

"Doesn't everyone?" Sitara stared at her. "You want something. They want something. Lamia wanted something."

"To guard her soul." Theo recalled the dove masquerading as one of Lamia's souls.

"True." Sitara breathed deep as if trying to calm himself. "She promised to release me when the threat against her was gone, and she'd hide her soul elsewhere. But I failed. You, the 'Unborn Hero,' destroyed her soul. When you killed her, her spirit came to me and vowed revenge."

"She had to be killed," Theo said. "She was destroying Dragon Village, the same as she and Zlo are doing now."

"Not my concern." Sitara shrugged. "I have to take care of myself first. When I become of no use to anyone here, then everyone's help and promises will end. So, let's turn this around. You want my help. Tell me, what can *you* do for *me*?"

"What is it you want?" Theo asked.

"I want," Sitara said through clenched teeth, "to be rid of this curse, to live a normal life, not one where I'm half man and half beast."

Theo looked Sitara up and down. A man stood before him, not the savage Vurkolak. "But … but I cured you, didn't I? I don't understand."

"Of course, you don't. You didn't cure me. You made everything worse." Sitara paced like a caged animal, growling like one, too.

"How?"

"Come with me, and I'll show you." Sitara walked toward a metal door covered with chains and locks at the back of the room.

"That's some tight security," Pavel said. "You must have treasures down there."

"That and something dangerous."

Sitara opened one lock after the other, dropping them onto the floor until he freed the door of its restraints. He walked down the steps in silence, leading them into a torch-lit room. Shelves filled with crafting tools lined the walls, and wooden barrels overflowing with precious metals and gems took up the bulk of the room.

"Oh, wow!" Pavel's eyes glittered like the lavish objects before them. "Look at all this jewelry. You work with gold and silver, too?"

Sitara turned around. "All metals turn into life in my hands. Upstairs, I make tools and weapons. Down here, is where I perform the more delicate work. This is what the Youdi require for their assistance. Golden trinkets to satisfy their vanity. And my most decorative war craft."

He picked up a sword, its blade etched with gold. Words. Charms, Theo thought, although he couldn't decipher their meanings. More charms, surrounded by sparkling gems, decorated its handle. Similar words adorned shields, helmets, and other weapons around the room.

"It looks like you're equipping an army," Theo said, a bitter taste in his mouth.

"Another request from the Youdi. But—"

"Oh, man." Pavel ran to the other side of the room. "That's so cool."

Theo looked where his friend stopped. An assortment of spears leaned against another wall. But what caught his eye—and Pavel's fancy—was a crossbow.

Sitara leaped across the room and guarded the weapon. "That's my real treasure. I crafted it so I can shoot five arrows at a time." He picked it up and aimed it at Theo.

Theo froze.

"No," Pavel shrieked and pounded Sitara's arm.

Sitara laughed and set the crossbow back on its shelf. "It's not loaded. It has two purposes, and killing your friend isn't one of them."

Theo wiped sweat from his brow. "Then … then what's it for?"

"I plan to repay the beast who took my family away from me." Sitara's gray eyes glowed as he ran his fingers over the weapon.

"The monster who resulted in my enslavement. Lord Vodnik, who ruined so many years of my life."

Theo shivered. "And what else do you use it for?"

"What I came down here to show you." Sitara moved aside straw and dust on the floor next to a kiln, revealing a metal ring. The blacksmith's muscles bulged as he tugged on it to lift a round cover. "It's in the room below. There's not enough space for all of you, so only Theo can come." Sitara grabbed a torch and disappeared down the opening.

"Don't go." Pavel grabbed Theo's shirt. "He might be tricking you. I think he's planning on killing you down there."

"Please let go. I have to know what I did to Sitara."

Sighing, Pavel released his grasp, and Theo followed the blacksmith down the wooden ladder. The air became dense and moist as he entered a small room carved out of the earth.

"This is what you did to me." Sitara pointed to the farthest corner of the room, although he needn't have bothered in the confined space.

Thick chains attached to handcuffs and ankle shackles lay sprawled across the floor. Their other ends had been driven into hefty stakes. Rust-colored stains soiled the floor and wall, along with long, deep scratches.

"What is this for?" Theo took a step back until he pressed against the ladder. *This couldn't be a punishment for me?*

Sitara picked up a chain and rattled it. "At the moment, I'm a man, but when the full moon rises, I turn into a beast."

"I … I only half-cured you?"

Sitara whirled around. "You gave me no kind of cure. At least when I was only that cursed Vurkolak, I lacked human thoughts and desires. Now when I shift, I'm caught between both selves. A being who can still reason, but with the blood lust of a beast."

"I …" Theo didn't know what to say. Another life he'd ruined because of the choices he made.

Sitara continued, "That crossbow your friend admires is for my apprentice. Every full moon, he sits in the room above, with the weapon pointed at the opening, while I chain myself here. I've ordered him to fire it if I escape, so I can't attack anyone."

"You want him to kill you?" Theo managed to say.

"Do you think I want to be caged in that dark hell hole again?" Sitara leaned his head against the wall. His voice cracked as he spoke. "I tore my way out of Devil's Throat on the first full moon after the cave-in. I did … unspeakable carnage to animals in the forest." He turned around slowly. "What if that had been people?"

Bile rose in Theo's throat. "Can't anyone help you?"

Sitara dug his fingers through his hair. "The Youdi have tried—and failed. If you want me to help you, find a cure. Before the moon rises tonight."

"Tonight?" Theo could think of only one person who had the skills to do that. And he was certain she wasn't happy with him. After all, he'd left her a prisoner in the fortress.

A door slammed above them and scrambling footsteps sounded in the upper room. Sitara's apprentice poked his head over the hole and shouted, "Master, soldiers are coming."

Chapter 14
Begging the Witch

RAGE BURNED THEO'S GUT, and heat scorched his eyes, a warning for everyone to beware. The apprentice had betrayed their location to the soldiers. Theo's intensified emotions woke his dragon spirit, who clawed to break free, the warrior hungry for revenge.

The boy pulled his head away from the opening. His voice quivering, he asked, "Master, what do you want me to do?"

"Run," Sitara shouted.

Run? Theo's fury ebbed. He took deep breaths to calm his dragon spirit. *The apprentice didn't bring the soldiers here. He's afraid of them.*

"Where?" the boy stammered.

"You know where." Sitara growled. "The tunnel. Hide in the place I showed you. Now, or they'll kill you."

Stomping came from the main workshop. A throaty voice boomed, "Sitara, bring us the red-haired boy. We know he's here."

"Theo, come on." Pavel reached his hand down the ladder. "We have to leave now."

Theo backed away from Sitara as far as he could. "Will you let us go?"

"Get out of here." The blacksmith waved Theo away. "Don't make me regret helping you."

As Theo scrambled to the top, he said, "We'll be back. We'll find a cure."

Sitara moved halfway up and grasped the metal cover. "Conceal the entrance when I replace the lid. I can't let anyone venture down here with the full moon so close."

Theo nodded and scattered straw around the cover and metal ring after Sitara set it in place.

In the upper room, more heavy, clanging footsteps made the ceiling shudder. Growling, howling wolves joined the commotion, along with the shrill voices of the Youdi.

"Zlo wants the boy alive," a deep voice boomed.

Theo recognized the speaker: Radan, Zlo's freaky-looking second-in-command. The beast had antlers and an anteater-like snout. But it was the bulging, icy-blue eyes that Theo remembered the most. Nothing but evil lay behind them.

"The fire's still burning, so they were here recently." That speaker's voice ended with a neigh.

Another enemy Theo didn't want to meet: Bor Stobor the Karakonjul. The half-man, half-horse creature not only smelled terrible, he also had a foul temper.

"Hurry, Theo. Over here." Diva waved her hands from a half-open panel behind a shelf. "I already sent Pavel after Sitara's apprentice, so we'll know the way."

Theo squeezed past the shelf and through the opening, pulling it closed behind him. Diva held a torch that lit a secret passage full of cobwebs and dust.

"Burn the smithy down," Radan roared upstairs. "That'll teach Sitara a lesson."

"No, you can't," a Youda screeched. Theo was certain it was their leader, Youda Stana. "We need the smithy."

Theo put his hand on the panel. "I have to go help Sitara."

Diva shook her head. "He'll be safe underground in the dirt. I heard everything he told you. It's the best place for him right now. We'll find a cure, then return."

Theo sighed. "You're right. Let's catch up to Pavel."

They followed scratch marks in the dirt that Pavel must have made. Theo scuffed them to cover their tracks. The narrow opening widened the farther they traveled, with passages veering off both sides of the rocky tunnel. In a short while, the marks ended at a solid stone wall.

"Where'd Pavel go from here?" Theo asked.

"There has to be an exit." Diva glued her ear to the wall. "I hear sounds on the other side."

Theo patted the stones and crevices until he touched a metal ring like the one that led to Sitara's chamber. "Found something."

He pulled the handle, which slid the stone wall aside. Daylight seeped into the passageway.

"You made it." Pavel rushed over.

Theo and Diva slid out of the opening, and the door closed.

"Where's Sitara?" Pavel asked.

"He wanted to stay." Theo told Pavel about his conversation with the blacksmith.

"Oh, man," Pavel said. "We'll fix his curse … and mine, but let's get out of here. We'll be safer away from the exit. Watch your steps and follow me. The path looks dangerous, but it's not."

They crossed a wooden bridge that spanned a gurgling spring. The path on the other side led up a steep, grassy hill. At the top, the door they'd exited appeared tiny, set at the base of a vertical rock wall. A wooded area grew right up to the stones. But from here, they could see in all directions.

Theo's heart ached. Smoke rose high in the sky in the direction of Vida Village. Radan *had* set fire to the smithy despite Youda Stana's plea not to.

Pavel dropped to the ground. "What's the plan?"

"Let me contact Sur to have the deer come here, then we can decide." Diva closed her eyes for a moment. "I can't connect with him. Something must be wrong."

"Oh, no," Pavel shouted. "My Whirl has to be okay."

"And Shar," Theo added.

"Don't worry. I'll try another way. They may have moved farther away looking for us when they saw the smoke." She withdrew a long, curved, silver pin from her belt and blew on the end. "That'll let them know where we are. Now let's talk about how to cure Sitara."

Pavel propped his elbows on his knees. "And me."

"Yes, both of you."

Theo paced. "Are you thinking what I'm thinking, Diva?"

"If it's that we need to see Baba Yaga, then, yes."

"Ohhh." Theo sat beside her. "We don't even know where she is. She might still be in the torture room in the fortress."

"I wish you had let her go." Pavel pulled his legs closer to his body.

"No." Diva shook her head. "Theo did the right thing. She betrayed us."

"I'm sure she found a way out by now," Theo said. "She is a witch after all."

"But she won't be happy to see you," Pavel said. "And she's the only one who can cure me."

"What about Kikimora?" Theo asked. "She—"

"No," Pavel screeched and jumped to his feet. "Never. I already have nightmares about her."

Theo craned his neck to look at Pavel. "But she removed the demon Lamia from me. If she can do that, she should be able to undo your curse."

Pavel shouted, "No, I'm never going back there."

"What if we can't find Baba Yaga?" Diva asked.

"Not even then." Pavel rushed away to the top of the hill.

Theo started to get up, but Diva shook her head. "Let him be for a minute. He'll come back when he's not so upset."

Theo dropped back to the ground. When had he lost touch with Pavel? Diva was the only one here who now understood Pavel. Theo even felt distanced from Diva these days. Before, it had felt as if the two of them had a connection, that she understood him even better than his sister, Nia, did. But now, the closer Diva and Pavel grew, the more alienated Theo felt.

"What about Sitara? Could Kikimora help him?" he asked.

"I doubt she's powerful enough to break the wolf curse."

"You're probably right. She's more likely to be brewing a new beer, rather than a powerful potion." Theo laughed.

"Then I guess we'll have to go to the Forest of Whispering Bells to see if that old witch escaped."

Pavel scrambled down the hill. "We have to get out of here."

Theo jumped up. "What's the matter?"

"Look." Pavel pointed toward the side of the cliff.

Wolves slunk out of the door, followed by several Youdi bearing bows and arrows. Behind them came Bor Stobor, soldiers, and finally Radan.

Theo tuned in his dragon senses to what they were saying.

Bor Stobor pranced around Radan. "We'll find them. They couldn't have gone too far."

"Our wolves will hunt them down," the grating voice of Youda Stana said.

Radan stomped to position himself in front of the group. "Use your wits if you have any. Use your magic. Do whatever you have to without killing the boy, but complete the mission or pay the consequences."

"Let the wolves loose," Youda Stana shrieked.

The wolves howled and ran as a pack over the bridge and up the hill. The Youdi screeched like deranged beings and sprinted after the animals.

Pavel trembled. "What are we going to do? There's nowhere to hide."

"Where are the deer?" Theo scanned the sky in all directions.

They weren't coming. Theo would have to fight to save his friends. His heart raced, heat built up in his chest, and power surged throughout his body. His dragon spirit woke and roared in Theo's mind. Theo calmed him. *Not quite yet. Let them come nearer, so they can't escape.*

"The wolves are getting closer," Pavel screamed.

Diva pulled out her whistle again and blew it several times. "Sur's coming. We've finally made a connection."

Whistling like the wind resounded through the branches in the forest below, while the panting and growling of the wolves grew nearer.

"There they are," shouted Youda Stana. "Get them."

"Hurry, hurry," Theo urged the deer.

He loosened his hold on his dragon spirit. If he became injured while fighting in that form, he could die. Then who would protect his friends? The deer would rescue them. It was the best recourse for now.

Sur broke through the treetops first, followed by Shar and Whirl. Their fireballs glowed violet with anger. Their hooves pounded the ground as they came in for a landing.

The wolves were several feet away.

"Shoot now," Youda Stana screamed.

A volley of arrows pierced the air.

"Quickly," Diva shouted as she hurried toward the deer. "Jump on while their running."

She vaulted and landed on Sur. Theo waited until Pavel had grabbed ahold of Whirl before he himself latched onto Shar.

The deer flew directly over the Youdi and wolves, and arrows continued to zip past them.

"Don't let them escape." Youda Stana ran frantically after the fleeing deer.

Pavel jeered at her. "Too late, you old hag."

Panting, Theo thought to Shar, *What happened? Why didn't you come right away?*

"Sur got word that Youdi had attacked the herd," Shar replied. *"We returned to check on them. Several had been wounded. One had a broken leg, and his wings were severely damaged. The Samodivi are tending to them. When we returned to the meadow to wait for you, they ambushed us. We barely escaped."*

Theo pressed his cheek against Shar's neck. *"I'm glad you're okay. Thank you for saving us."*

"I could sense your distress. Sur felt Diva's, too. And Whirl was going crazy with worry for Pavel. We came as quickly as we could."

Theo and his friends were getting closer to freeing Zmey. They had a good idea where the dragon king was. They had a possible solution to defeating the monster that guarded him. They knew someone who could cure the blacksmith, so they could accomplish that goal. Now, if only the witch would cooperate. They needed to free Zmey and destroy Lamia and Zlo, so everything would be restored in Dragon Village. Order would reign, and nature would be reborn.

"Have you seen Baba Yaga around?" Theo asked Shar.

"No, we haven't seen her flying in her mortar, and her hut's gone into hiding. I'm sure she's up to no good."

Smoke darkened the sky over Vida Village, and the wind swept ashes their way as they traveled toward Baba Yaga's property. Theo could no longer tell what time it was, but the day was dwindling. They had to find the witch and convince her to help them before the moon rose.

After a short flight, they landed in the grove where Baba Yaga lived. Her hut was nowhere in sight, but the eyes in the skulls atop her fence of bones began to glow red in their presence.

"The bells in the trees are silent," Theo said as he slid off of Shar. "I wonder if that means she's not around."

"Maybe she's taking a vacation after being imprisoned," Pavel said. "Since her hut's on chicken legs, she could be moving around to find a sunny spot."

Theo laughed. "Like a Florida snowbird. How long should we wait to see if she's—"

Crashing and snapping of branches erupted in the forest. The witch's hut danced into view. It stopped in the middle the gated area, dug its chicken feet into the ground, and slammed its door wide open.

Pavel took a step back. "I wonder if she's inside."

"I'll go check," Theo said.

"Maybe I should go first to see if she's in a friendly mood since she's likely to be angry with you, Theo." Diva took a jar from her pouch. "This will be a good way to get her talking."

"Is that some kind of truth serum?" Pavel asked.

"No, it's smil, a flower available only around Samodivi Lake."

Theo came closer. "What do you use it for?"

"Anything from a love potion to curing depression."

Pavel covered his mouth, but he wasn't able to hide his snicker. "You think the witch is depressed because no one loves her?"

"Her cat might," Theo said.

"But only when it wants food," Pavel replied.

Diva rolled her eyes. "Boys, get serious."

"Sorry," Theo and Pavel said together.

"I'm going to see if the witch is inside now." Diva approached the hut, calling out, "Baba Yaga?"

The door slammed shut the moment Diva set foot on the steps.

"I guess she doesn't want to talk with you, either," Theo said as Diva returned.

The bells in the forest began to chime with a frenzy. Sounds like a car backfiring came from the forest, followed by cursing. Baba Yaga flew out of the woods in jerky motions, black smoke puffing from the back of her mortar. She slammed into her herbal garden and staggered out of her vessel. Her cat, Kotka, flew off of her shoulder and hid in bushes near the fence.

"Old piece of trash you are, Chutura." Baba Yaga kicked the wooden mortar. "You're broken. Dang doorbell's broken. Ain't nothing working here anymore."

Diva leaned close to Theo and Pavel and whispered, "She's in such a bad mood, you need to let me do the talking."

The witch turned in their direction and stormed toward them. "What're you doing here trespassing? Can't you read?"

"Read what?" Theo said, and Diva poked him in the side.

"My sign, my sign. Are you stupid?" Baba Yaga pointed her pestle toward the gate. "If you trespass, I'll put you in my soup."

Diva cleared her throat. "You might want to look again."

"Huh?" The witch glanced over her shoulder toward the empty gate. "Dang it."

She hobbled toward the gate and dug in the high weeds, finally pulling out a sign with peeling yellow paint. The sign swayed as she looped it over a finger bone on the gate. A childish drawing of a skeleton and crossed bones over a flaming cauldron stared back at Theo and his friends.

"There. See?" Baba Yaga sneered. "Now, begone from my sight."

Diva approached the witch. "We need your help."

"Of course, you do," Baba Yaga shouted. "You always come to me expecting help. But I'm tired of getting the lot of you out of trouble. Go away. I'm so angry I can't promise to restrain myself from hurting you."

She roared and walked toward her hut, but turned around sharply and stalked toward Theo. "And you, especially you … How dare you come begging me?"

"I … I …" Theo backed away and bumped into the fence. A skull came loose and fell at his feet.

"I expect an apology." The witch pointed her crooked, bony finger in his face. "Or you can replace the head you broke on my fence."

"Apologize for what?"

She pressed her nose close to his face. "Did you think I enjoyed standing in a barrel like aging cheese, waiting to be live bait for rats?"

Her breath made Theo's stomach turn upside down and his eyes water. He turned his face away and said, "How'd you escape?"

"My Kotka used her claws to open the locks. She was hungry."

Pavel laughed and said, "Told you."

Baba Yaga whirled around. "Oh, you, human boy. I'll deal with you next." She turned back to Theo. "Well, I'm waiting. Tell me how sorry you are."

"I'm sorry you betrayed us, and we were forced to leave you behind."

"Blah, blah, blah … Do I look stupid, dragon boy?" The witch blinked her glowing yellowish eyes.

"We had to rescue Kosara. She ensures harmony in Dragon Village and makes sure the soil and spirit of the land are protected." Theo spread his arms wide. "This includes your place and garden."

Baba Yaga spread her own arms in an arc. "Well, the priestess has been rescued, but I don't see much of an improvement. And here you are wanting something from me to make things better."

Theo remained silent. *What can I say to that?*

"Well, cat got your tongue?" Baba Yaga cackled, displaying her sharp iron teeth. "Now there's a thought. Well, what do you want from me this time?"

"We need your help with a curse," Theo said.

"Make it or break it?"

"Break it."

"It's easier to make one, but I do like a challenge. Let me think." She plucked a hair from her chin, examining it. "Nope, not interested. Now get out of here."

"Wait, please help me." Pavel tugged on the witch's sleeve.

She turned to look at Pavel, sniffing him. "What uroki do you have, tasty one?"

Pavel stepped back. "One that gives me nightmares about your friend Kikimora."

"He he, ho ho. Kiki would find that humorous." Baba Yaga hopped around like her chicken hut. "And how did you get cursed?"

"Zima got angry with me," Pavel said. "He had his faceless doll curse me."

Baba Yaga snarled. "Oh, that one."

"He didn't do it on purpose," Theo said. "He doesn't even know he actually cursed Pavel."

"Words have power." The witch spat on the ground. "He may not have thought he cursed your human friend, but Kukeri have magic. All that nasty creature had to do was speak the words with enough intent for them to take effect."

Pavel placed his hands together. "Can you help me, please? You might be ugly and stinky and mean, but you're the most powerful witch ever."

She preened as if all of Pavel's words were a compliment. "Can and will. Just to spite that Kuker beast. Tell me exactly what he said."

Pavel said, "Kikimora doll, kikimora doll, remember that face. Remember that boy. Haunt his dreams. Give him no peace."

"Ho ho. Good one. Well, what will you give me for payment?"

Pavel patted his backpack. "I have all kinds of things in here that you'll never find in Dragon Village."

"Come along, then. I'll fix you right up." Baba Yaga grabbed a skull from the fence, giggled, and waved it like a torch as she hopped toward her hut.

Pavel crept silently along behind her hunched figure.

Theo followed and whispered, "Are you sure you trust her?"

"I don't have a choice."

Baba Yaga whirled around at the steps and put her hand out to Theo. "You stay here, dragon boy. What I'm going to do ain't for you to see."

"But—"

Pavel shook his head. "I want to do this by myself." He walked up the steps behind the witch and disappeared into the hut without a backward glance.

Chapter 15
The Dragon's Lair

THEO KEPT HIS EYES glued to the door on Baba Yaga's hut. Every minute his friend was inside—alone—with the witch felt like an eternity. Pavel's feelings about the witch had always ranged from fearful to snarky. In his current state of mental health, anything could happen.

As the sun began to set, Theo couldn't stand still. He walked all around the hut, trying to peek in the windows, but the chicken legs kept moving, preventing him from seeing anything except the entry. With a sigh, Theo returned to where Diva sat on the ground outside the bone fence.

"What do you think she's doing?" he asked.

"Removing his curse."

"I know, but—"

The door slammed open, and a smiling Pavel skipped down the steps. Theo wondered all the more what had happened between his friend and the witch. Whenever Theo had been inside the witch's hut, he'd wanted to get as far away as possible. He certainly never had a smile on his face as he left.

"Hey, guys." Pavel waved to them. "Come on in. The witch said she'd help with Sitara's curse, too."

Theo looked at Diva.

She shrugged and got up off of the ground. "Who knows why she changed her mind."

When Theo reached the foot of the stairs, he asked Pavel, "What happened? Why'd she say she'd help?"

Pavel shook his now less bulky backpack. "She got lots of new toys."

"But—"

"Don't worry, nothing dangerous and nothing I can't live without while we're here." Pavel took a step up. "You know, she's quite funny. I was laughing so hard at her trying out my devices." He leaned closer. "I even gave her my extra toothbrush and toothpaste. Told her it would make her teeth sharper."

Theo let out a half-hearted laugh as he leaned against the stair railing, his mouth open, trying to digest his friend's words. Pavel wasn't terrified of Baba Yaga any longer. What kind of magic had she performed in there? Or had Pavel done the magic? Theo had lost all hope they could cure Sitara, but then Pavel had worked wonders with the witch, making her change her mind.

"Come on, children," the witch yelled from the doorway. "Stop dawdling. Time's a wasting."

Theo tramped up the steps behind Pavel, with Diva following. The door closed with a slam behind her. A bright light flashed on and off, swirling around and making the creepy room even eerier. Theo found the source, an LED road flare, like the one Pavel had given to Lord Vodnik for his help. Pavel must have brought two on this trip.

"Don't touch anything," Baba Yaga said as she sat in a chair—the only one available—in the center of the room.

"How can we?" Theo squinted. "I'm being blinded and can't find anything. Pavel, will you shut that thing off, please?"

Pavel pushed a button on top, and the room stopped swirling. Now, ghastly light from the glowing eyes of the skull torch lit the room instead.

"I'm not sure that's any better." Theo blinked away the dots in front of his eyes.

"Picky, picky." Like performing a holy ritual, the witch got up and lit candles around the room, then sat back in her chair. The candlelight made the wrinkles on her face look like deep canyons. "The rest of you can sit on the floor or stand. I don't care which, as long as you don't stay too long. Tell me what you want."

"We need you to break Sitara's curse—permanently," Theo said.

"He he, ho ho." Baba Yaga held her stomach as she laughed. "Your human friend told me you'd really messed that up."

Theo looked at Pavel, who mouthed, "That's not how I said it."

"And now you want me to fix your problem. He he, ho ho," the witch continued. "Well, I can do it."

"Thank you. We—"

"Wait a minute. I'm not done." Baba Yaga picked at her hair and removed a bug, which she crushed between her teeth. "What are you gonna give me for my services?"

"What?" Pavel said before Theo could answer. "I gave you a bunch of stuff already. You said you'd help."

The witch smirked. "I meant I'd *talk* with the dragon boy. *He* still has to pay his dues."

Pavel grumbled under his breath and walked over to stand by the door.

Theo felt bad for his friend, falling for the witch's tricks, and angry at Baba Yaga for taking advantage of Pavel's trust. "Maybe I'll go ask Kikimora instead. She was kind to me."

Baba Yaga cackled. "You think she can do that? Who do you imagine introduced magic to her? She's like a beloved daughter to me. I taught her well, but no one, no one I tell you, is a more powerful witch than Baba Yaga. I am the witch of witches."

Theo stepped toward the door. "She got rid of Lamia from me. I'm sure she could cure a Vurkolak."

"Kiki didn't know how." Baba Yaga got up and walked to a shelf. "Why do you think I went inside first? To tell her what to do."

"No," Theo shouted. He didn't want the witch to be their only resource.

"Did you really think she didn't want company?" Baba Yaga snorted with laughter. "She's so lonely, she'd let that nasty Lord Vodnik visit her if he came by."

"Why lie about all of it, then?" Pavel asked.

"Why, genius boy? I wanted an excuse to visit my dear friend. And it's always hilarious to play jokes on everyone."

Pavel swung his head slowly from side to side. "That's just … so wrong."

"Wrong for you is right for me." She poked at a book on the shelf. "This one? No, maybe this one." She removed one with a dark blue cover and gold inscription. Dust and feathers flew around the room. "What are you doing here in my library?" She reached in among the books and pulled out a squeaking mouse. "Kotka, oh, Kotka?"

The door flew open, narrowly missing Pavel, and the purple cat came flying in. "Mrawl."

"Here, my lovely." Baba Yaga threw the mouse by the tail over Theo, straight into the cat's claws.

"Gross," he and Pavel both said.

"Cat's gotta eat." The witch licked her fingers and flipped through the book's pages. "*Tuk, tuk ... shah shah ... tazi, ne ne tazi.* Ah, here, 'How to reverse a Vurkolak curse.' Yes, I thought *Moon Magic* was the right book."

Diva crept closer and looked over Baba Yaga's shoulder.

The witch slammed the book shut. "Not for your eyes." She turned toward Theo. "So, dragon boy, what's your answer? What will you give me to help?"

"You want more gold?"

"*More* gold?" Baba Yaga snorted. "I've had enough of gold. Besides, I ain't got the gold I was promised for tricking those Youdi." She stared down her crooked nose and looked at Diva. "Nor my new mortar your sisters promised me. I still have to ride around in my old, decrepit Chutura."

Diva stood straight. "Unlike you, my sisters have been rather busy trying to save Zmeykovo if you haven't noticed. You know they'll give you one when they have a chance."

"Certainly hope so. Old thing's falling apart. But back to you, dragon boy." She faced Theo again, casting glances at his backpack. "What's my payment? I don't do favors for free. I want something magical."

"I don't have much of anything in here. Pavel's the gadget person." Theo opened his backpack.

The witch grabbed it and pulled out clothing and odds and ends. "Hmmmph. Nothing interesting. You'll have to do better than that."

"What I'm going to have to do is sterilize everything that touched your floor," Theo grumbled.

"The castle." Baba Yaga clicked her long, sharp fingernails. "There has to be something special in Zmey's treasure hoard. Take me there."

"How?" Theo clenched his fists. "I don't know where it is."

"I do," Diva said. "But we'll have to blindfold the witch so she doesn't come and go as she pleases."

"And cover her ears," Theo said. "We don't want her hearing anything. Maybe even gag her so we don't have to listen to her jabbering all the way."

"And make her ride with you on Sur," Pavel added. "She might have a tracking device on her mortar."

"Great idea." Theo smiled at Pavel.

Theo snickered, hoping Sur would make the ride bumpy to pay the witch back for trying to poison him and Whirl once before. *Let the old witch cling to the deer, without the security of her vehicle around her. It'll be like traveling in a jeep without its doors.*

"All agreed," Diva said.

Pavel looked out the window. "We better hurry. It's already getting dark. The moon will be up soon."

They led Baba Yaga outside. She sputtered as Theo bound her eyes and ears. Before Baba Yaga could get any words out, Diva gagged the witch and tossed her onto Sur.

The deer pawed the ground, and his fireball turned purple.

"I know. I'm sorry." Diva ran her hand down his side. "I don't want to ride with her either, but we have to do this."

They traveled through the crisp air toward Cherna Mountain. Soon a waterfall that fed a lake appeared in the fading light. The last time they'd been here, Zima had frozen the lake so they could cross. Now, Diva guided Sur to a meadow near the cliffs. She slid off the deer and pulled Baba Yaga down with her. Theo and Pavel landed and followed Diva along a path near the thunderous waterfall. Before they reached the water's edge, Diva disappeared between two boulders. The boys kept on her heels as she meandered one way then another through dark passages. It felt like hours before they left the tunnels and entered a vast cavern.

Diva released her grasp on Baba Yaga and lit a torch on the wall.

The room glittered and sparkled. Gold. Crystals. Gems. A mountain of treasures lay before Theo, just like he'd always imagined a dragon's hoard to look like.

"Oh, man." Pavel stooped to run coins through his hands. "Theo, you're rich."

"Diva, how did you know this was here?" Theo asked.

She grinned. "Samodiva secret."

"Someone could help me." Baba Yaga had pulled the gag down and was fumbling with the restraints on her eyes and ears.

Diva removed the cloths, and the witch's eyes lit up. She scrambled around, picking up one item after the other. "This? No. Maybe this one." She stuffed her pockets full of gold while saying, "This is payment for helping you with the Youdi."

"Fine. Just please hurry," Theo said. "We have to get back to Sitara before the moon rises."

"Pfft, wouldn't worry about that if I were you. I can't perform the ritual until midnight." Baba Yaga handled more treasures.

"Theo." Diva's words forced him to look away from the witch. "We'll need gold, too, for Sitara to melt so he can guild the water buffalo's horns."

He tapped his forehead with the back of his hand. "You're right. Will you keep an eye on the witch for me while I get some?"

"Sure."

Wanting to be away from Baba Yaga and her gluttonous ramblings, Theo walked toward the far wall. He scoured through objects until he came across a pile of golden nuggets. Glad he didn't have to destroy coins or finery, he gathered up handfuls of the rocks into his backpack. He glanced back to the center of the room, where the witch still scrambled through Zmey's wealth.

I guess she won't be done any time soon. He sighed. They really did need to hurry.

He tuned her out and continued to examine his father's treasures. *Where did he get all these things?* Had they been stolen through the ages? Tribute from subjects? Gifts from Bendis? So many more questions Theo wanted to ask his father.

A scratching noise brought him out of his thoughts. *Where did it come from?*

Theo focused his dragon hearing on the sound. Scraping and whispers. They weren't in this room, but on the other side of the wall. He pressed his ear against the cold stone, but it was too thick for his senses to penetrate.

Who's over there? Has Lamia found us even here?

He scanned the walls. *There has to be another way out of here.* But he found nothing.

"Oh this, this." Baba Yaga finally screeched as she picked up a crystal ball. "See how it sparkles. Here's my payment."

Theo hurried back to where Diva was standing. "Can she do any damage with that?"

Diva shook her head. "Not to my knowledge."

"Take it, and let's get out of here," Theo said. If they'd been discovered by their enemies, they had to get out quickly.

"Now I can see the future." Baba Yaga danced around. Coins clinked under her feet. She stopped short. "Hmmm. You gave it to me too easily. I have to test that it's real." The witch bit into the globe with her sharp iron teeth.

With a loud crack, the crystal ball shattered.

"Fake. It's fake. I want something else." Sobbing, she dropped to her knees and put her head into her hands.

"Sorry, no returns," Theo said. "A deal's a deal."

Pavel scooped up the crystal fragments from the floor and examined them. "Ah, witch, if you don't want them, I'll take them."

Baba Yaga uncovered her head, her eyes as dry as a river bed in a drought. "Why would you want that broken thing?"

"Look." He held his cupped palms toward her. "Priceless diamonds."

Before Theo could blink, the witch sprang up and snatched the gems from Pavel's hands. "Mine. All mine. A deal's a deal."

Pavel jumped back and rubbed his hands on his shirt. "Maybe you can use them as new teeth. Better than those ugly iron ones."

The witch stuffed the gems into her pockets and looked again at the pile of treasure.

"No, nothing else." Theo stepped in front of her. "It's time to keep your promise and cure Sitara."

"Of course." Baba Yaga grinned and took a step toward the passage. "Go get him, and I'll meet you at my hut."

"Not so quick." Theo pulled the witch back. "Diva, tie her up again, please, so we can get out of here."

Baba Yaga grumbled while Diva bound her eyes, ears, and mouth. They hurried down the passageways and exited by the boulders.

Night had fallen, and the full moon glistened on the waterfall.

They were too late. Sitara must have already changed into a Vurkolak.

Chapter 16
Ritual Beneath the Moon

THE FULL MOON HID behind a cloud. Theo and Pavel used the opportunity to dash into Sitara's smithy. This time, stealth triumphed over openness. Not that anyone was around. The fire earlier in the day must have terrified the residents. Even now, the odor of charcoal filled the air, and ashes dusted everything. Or perhaps the soldiers had forced a curfew on the villagers. Or—horror of horrors—Sitara had managed to escape and was terrorizing Vida Village. But if that were the case, then the screams of victims would fill the air, not the silence that greeted Theo and Pavel.

"I think we should have had Diva come with us," Pavel whispered after they slid inside the shop.

"And trust that Baba Yaga would do as she promised?" Theo asked.

Pavel sighed. "I guess you're right. Someone had to keep an eye on the witch, and it wasn't going to be me."

Theo crept toward the stairs at the back of the room. "Let's find Sitara and get out of here. I hope he's okay."

The stairs creaked as Theo made his way down. Although the barrels filled with precious metals and gems had been overturned, the room remained free of the scorch marks that ravaged the upper area. Had the Youdi protected this room despite Radan's command to burn down the building? The shelving blocking the tunnel had been hurled aside, and the opening looked as if it had been blasted open with dynamite. How else could Bor Stobor and the other massive creatures squeeze into the tunnel Theo, Pavel, and Diva had escaped through?

Theo took steps toward the cover behind the kiln. He kneeled and whispered as loudly as he dared, "Sitara, we've returned to help you."

A rustling came from Sitara's self-imposed prison, but no other sound.

"Do you think he's still down there?" Pavel asked as he came closer.

"No one's disturbed the cover, so I think so." Theo swept away straw and tugged on the ring, but it didn't budge. He stood, bent over, and tried again. "Too heavy. Will you help me?"

"Sure." Pavel gripped the ring, and together they inched off the cover.

"Sitara?" Theo called down the hole.

The beast below them roared. "Get out of here before I rip you to shreds."

"I have to go down and talk with him." Theo dropped his backpack and sword onto the floor and placed a foot on the first rung of the ladder.

"No, don't." Pavel pulled him back. "He'll kill you."

"I have to try." Theo looked at the crossbow. "Do you know how to use that?"

Pavel nodded. "I can figure it out."

"Good. Get it ready to protect yourself if I fail." Theo scrambled down the ladder before Pavel could protest again.

A huge wolf-like creature lunged toward Theo from the darkness. The man-beast thrust his claws forward, straining at the chains wrapped around his torso and those binding his hands and feet to the stakes. Snarling and baring a mouth filled with bloody fangs, he growled with a gravelly voice, "I told you to leave."

Theo pressed back against the ladder. He had to be brave and try to reason with the monster. His dragon spirit woke, clawing at his insides to be released to fight the beast.

Sitara's a friend, Theo reminded himself. *Not an enemy.*

But the wolf-like creature in front of him didn't act friendly. His glowing gray eyes were riveted on Theo. The hatred that shone out of them now was a hundredfold more frightening than it had been the first time Theo had encountered Sitara in beast form. Whereas before, only a caged animal had stared back at Theo, this time that monster exhibited the intelligence of a man. Sitara fought for more than survival. He sought revenge. Against the person who had made him this way.

Under the surface, Theo sensed something more than an enraged beast. Sitara struggled against the monster within him that craved blood and destruction. Humanity, the kind that desired to create rather than destroy, emanated from the man-beast. A kind, human soul lay hidden beneath the façade of the monster.

We can save him, but how do we get him out of here?

Keeping his distance, Theo said, "Sitara, Baba Yaga knows how to cure you. She's waiting. Will you—can you—come peacefully with us?"

"Do I look like I can? I crave blood. I yearn for flesh." Sitara foamed at the mouth. "If you take me out of here, not only you, but everyone in Zmeykovo will be in danger. Get lost! Leave me alone. You're too late. Let this monstrous body of mine rot in this hole."

"No." Theo wiped his sweaty palms against his shirt. "I won't let it be too late. We'll free you from this curse."

But how? When they'd encountered the Vurkolak in Devil's Throat, Diva had put him to sleep with herbs mixed with sulfur. Theo didn't have that, but maybe …

"Pavel," Theo called up the hole, "do you have any lavender leaves on you? Like what Diva used in the tea to relax you?"

Pavel poked his head over the opening. "Lavender? Not the leaves, but I have a vial with some tea." He handed it down. "I don't really think this is the time to have a soothing drink, though."

After Theo explained what he wanted it for, Pavel tapped his lips with his fist. "That's not enough to put him to sleep. It might relax him a little, but we don't want him unconscious. How would you get him up the ladder? He weighs more than an elephant. We'd need at least six people to move him. Let me think."

Pavel disappeared. Scraping, pounding, and scratching came from above. Finally, Pavel said, "Aha." He peered over the top of the hole again. "I have an idea, but you might not like it."

"Anything, if it helps us get Sitara out safely," Theo replied.

Sitara growled. "I told you to leave. I'm beyond hope."

"We're not giving up." Theo glanced over his shoulder, then looked back up at Pavel. "What's your idea?"

"This." Pavel slid Theo's bow down to him.

"You want me to shoot him?"

"No." Pavel shook his head. "Remember when we were hiding in Lamia's garden, and your bow turned into a snake?"

"Yeeeess." Theo *didn't* like where this was going. "And …"

"Well …" Pavel took a deep breath and spit out his words quickly. "I think you need to make the bow turn back into a cobra and hypnotize Sitara."

Theo definitely didn't like that idea. "I …"

Pavel pushed himself away and muttered, "I knew you wouldn't like it because it's my idea."

"No, that's not why." Twice before Theo had turned the snake into a bow, but never the other way around. He climbed halfway up the ladder and looked at Pavel slumped on the floor. "I just don't know how to do that. Do you have any gadget in your backpack we could use to try to hypnotize Sitara?"

The blacksmith growled, and Theo sensed a hole burning in his back.

"No, Baba Yaga has all my cool stuff," Pavel said. "I wish Diva was here. She knows how to deal with animals."

"Sitara's not an animal. He has a monster's appearance, but inside he's human."

"I still think my idea would work." Pavel drew closer. "Last time, you talked to the snake and asked it to turn back into a bow. I really, really, *really* think you could ask the bow to turn into a cobra."

"Okay." Theo gulped and descended the ladder. "I guess we won't know until I try."

Theo caressed the ebony bow, the one the priestess Kosara had given him, the same bow that had once belonged to his mother. What would Kosara tell him to do? Perhaps she'd say he had to call the soul of the snake inside the bow and ask for help. He felt silly talking to an inanimate object.

Can I do this silently? Can I just imagine what I want the snake-bow to do?

He closed his eyes and pictured the bow changing shape. Its smooth surface wavered in his hands. Theo opened his eyes and froze at the sight of a black cobra with glazed eyes piercing into his soul.

"Pavel, it worked," he whispered.

"I see that," Pavel said. "Now try to have it hypnotize Sitara."

Sitara continued his low growl, but he'd ceased struggling against his restraints.

"Do you understand that I'm trying to help you?" Theo stared into the blacksmith's glowing eyes, but discerned no emotion. Hoping that Sitara was fighting his animalistic urges, Theo spoke into the cobra's mind. *"Please help us. Relax Sitara so he won't attack and he'll do what we ask. Please."*

The cobra twisted its body around so it was facing the blacksmith. It undulated across the floor, just out of Sitara's reach. Back and forth it swayed its head in a mesmerizing dance. A glow radiated from its eyes until it locked with Sitara's. The blacksmith's grip on his chains loosened, and he followed the cobra's movements. Little by little, the wild glare in Sitara's eyes dimmed, and his head fell forward, limp.

Theo uncorked the vial of lavender tea and approached the blacksmith. "Sitara, are you awake?"

The blacksmith nodded and raised his head. His eyes held a faraway look, and drool ran down his chin, but it was those sharp teeth that Theo wanted to avoid.

"Will you drink this?" Theo held out the bottle in his shaking hand. "It'll relax you for a while longer, until we can get you to Baba Yaga's house."

Again, Sitara nodded without taking his eyes off of the swaying cobra.

Theo crept closer while the cobra continued its hypnotic dance. He tripped over the tip of the snake's tail, and the vial slid from his grasp. He grabbed it and squeezed it tight before it had a chance to smash on the floor. Sitara stood frozen, his mouth slightly open, letting out a stream of corpse-like breath. Theo mustered up courage and brought his trembling hand closer. The hairs on Sitara's face tickled Theo's hand as he poured the liquid into the blacksmith's mouth.

Theo backed away. "Swallow it, please."

For a third time, Sitara nodded. He audibly gulped. Then, to Theo's horror, the blacksmith swayed and landed unconscious on the ground. The chains attached to his arms and feet clanked as they struck rocks in the soil.

The cobra pulled away and slithered to a corner of the room.

"Ah, Pavel," Theo shouted, "we have a problem or two."

Pavel looked into the opening. "What? It didn't work?"

"No, it did work, but—"

"It did?" Pavel's voice held a hint of surprise. "I mean, of course it worked. I knew it would. So, what's wrong?"

"It worked too well. Problem one. Sitara's on the floor, and we'll have to get him up the ladder somehow. I wish the Kukeri were here with their superhuman strength. Another problem is I don't know where the key to unlock his chains is."

"I'm coming." Pavel scrambled down the ladder rungs. "Phew, it's stinky down here. Moldy and bad breath." His smile faded at the sight of the huge sleeping Vurkolak. "Are you sure he's not going to wake up?"

"He's out like a drunk," Theo said. "I think the combination of the cobra's hypnosis and the lavender will work for hours."

"Are you sure?"

"Is anything ever a hundred percent certain?" Theo replied. "Any ideas on how to lift our heavy friend?"

"There's not much down here to work with." Pavel fiddled with his glasses. "Why don't you look for the key while I think."

"Okay." Theo approached the coiled snake with slow steps.

It raised its head, staring at him.

"I guess I should turn you back into my bow first. Please stay still and don't strike me." He grasped the back of the cobra's cold head. Its scales hardened into a smooth ebony bow. "Glad to have you back this way again."

On the ground where the snake had lain glittered a thick key. Sitara must have kicked it as far away as he could after he'd chained himself. Theo picked up the key and returned to where Pavel was kneeling next to the blacksmith. "Found the key. Any luck with ideas about getting Sitara up the ladder?"

"I think we can just ask him to go up. Hypnotists make people do all kinds of things while they're asleep. Watch." Pavel stood and snapped his finger and said in a commanding voice,

"Sitara, stand up and climb the ladder. Wait for us in the jewelry room."

The blacksmith got to his feet. He stepped forward but growled as the chains restrained him.

"Oh, sorry." Theo unlocked Sitara's bounds that tethered him to the stakes and unwrapped the rusty chains from around the blacksmith's body. He kneeled to unlock the shackles on Sitara's feet.

"Maybe you should leave those and the ones on his hands right now," Pavel said. "To make sure we're a little protected if the hypnosis wears off. He can still move around enough, but we can stop him if he tries to attack or escape."

Theo looked up at the blacksmith. "Is that okay? We'll free you completely after Baba Yaga cures you."

All he got was a growl in return.

"I guess I'll take that as you're not happy about it but agreeable." Theo stood and moved out of the way. "All set now."

Sitara mumbled something sounding like "annoying kids" as he climbed the ladder. Theo and Pavel followed and led the way back to the meadow where they'd left their deer.

"How do we ride?" Theo asked. "Three of us and two deer."

"*I'll carry the blacksmith,*" Shar thought to Theo. "*I can manage him if anything goes wrong. You and Pavel can ride together on Whirl. Although he's larger than I am, he wouldn't know how to deal with such a creature.*"

Theo caressed his companion's neck. "*Are you sure?*"

Shar snorted in reply and positioned himself near the blacksmith.

"I take it you're riding with me," Pavel said as Sitara mounted Shar. "There's no way your deer can carry him and you."

Theo nodded. "It's Shar's idea. Let's get back to Baba Yaga's house quickly."

Pavel got on his deer. After Theo slid on behind him, the deer took flight. "Thanks for all your help, Pavel. That was a great idea to use the cobra to hypnotize Sitara."

Pavel laughed nervously. "Save your praise until we get to the witch's. You never know what might go wrong before then."

They flew in silence the rest of the way. Soon, the eerie glow of the witch's skull fence lay beneath them, and the deer descended. Theo's breathing increased, and he bit his lips. Time slowed as he recalled his involvement in all the events that made Sitara what he was today. Stabbing him, which turned him into a man—or so Theo thought at the time. Leaving Sitara in the cave because time was running out to rescue Nia.

Could I have changed anything to save Sitara and not jeopardize my sister?

He couldn't keep torturing himself about it. What was done was done. He was bound to make mistakes. As long as he took the steps to right them, he was doing what he should and could. Now, his only hope was that the witch would do as she'd promised.

The deer landed within the fenced-in area. Diva stood near Baba Yaga, who was holding Kotka.

"I see you've brought the Vurkolak. Sedated, too. Nice job." Baba Yaga cackled. "Now part two, breaking the spell." She turned toward Sitara and pointed toward a black cauldron filled with steaming, boiling water. "Go lie close to the fire. You need to be inside the circle of white sulfur stones."

The blacksmith remained seated on Shar, staring into space.

Theo approached him. "Sitara, please do whatever the witch asks."

Sitara slid from the deer and settled on the ground on his side, facing the fire. The flames danced across his fearsome wolf face.

"Should I arrange the stones?" Pavel asked.

"No, boy. I took care of it, but you can pour more water into the cauldron and keep the fire going. It's almost midnight, and we don't want it to go out. Now, you …" She turned back to face Theo. "There's the matter of a small rental fee for the cauldron."

"What? No." Theo got into the witch's face, regretting being so close as soon as her foul breath hit him. "That was not part of the deal. No changing the terms now."

"All right, all right. Can't blame me for trying."

"Do you have everything you need, so we can get this ritual going?"

"You're a smart dragon boy. Does it look like I have everything I need?"

Theo shook his head. "How would I know? You're the one with the book. Stop wasting time."

"I am missing something." The witch scratched her chin, then smacked her lips as she looked at Pavel. "Ah, that's it. To break the curse, I need the blood of a young human boy …"

"No way." Pavel scooted away from the cauldron and rushed to Diva's side.

Diva scowled. "Witch, stop tormenting my friends. You need the blood of a black hen, which we got earlier from your friend Kikimora. The only thing we're waiting for is special herbs my sisters are sending."

"This is why I keep peace with the Samodivi. They supply me with herbs available only in their forest. We have a great business relationship. They give me what I need, and I don't harm them." Baba Yaga cackled as she hobbled to the fire and tossed more wood onto it.

"Diva, how did you let your sisters know we needed herbs?" Theo asked.

"I spoke to the birds, and they got the message out. Someone should be arriving any moment." She looked toward the canopy of trees. "There, see. I think it's Boo."

A faint outline of a bird flew in front of the full moon. It quickly grew larger as the bird approached the group. A magpie swooped down and circled the cauldron before landing on Theo's shoulder. A small cotton bag dangled in the bird's beak.

Diva took the bag. "Thank you, Boo."

"My pleasure. My pleasure."

"Boo." Theo patted the magpie. "I've missed you. I'm so glad you're okay."

"The lovely Samodivi have much for me to do. I'm their messenger." Boo hopped from foot to foot and preened his feathers. "Can't stay. Must return to help them fight the demons."

Without another word, Boo zipped off into the sky and soon became a small dot. Sadness overcame Theo. His scared little friend had become so brave and important, helping protect Dragon Village, while Theo himself kept endangering his friends.

Things are going to change now.

He held out his hand for the bag of herbs, which Diva gave him, and he marched over to Baba Yaga. "Here, you should have everything you need now. Start the ritual before we run out of time."

The witch jumped back. "Okay, okay. No need to yell." She took the herbs and opened her spell book. "Let's see. A little of this, some of that, and a pinch of this. Got it." She slammed the book shut, opened the bag and added herbs into the boiling water.

Pavel sniffed the air. "That smells like beer. Did you mix up the recipe?"

"No. First, I'll make beer." She twisted her head around and licked her lips as she looked at Pavel. "Then I'll roast a smart boy on the coals to make a tasty meal. I see some tender meat right in front of me."

"Leave him alone," Diva said. "Do you want me to add the chicken blood to your potion now?"

"Yes, yes. That's next." While Diva came over and uncorked a vial, Baba Yaga pulled out white, yellow, and purple crystals from a pocket and arranged them in a circle in between the sulfur around Sitara.

"Is that it?" Pavel asked. "I expected more fanfare."

"Of course, that's not all." Baba Yaga snorted. "I need all of you to hide in the bushes while I add the final ingredient. You, too, Kotka. The moon is at its peak. I just need to …" She reached into another pocket. "Where's my silver wand? I can't complete the ritual without it."

"Go look in your hut," Theo said. "Diva, will you go with her to keep an eye on her?"

"No, no. There's no time to look." Baba Yaga paced. "I need something silver now, or the ritual will be ruined."

"Theo, your sword?" Pavel said.

"Yes, give it to me." The witch snatched it from Theo's scabbard before he could protest. "Now, everyone, get away from the cauldron so I can finish." She pointed with the sword to the bushes.

They all scattered to safety.

Baba Yaga opened the book and muttered her spell. Theo strained to listen, but couldn't hear the words. The witch finished her incantation and threw more herbs into the cauldron. Green steam blasted out, straight up into the air.

With the sword, the witch drew circles around the crystals. A soft purple light grew from them and mixed with the green steam. Together, they thickened into a fog that covered Sitara. The witch continued to draw circles, faster and faster.

The light of the moon brightened as if zooming toward the fog.

A loud roar split the night. Theo grabbed Pavel's and Diva's hands. They all looked at each other in fright when a second terrible roar erupted from within the thick fog.

Chapter 17
Dressing for Battle

JULY 2

BABA YAGA STOPPED creating circles with the sword and aimed the weapon toward the thick fog as if preparing to defend herself. Theo clenched Diva's and Pavel's hands tighter. What if Sitara attacked her? The witch was annoying, but he didn't want harm to come to the old woman. He released his grip and took a step toward the grove. Diva pulled him back and shook her head, whispering, "Wait."

The figure of a young man emerged from the dissipating fog, swayed, and fell to the ground. Baba Yaga stood over the man and touched him with the tip of the sword. She mumbled more words that Theo couldn't distinguish.

They waited for what felt like ages before the witch yelled, "You can come out now."

With hesitant steps, the trio approached the grove. Sitara's body lay by Baba Yaga's feet.

Theo kneeled and felt for a pulse. "You killed him?"

"Well, the monster's gone, the curse broken, as I promised, dragon boy," the witch spat back. "Always a risk with these kinds of spells."

"That wasn't our deal." Theo sprang to his feet and clenched his hands into fists. His dragon spirit roared inside him, once more begging to be released.

"The devil's in the details. Isn't that what you'd say?" Baba Yaga cackled. "Or, rather, the witch is. I'm not quite the fool you think me to be."

Theo brought his fist to her face. "I ought to—"

"Uh, Theo." Pavel pulled Theo's hand away. "Look."

The blacksmith's muscles twitched, and he let out a deep groan. He pulled himself up off of the ground and slowly opened his eyes. "What a nightmare." He lifted his arms to rub his shoulders, stopped, and stared at the shackles. "Why am I handcuffed?"

"Sitara, you're alive." Theo dropped to his knees by the blacksmith. "Don't you remember anything?"

The blacksmith cupped his face in his hands. "It's … it's coming back. Not a nightmare. All real." He moaned.

Diva and Pavel stood behind Sitara and each laid a hand on his shoulders.

"He he, ho ho." Baba Yaga hopped around. "What a great trick. You shoulda seen all your faces. Don't forget this is Zmeykovo, the land of beasts, fairies, and talented witches. Anything is possible here."

Theo ignored the witch and unshackled Sitara's arms and legs.

"Do you think he'll turn into a wolf again?" Pavel asked.

"No, I'll give you a ten-year warranty," Baba Yaga said. "After that, you must come back and use my services again."

Theo leaped to his feet and held back from strangling the witch. "Enough of your nonsense. Don't make an enemy of me. Our agreement was a permanent cure."

The witch paled. "Fine, dragon boy. Can't even take a joke."

Theo backed away, a sneer on his face. He wanted to wash his hands from being so close to the disgusting witch. She was foul on the inside and outside. He felt sympathy for many of the other beings in Dragon Village, but had no compassion toward Baba Yaga. He doubted she became this way because of circumstances. She must have made herself this way and thrived on the power she exerted over others. Or, at least that's how it appeared. Those with power should do what they could to make the life of the defenseless better, not worse. The powerful should try to empower the downtrodden, not enslave them.

He turned his back on the witch and held out a hand to Sitara. "Let me help you up."

Sitara took hold. Theo felt energy surge through him, and he pulled the blacksmith up with ease.

"Thank you." Sitara breathed in deeply of the cool night air. "I feel free. Not only of the curse, but the raging anger that overpowered me all the time. I owe you my life for not giving up."

"Oh." Baba Yaga crept closer. "An extra benefit from the cure. I think I deserve something more for that."

Theo spun around. "No. You. Don't."

The witch backed up.

"And ..." Theo stepped closer as Baba Yaga continued to retreat to her hut. "Where's my sword? Did you think I'd forget?"

"I … I …" she spluttered.

"Theo, here it is." Diva came closer, sword in hand. "She hid it in the bushes."

"Thanks." He took his weapon. "Let's get out of here. I can't think straight around the witch."

Diva rested her hand on Theo's forearm. "Try to relax. You're letting your anger consume you."

"I know. I'm just so frustrated." Theo closed his eyes, inhaled, and held his breath as long as he could. He opened his eyes and shook his head. "Everything's gone wrong. Sitara's shop is destroyed, and we now have no way to defeat the Water Bull."

"That's not true." Sitara joined them. "My shop is destroyed, yes, but I was smithing long before I had all the tools to make it easier. I'm sure I'll be able to scavenge enough equipment and materials to make the golden horns, well, horns tipped with iron, and other protections your bull will need. I owe you that much for what you've done for me."

"You can?"

"Absolutely. Bring me to your bull so I can get a sense of his size and what I'll need. I'll also make a cast of his horns so I ensure they fit snugly."

They mounted their deer, with Sitara riding on Sur with Diva. Theo's mind was in a haze for the next couple of hours. When they arrived at the Kukeri sanctuary, he went through the motions of greeting Zima and Jega and nodding at their thanks for finding a male buffalo to fight the Water Bull, even though Theo had nothing to do with that. The Vodnik Sly had been responsible for providing them the animal. Theo sat at the base of a tree while Sitara formed a cast made of mud around the bull's horns and Jega dried and hardened it with his fire power. When Sitara was ready to return to the smithy, Theo gave him the gold nuggets and tried to convince the blacksmith to let someone go with him. But Sitara refused, saying he knew what he was doing, and everyone else would get in his way.

"I'll be back later this morning." Sitara climbed onto Sur's back. "The Water Bull is most active around noon, so you'll have your best chance of engaging with him if you get to Rabisha Lake by then."

As the blacksmith disappeared into the moonlit sky, Diva pulled Theo aside. "Out with it. What's wrong?"

Theo shrugged. "I guess I'm just focused on the upcoming battle with the Water Bull."

"No, it's more than that. I know you. Tell me."

Theo poured out his heart, repeating things he'd said to her before. He talked about his conflict with Pavel. His struggle with being a leader. All his mistakes and unworthiness. And even his feelings that he and Diva were becoming alienated. "On top of it all, I feel guilty I haven't even thought about my family in Selo for a while. I'm worried about them and know they must be frantic about me, but I've had to shove that into the back of my mind, so we can complete our mission."

"You worry too much. Worrying never solved a problem. Action does."

"Yah, but—"

"No, let me finish." Diva grabbed hold of Theo's chin and turned his face so he was looking into her eyes. "Pavel and I will always be your friends, and your family will be fine. Your mom survived when both you and Nia were gone before. Now, she has your sister there, so she's not alone. Okay?"

Theo shrugged. "I guess so."

"Change is a part of life. A part of growing." Diva released Theo's chin and smiled. "Every great leader has learned from the things he does wrong. If you think you're making mistakes now, that means you'll know how to relate to people better later on. You'll understand their problems and try harder to fix them."

"Then I'm going to be very wise someday, because I'm certainly making a lot of mistakes now."

"The way you deal with adversity will shape you into the person you will become."

"What do you mean?"

"Like nature itself. You can consume adversity and be strengthened, or be consumed by everything that goes wrong and let it eat you alive."

Theo thought about Diva's words. His aunt, Lamia, was the perfect example of the latter. She had alluded to bad things that had happened to her. She let those events make her bitter. On the other hand, Diva, too, had suffered. When Theo had first met the Samodiva girl, she had lost her sister, killed by the Harpies. That didn't fill Diva with thoughts of revenge. She saw the whole picture, how Lamia had manipulated the Harpies, the strong bending the will of the weak. Theo would not be like his treacherous aunt. He would model his actions after Diva's, and make the bad into good.

"Hey, guys," Pavel shouted from next to a campfire, "Jega made breakfast. Stop talking and come and eat."

Theo laughed. "It's nice to have Pavel back to normal and thinking about his stomach again."

"See, one problem solved." Diva looped her arm into his. "Let's go."

Theo's mouth watered at the aroma of strips of meat sizzling on a pan in the fire. "Jega's cooking bacon?"

"Not real bacon," Pavel said with his mouth full. "Jega had meat stored away. I had him slice it into thin strips. No fat, but it's real crispy. And eggs. Chicken ones this time, not lizard. He even scrambled one for me. Plus, he made toast from bread. And last, but not least, milk." Pavel waved a cup. "From the cow."

"That all sounds like a continental breakfast at a four-star hotel." Theo sat next to Pavel and grabbed a plate and food.

They sat eating and talking until the rosy glow of the sun made an appearance. Satisfied, Theo leaned against a tree. It was a nice break to have fun for a while. If he hadn't known what to expect from the rest of the day, he would have thought they were all a bunch of kids out camping during summer break. Best friends forever. He closed his eyes and thought about home. What would Mom be cooking this morning? Would Nia take any time away from home to visit with her friends? What was happening—?

"Theo, wake up." Diva nudged him. "Sitara's back. We're getting ready to leave."

A warm, bright day had replaced the rosy glow of the morning. The sun had not yet peaked, but it was close. Theo's moment of relaxation and pretending everything was normal was gone. It was time to venture to Rabisha Lake and battle the Water Bull.

"I can't believe I fell asleep." He yawned and stretched as he stood and felt more relaxed than he expected. Voicing his concerns to Diva earlier had lifted the dark cloud of anxiety that had been smothering him. He could now face the challenges ahead with the hope of succeeding.

Theo approached the cart, which the Kukeri and Sitara were loading with iron-tipped arrows and spears and the gear the blacksmith had made to cover Lucky's body to make him invincible: a helmet, shields, and an attachment for Lucky's feet, with long spikes jutting out.

"And now for the most important weapon." From a crate he'd brought back with him, Sitara lifted out two golden horns, their pointed tips edged with iron. "The masterpiece to turn the bull into a warrior." He placed them over the bull's horns, and the gold sparkled in the sunshine.

"Amazing." Pavel came forward and touched the metal into which what looked like charms had been etched. "These are even better than what I imagined they'd be."

"How did you have time to do all that?" Theo asked.

"I'm a master." Sitara shrugged as if that said it all. "The Youdi must have made sure my shop only looked destroyed. Everything I needed was there and in usable condition."

Zima loaded Kukeri bells and masks into the cart, along with additional spears, and then harnessed the buffaloes. "Is everyone ready?" He scanned the group. When he got to Pavel, he snickered. "Maybe the baby should stay here."

Pavel scowled. "I'm not a baby. I can fight as well as the rest of you. I have Theo's magic bow."

"Maybe so," Zima said as he pointed to Pavel's face, "but you have milk around your mouth like a baby."

Pavel wiped the residue from his face. "Now I'm ready to go."

"That was the best breakfast I've had in a long time, Jega," Theo said to ease the tension. "I'll rate your cooking with seven stars." He took a piece of remaining toast that Pavel hadn't devoured and put it into the top of his backpack.

"A snack for later?" Diva asked.

"Not for me." Theo shook his head. "In case Boo comes by again. He's always hungry like Pavel."

"Don't worry." Diva gave him a nudge. "Boo hasn't deserted you. My sisters said he's been a great messenger. They need him more than we do at the moment."

"Everything's ready," Zima said. "Pavel, do you want to ride in the cart?"

"Huh?" Pavel stared at the Kuker, as if waiting for another snarky remark. "I told you I'm not a baby."

"No, not for that," Zima added. "That was meant as a joke. I'm healed, so I can walk with Jega."

"Uh, no." Pavel backed away. "Baba Yaga got rid of my curse. I'm fine. I'd rather stay with Diva and Theo."

"I'm sorry." Zima cleared his throat. "I really did not intend to curse you. You annoy … annoyed me, but I meant you no harm."

"Oh, ah, thanks. Apology accepted." Pavel scurried away toward Theo and Diva and whispered, "Has the ice man begun to melt?"

"I think he's trying," Theo said. "Give him a chance. I did tell you earlier that he didn't curse you on purpose."

"Sitara," Zima said to the blacksmith, "are you joining us?"

The blacksmith shook his head. "I need to recover my energy. I did bring one final item to help you, though." He lifted his five-arrow crossbow from the crate and held it toward Pavel. "I know you have Theo's magic bow, but I want to lend you this if you'd like to use it. The arrows have been tipped with iron. It's a weapon forged to defeat a beast."

"Oh, wow. Really?" Pavel stuttered.

Sitara nodded. "Without your help, I wouldn't be rid of my curse. Please, take it with my wishes for your success."

"Sure, I'd love to use it." Pavel took the crossbow from Sitara's outstretched hand. "Thank you." Then he turned to Theo. "You don't mind if I use this instead of yours, do you?"

"Not at all. Use whatever will protect you the best. We all want you safe."

Zima climbed onto the driver's seat. "If everyone's settled, put your weapons in the cart. The extra weight won't hurt the buffaloes, now that we have a second one. Then, let's get going so we can arrive by midday."

Pavel caressed the crossbow, put it and the bow and arrows into the cart, then hurried to hug Whirl. "We'll see you later, pal."

Theo and Diva likewise loaded their weapons and gear into the cart and said goodbye to their deer. Then, everyone set off for Rabisha Lake. They bypassed the forest of demons on this southern route and traveled in a more easterly direction. The journey was trouble-free for once and quick with two buffaloes pulling the cart. In no time, the cliffs called Magura Hill appeared, and the expansive lake shimmered at its base. Across from it, in the center of the cliffs, a forest of oaks proudly displayed their branches. Somewhere beyond that, Zmey suffered in a prison.

We're coming, Father. Soon you'll be free, Theo thought.

Zima stopped the cart a short distance from the shore. He climbed down, moved aside branches, and led the animals into a grove of trees surrounded by boulders. There, he unhitched the buffaloes. "We'll assemble the bull's armor here before we bring him to the lake. This spot will keep Milka protected while we battle the Water Bull."

Jega grabbed a shield. "Theo, can you get the other one?"

Theo struggled to lift the shield engraved with a fire-breathing dragon. Pavel came to his assistance, and the two of them slid it to the edge of the cart, where it crashed to the ground.

Theo breathed heavily and leaned against the cart. "How did Sitara manage to carry all this stuff by himself? I can't even lift one."

"Think about poor Lucky," Pavel said. "He's not so lucky to have to wear this."

"No need to worry. The bull is strong." Jega returned and hefted the fallen shield to his shoulder. "Sorry about that. I forgot how heavy these were. Can you two bring over the bindings and smaller pieces instead?"

"Sure thing." Pavel grabbed a handful and whispered to Theo, "I'm glad Diva didn't show us up and lift that shield."

Theo laughed. "Me, too."

Diva poked her head over the side of the cart. "I'm too busy making Milka comfortable to worry about your male egos."

Pavel's face reddened, and he trudged away. "Uh, let's get this stuff to the Kukeri before they start complaining."

Zima and Jega assembled the many pieces Sitara had forged for Lucky. Soon, metal gleamed off of the buffalo, making him look like a mechanical bull, ready to take a cowboy on a wild ride. But, the iron-tipped golden horns distinguished him from the norm, making him more suitable for a god to command. And bells decorated the bull's newly formed armor.

Pavel strode around the animal, stopping to tap his shoe against the spikes jutting off of Lucky's front feet. "Man, I wouldn't want to get pierced with those. They'd go right through me."

Jega stroked the beast's horn. "Our boy is magnificent, a real warrior. And a dangerous one."

Lucky shook his head, and bells strung along his golden horns clanked.

Finally, the Kukeri attired themselves with their belts, each bell on them looking as if it weighed twenty pounds. Last of all, they donned their hair-covered wooden masks, carved to look like a frightful beast with fangs and blood-red eyes.

Pavel approached Jega. "I see Zima is dressed for a ritual this time, instead of just you."

"Yes." Jega covered a bell with his hand as if protecting it. "These are special bells, blessed by Kosara herself. We use them only here in Zmeykovo, where evil is more potent than in the human world because of all the magic that abounds here."

Zima cleared his throat. "Everyone, grab your weapons. Let's conquer the beast."

Chapter 18
Battle to the Death

BELLS JANGLED AND CLANKED, drowning out the tweeting of the birds, as the Kukeri led the bull, dressed like a gladiator, to the lake's edge. Theo, Pavel, and Diva spread out behind them, keeping an eye on the sparkling, yet still, water.

"We must be early," Pavel said. "With Daylight Savings Time and all. Or would that make us late? I always get confused. I think it's springing ahead and falling back. That would mean if it's really noon on standard time, then it would be 1 PM savings time. Or do you do that here?"

Jega stopped and looked backward. "We do not manipulate time here the way you do in the human world. Time is what it is. She will come when she chooses. The beast will arise shortly."

Pavel glanced at his tiny shadow. "Yah, I guess it's not quite noon yet." His stomach gurgled, and he cupped his hand into the water. "Man, I'm starving. Jega, did you bring the Ribotron I traded with you? I bet this is a perfect place to fish. Must have good-sized ones. Unless the Water Bull eats them all."

"No, my thoughts were on war, not food." Jega laughed. "It's not a good idea, unless you want to catch the Water Bull that way instead. But I doubt he'd fit into such a small plastic tube."

Zima placed his hand on his head. "What nonsense you two speak. Have you forgotten our plan already? We must make the Water Bull angry so he comes out of the water. If he sees another bull here, the Water Bull will think the buffalo is trying to become the ruler of Rabisha Lake."

"Does Lucky really have to fight?" Pavel approached the buffalo.

"Do you think the Water Bull will move out of the lake and find a new home if we ask him?" Theo lifted his hands in a questioning manner and spoke in a harsh tone. "No, he won't. He's a monster, and we fight monsters."

Pavel's jaw dropped, and Theo played back in his mind the words he had just spoken. It was more than the tone. *Is my dragon spirit making me become insensitive to the needs of others—just because they're called monsters? Who am I to judge? What do I really know about the Water Bull except what legends and Zima's history book say?*

The ground rumbled and the water rippled, tearing him from his thoughts. Everyone held their weapons poised toward the lake.

But still, the Water Bull did not appear, and the water returned to a calm surface.

"He must know we're here." Theo paced the shore.

"I guess we'll have to make him angry," Pavel said. "Diva, do you have a red scarf?"

"No." She looked at him with a puzzled look. "Why?"

"In Spain, they wave a red scarf in front of a bull to make him angry, so he'll charge." Pavel shook his head. "Or maybe the Water Bull is still asleep and was just rolling over."

"Then let's make some noise and wake him." Jega jumped around, chanting, while the bells on his belt clamored.

Zima joined in. Theo watched in amazement as the Kukeri danced around Lucky like shamans, with lots of jumping, flipping, and shaking. He had no clue how they could do that with all the weight they carried on their belts. But he was certain their terrifying masks and antics were enough to frighten any demonic creature back into its dark hole.

A whirlwind spun in the middle of the lake, forming a waterspout that shot straight up into the air. The massive stream rose so high that, like an enormous sponge, it quickly absorbed the light and darkened the sky. Thunder boomed, and lightning crackled, covering the summit of Magura Hill like an electric net. Huge chunks of hail spewed from the sky, coating the hill and beach white, but just as quickly melted. The spiraling water on the lake changed direction and surged toward the shore like a tidal wave.

"Run for cover," Pavel yelled as he raced toward the trees and scrambled up one's branches like a squirrel.

The others followed without hesitation.

"Lucky." Pavel screamed. "Run!"

The bull remained steady, pawing the ground, as if anticipating a long-desired battle.

Water flowed onto shore like lava, covering rocks, sand, and everything in its way—including the bull. Rotten tree branches, stones, and other indistinguishable debris from the bottom of the lake rushed forward like a battering ram, slamming into the grove.

When the lake's assault receded, small silverfish caught in its wake flopped on the sand. Lucky, however, remained standing his post, like a true gladiator.

"Where's the Water Bull?" Theo asked as he climbed down from the tree. "An earthquake didn't cause that, did it?"

"Look over there." Diva pointed toward the spot where the waterspout had first appeared.

The lake shook once more, and the hideous head of the Water Bull surfaced. The beast tore toward the shore.

Pavel rubbed his eyes and cleaned his glasses. "I-I guess I was wrong. That creature is very real."

"I was hoping it was all just a fairy tale, too," Theo said.

Sunlight returned and gleamed off Lucky's golden horns. The Water Bull roared, causing rocks from Magura Hill to crash into the lake. The monster changed direction and headed straight toward the buffalo. The Water Bull's bloody-red eyes glowed, and algae covered his four dangerously sharp horns.

Pavel dashed toward the animal. "We have to help Lucky."

The Water Bull roared again, fiercer than before, and birds scattered from the trees. For a moment, all was silent except for the splashing of water.

By the time Theo and Diva joined Pavel, he had already loaded the five-arrow crossbow and was pointing it in the direction of the Water Bull. The Kukeri brothers had spread out a little farther down the beach, one on each side of Lucky. The clanging of their bells added to the cacophony.

The Water Bull stopped in the lake, shook his head at each intruder, and roared again.

Time seemed to slow as both sides ceased moving. A deadly silence fell over the beach.

Go away. Go away. Theo forced the thought out toward the Water Bull. *We don't really want to hurt you. I just have to get to my father, and you're blocking the way.*

As if hearing Theo's mental plea, the Water Bull slowly turned his head in Theo's direction. The creature did not return a message. Instead, anger, fear, hatred—Theo couldn't tell which—glared back at him from the monster's red eyes. This was the look of a being that understood what he was doing, not a creature driven by his nature. The Water Bull snorted, pawed the ground beneath the water with his long-spiked, hoofed front feet, then surged forward like an avalanche straight toward Lucky.

Dragon spirit, don't let me down now. Theo concentrated on shifting into his physical dragon form, hoping his dragon spirit would still be able to assist him that way. This wasn't a spiritual battle, like the one he'd had with Lamia. Theo needed a corporal form to attack the Water Bull.

Theo shifted so quickly and painlessly, it took him a moment to realize he'd even changed. The Red Dragon was here to protect Lucky. Theo let his dragon spirit roar, exhilarated to have finally been let loose—even if it was in a physical form.

Even that didn't deter the Water Bull. The creature sped forward on his front hoofed feet, while his back lizard feet dragged behind, the beast using his tail to push himself onward.

That will be his downfall. He's a creature best-suited to water. Theo looked toward where Diva stood armed with her bow and arrow. *"Diva,"* he thought to her, *"we need to pull back and take Lucky farther inland."*

She nodded and shouted, "Pull back, away from the water."

A puzzled look from Zima made her nod toward Theo. The Kuker gave Theo a quick look, shrugged, then nodded. The two brothers coaxed Lucky farther from shore.

Will that be enough? Theo wondered. *It'll have to be. There's no time to retreat any farther.*

Diva shifted into a hawk and lunged at the Water Bull. *"I'll slow him down a little,"* she sent back to Theo. *"Every step counts."*

Pavel kept pace with them, continuing to point the arrows at the Water Bull.

"I'm coming in, Diva," Theo thought to her.

She swooped out of the way of the Water Bull's pointed horns with the grace of a ballet dancer.

Theo let off a stream of fire that struck the Water Bull in the chest. The monster bellowed and stopped his advance, but he'd already reached the shoreline. One more step, and the creature would be completely out of the water. Theo hovered in front of his enemy, just out of reach of his horns and spiked feet. The flapping of Theo's wings stirred up the smaller debris the tidal wave had hurled onto shore.

The Water Bull snorted and pawed the ground. A low rumble came from his throat at the retreating buffalo. As the Water Bull jerked his head to look at everyone, water droplets fell from his silver scales. His gaze stopped at Lucky.

The buffalo dug deep into the sand and lowered his head. Lucky was ready to fight, despite the fact the Water Bull stood twice his height.

Without warning, Lucky lurched forward.

"Lucky, no," Pavel screamed, but held off shooting.

Lucky huffed and stopped mere steps in front of the Water Bull. The two animals stood looking each other down.

Does he know he has to get the Water Bull out of the lake? Theo wondered.

The buffalo thrust his head forward, tips of his horns missing the Water Bull by inches. Grumbles and grunts came from the two beings, as if they were taunting each other with words. How Theo wished he could understand what they were saying.

"Come on, you two, *fight*." Zima thrust his spear against the Water Bull's thigh, but not through the skin.

The enraged beast turned his head and clipped Zima on his hand with one of the horns. The Kuker pulled his arm back and shouted, "Then fight, you monster. Show us you're not afraid. Give me a reason to—"

But before Zima could finish, the Water Bull swung his head back, rushed toward Lucky, striking the buffalo and piercing one of his front legs. Blood spurted out of the gash and soaked the ground. Bellowing, the Water Bull drove his front hooves into the ground and sent a wad of sand sailing toward Magura Hill.

Jega hurled a spear at the monster while continuing to dance to divert the beast's attention from Lucky. Next, Diva flew at the Water Bull and pecked at his scaly skin, but her efforts achieved nothing. Pavel re-aimed the crossbow, but everyone was in the way.

My turn, Theo thought, and he crashed into their enemy, knocking the beast to the ground with the force.

Getting to his feet, the Water Bull roared and once more charged Lucky. Much to Theo's surprise, the beast burst forward like a fox despite his short back legs. He struck Lucky on his side and crushed one of the shields. Tossing his head, the Water Bull roared and came in to strike Lucky's neck, but the buffalo lowered his legs and received a blow on his helmeted head.

Zima hurled himself onto the beast's back and stabbed him in the neck with his spear. The Kuker's bells, all the while, crashed into one another. The beast tossed and bumped until Zima went flying into the lake.

Nothing hurt or slowed the beast.

Until …

Pavel let loose the five iron-tipped crossbow arrows. They slammed into the Water Bull and stuck from his scaly chest. Howling, the beast fell to his knees and dug in the dirt, trying to stand.

"Now, Lucky. Do it, please." Pavel pleaded with the buffalo.

Jega began jumping and screaming, "Hurry, he's getting up."

The Water Bull turned his head toward the Kuker for a moment, the animal's eyes riveted on the sparkling bells.

Lucky made his move. He lowered his horns and, limping on his wounded front leg, ran straight toward the beast's heart.

Chapter 19
Nightmare in Dubrava Forest

LUCKY STRUCK THE WATER BULL with a force that sent them both skidding down the shore. Howling, the Water Bull dropped to the sand when Lucky pulled out his horns. Blood gushed from the wound. As the Water Bull crawled toward the lake, he left behind a trail of red in the sand. Lucky grunted as his defeated enemy floated to the middle before his head sank beneath the waves. The lake calmed, and the red-tinged water ebbed like ocean tides.

Theo regained his human form and ran to the shoreline to make sure he wasn't imagining it. But there it was. The water was truly seeping away. "What's happening?"

Zima came to stand next to Theo. "The Water Bull is taking the water with him. My book says that when the lake becomes red with his blood, he'll move on to become the master of another area."

The two of them gazed at the water as the level got lower and lower. By the cliff edge, a rocky ledge appeared.

Theo pointed toward it. "That must lead to the forest." At least, he hoped that his guess was right.

"I can't see what you're pointing to, but I'll trust your dragon eyes."

"Zima," Jega shouted. "We have to help Lucky. He's bleeding badly."

Zima and Theo left the shore and made their way back to where the buffalo had dropped to the sand.

Diva examined the bull's leg. He lowed and tried to kick out at her while she coated his wound with sand to staunch the worst of the bleeding, but she held him steady. "This will help for now, but we have to get him back to the cart, so I can see what medicines I have left."

As gently as he could, Jega dragged Lucky back to where they'd left the cart, but the animal struggled to break free. Finally, they arrived. Everyone helped remove Lucky's golden horns and war attire, and the buffalo dug his hooves into the grass.

While Diva searched in her pouch, Pavel caressed the bull's face. "You're going to be okay. We'll take care of you."

The bull calmed, and Milka approached and licked his nose.

Theo laughed. "See, even Milka says her kisses will make you better."

Diva removed strips of cloth, an ointment, and a container of water. She cleansed the wound and applied the medication. "This won't cure him, but it'll ease the pain and stop the bleeding. We're going to need my sisters to bring a better remedy."

"How are we going to get in contact with them?" Jega paced by the buffaloes. "We can't drag Lucky around looking for them."

"With this." Diva pointed to her silver falcon-shaped barrette, stretched out her hands, and whistled.

Birds left tree branches and flocked toward her.

"Find my sisters, please," Diva said to her attentive audience. "Tell them to come here. We need to cure a gash on Lucky's leg."

The birds scattered, each flying in a different direction.

"I'll wait here with Milka and Lucky." Jega wrapped an arm around each of the buffalo's necks. "Then I'll return them to the Kukeri sanctuary, and inform Sly he can retrieve Lucky."

"Milka's going to miss him." Pavel gave the female a sad look.

"Perhaps we can work something out with Lord Vodnik at a later date," Zima said. "But right now, we can't let him know we even borrowed the buffalo. Even I don't want to mess with him."

"Thank you for helping us, Lucky." Pavel stroked the bull's cheek. "I'll miss you."

"Let's get going then, if everyone is ready." Zima took off his Kuker mask and belt of bells and grabbed weapons from the cart. "Take what you need. We have a long hike to get to the cliffs."

"It's too bad the water went down." Theo gathered his backpack and sword. "We could have swum across quicker than doing all that walking."

"When you find your father," Jega said, "bring him to the castle. The last time I talked with Sava, she said the Samodivi and some villagers had been restoring his home."

"What about Zlo's guards?" Pavel asked as he grabbed the black bow.

"Gone." Jega shrugged. "They all left and never returned."

"I don't like the sound of that," Theo said.

"Me either," Diva replied. "It sounds like he's getting closer to opening a portal to the human world. We have to hurry."

Devoid of his Kuker bells, Zima led the group in silence toward the cliffs. Theo couldn't help but be a little annoyed that Zima always took the lead. If Theo had been quicker, he could have started out first.

I should be more decisive and take the initiative. He vowed that he wouldn't let his hesitation turn into jealousy. He admired Zima. The Kuker knew how to lead. That's why Mraz had given Zima that role. For now, Theo would go with that, but soon, he'd make sure he was the one making the snap—but right—decisions.

They walked for hours, with groans escaping from both Theo and Pavel, before they reached the cliffs. As Theo had thought, the receding water had revealed a rocky path along the former shoreline. The stones had been worn smooth by erosion, so the four of them passed over the ledge easily. By the time they reached the dense oak forest, sunlight had dimmed. The air in the enclosed area was cool and comforting after the long hike.

"I think we should rest here for the night," Theo said. "We can look for the cave entrance when it's light out."

No one objected, and Pavel plopped down onto a pile of straw. "Thank goodness. I'm exhausted."

Theo, proud of himself for making that quick decision, surveyed the area and sent out his dragon senses. Everything was peaceful, and birds sang their evening goodnights to one another. Some of the trees had withered in the dense forest, and should be thinned out so the others could grow healthier.

"Hey, look at these rocks." Pavel picked up one and held it out to Theo.

The stone had long streaks pierced through it, as if someone had shot them with a syringe filled with acid.

Theo took the rock and turned it around, then gave it back to Pavel. "Odd. There are a lot of them around. I wonder what kind of erosion happened here."

"Don't know. Maybe just porous." Pavel peered at it. "I'm not sure what kind of stone this is. But too bad it doesn't have a nice hole through the center. I could have had myself a hag stone."

Theo did a fake gasp. "You want to rely on protection amulets now?"

"With everything that happens here, I think everyone needs one."

"True." Theo yawned and stretched out next to Pavel on the straw.

Grotesque, dark shadows floated through tree branches in the fading sunlight. They disappeared the moment Theo looked in their direction.

Just shadows. I can't worry about them now. Too tired. Theo closed his eyes.

The next thing he knew, darkness surrounded him, and the night had gone deathly quiet. He opened his eyes and looked for Diva and Pavel, but his friends were nowhere nearby. He got up off of the straw and leaned against the tree. Now black, empty space lay beneath the branches where Pavel had been before. Had he fallen? Theo scanned the area. Deep down in the bottom of the chasm a bonfire burned. A misty form of a woman appeared in a white wedding dress, veil, and necklace of golden coins. Some girls in his village still dressed like that. They said they were a dragon's bride. The woman below laughed and took the hand of a man, who appeared out of the mist beside her. She removed her veil and kissed the man.

Theo blinked. It was his parents. Zunitza and Zmey.

"Mom, Dad," he shouted, but neither turned in his direction. "I must be sleeping, but such a lovely dream."

The couple danced around the fire, while they laughed and held each other close. Theo sensed their love for one another, and his body relaxed within the pleasant sleep.

But then, pain crossed his mother's face. She pulled away from Zmey, and tears streamed down her cheeks. Her makeup blackened the golden coins, which sizzled and curled into grotesque shapes. Zmey reached for Zunitza, but she ran, stretched out her hands, and dove into the fire.

Theo's dream self had to do something. "My mother's going to burn alive." He struggled to spread his arms and give birth to his wings, but failed. Something squeezed his body, and needle-like pricks pierced his shoulder. He couldn't breathe.

He opened his eyes. His startled reflection appeared within four pupils that stared back at him. The top set of eyes appeared to be those of the living, but the bottom pair made Theo's heart race. Bloody, soulless orbs. Looking at the monster was like looking at two beings in one, a human trapped within a demon.

This was real. The pain too debilitating to still be a dream.

"Diiiiva, Paaaavel," he screamed.

The creature sitting on Theo's chest pulled back and hissed. Theo got a better look at the black ape-like being suffocating him with its broad feet. Sharp talons emerged from its skinny, hairy hands, and the demon's long, pointy ears twitched.

Theo sent a desperate message to his dragon spirit. "*I can't move. Help me if you can.*"

He tried forcing his arms up, but they remained stuck to the ground. His dragon spirit didn't respond. He was as paralyzed as Theo was. The creature grabbed Theo's ears and screamed with ugly sounds, like thousands of hungry crows.

"Coming," Diva yelled and was at his side in a moment. "*Vurvi si zul duh.* Go away, bad spirit," she shouted at the monster.

It twisted its head toward her, then screeched as if in pain. The creature leaped off Theo, vaulted into the tree, and hung with one arm from a branch, while it covered its face with its other arm.

Freed of the monster, Theo pulled himself up from the ground, grabbed his sword, and leaned against the trunk while keeping the creature in sight.

Theo panted. "Why was it afraid of you?"

"Not now. Another Mora's attacking Zima." Diva sped toward the Kuker, who had settled down a short distance away.

Pavel awoke with a scream, unable to fight off another creature that clung to his chest.

The new Mora had been so quick. Pavel had been fine a moment before.

Theo swung his sword to slice through the creature, but it dissolved into a black mist before the weapon reached it. Above him, the Mora that had attacked earlier continued to sway on the branch and screech. It thrust its hand out and snatched the sword. When Theo reached for his bow, the Mora in the tree jumped onto his back and started biting his shoulder again.

Screeching, Theo grabbed one of the strange rocks and pounded the Mora's head.

The creature immediately released its grasp and disappeared in a puff of smoke.

Pavel screamed again. The Mora had returned and glued its face to his chest. Theo hurled a rock at his friend's attacker, and that creature also disappeared, leaving only a wisp of black smoke.

"Pavel, are you okay?" Theo kneeled at his friend's side and helped him sit up.

Pavel nodded while he took a deep breath. "What was that nasty ugly thing? It was suffocating me. And why … was it sucking on me as if I'm a cow?"

Diva approached with Zima walking unsteadily while leaning his hand on her shoulder.

"It sucks your blood until your breasts swell and drip milk," Zima answered.

Pavel turned red. "But, but, I'm a boy."

"They don't care." Zima rubbed his neck, now covered with blue dots like the ones on Pavel's chest and Theo's shoulder. "The one that attacked me pierced my throat with its tongue. Jega would find humor in that. He'd tell me I should have kept my bells with me, and he would have been right for once."

"Does it attack only boys?" Pavel asked. "It didn't bother Diva."

"No, they mostly attack children," Diva replied. "I don't know why they left me alone. They seemed afraid of me." She brushed a loose strand of hair from her face.

"You can be scary, but I think maybe that's why." Theo pointed to the barrette her sisters gave her for her birthday. The black bead eyes were glowing.

Diva scowled at him, but removed the barrette. "Strange. Why would they be afraid of that. I can't imagine the glow would bother them. Their own eyes are fiery."

"Let me see it, please." Pavel held out his hand, and Diva dropped the barrette into it. "Look, the black eyes aren't beads. They look the same as these stones."

Diva sat next to Pavel and examined both objects. "I think you're right."

"Those stones were the only thing that I used that drove them away, too," Theo added.

Zima smirked. "I know what they are."

"What?" Everyone looked at him.

"They're made from—"

A winged donkey burst out of a tree and latched onto Pavel's back, and he screamed. Diva snatched back the barrette and aimed it toward the creature. It shrieked as it closed its eyes and flew off into the woods.

"What was that thing?" Theo asked.

"Another Mora," Diva said. "They're shape-shifters and can appear as anything. They're well-known for turning into straw to hide."

Theo glanced at the straw he and Pavel had slept on, before turning his attention to scanning the trees with his dragon senses. No traces of evil lingered. "Looks like they're gone, at least for now."

"I guess we shouldn't have expected things to go smoothly," Diva said. "Lamia must know by now that we defeated the Water Bull and know where Zmey is. She'd have sent someone—something else—to try to stop us."

Pavel shuddered as he put a couple of the strange rocks into his backpack. "I guess I have my talisman now. I wonder what we have to expect next?"

"How are we going to protect ourselves from the Mori?" Theo yawned. "I'm exhausted. I can't stay awake all night."

Diva smiled. "I could let you wear my barrette."

"No, thanks."

"There are other ways to protect yourselves from them," Zima said. "Jega and I have run across Mori often in the human world."

"What do you suggest?" Theo asked.

"The best way would be to be inside a shelter and put a key into the door. The Mori can't pass through the keyhole that way." Zima looked around. "I doubt we'll find any shelters in this forest. So, it'll be wise to draw 'the paw of Mora' onto each of us. It's a way to ward off evil creatures like Mori. Are you familiar with that, Diva?"

She nodded. "That's a good idea. Let me make some mud to draw it." She dug in the moss, revealing black earth, which she poured water on.

"We'll just have to make sure no one slaps the Mori with a broom." Zima snickered.

"What happens then?" Theo asked.

"Humans paint these symbols on the bedroom door or window and lean a broom against the bed. If a Mora does manage to get in, they can whack it three times with the broom. It'll leap into the drawing, then collapse dead on the floor. So, I don't think you want one jumping into you if the sign's painted on your clothes."

"No, no. I've had enough of spirits jumping into me." He shivered remembering how Lamia had once possessed him.

"All ready, everyone." Diva took a glop of mud and, with one continuous motion, drew a pentagram onto Pavel's shirt. She repeated the procedure with Theo and Zima.

"Thank you, Diva." Theo yawned and settled down on the ground again—away from the straw.

"Hey, Zima." Pavel picked up one of the strange rocks. "You were going to tell us about the stones. How do they get this way?"

Zima laughed. "The Mori urinate on them."

Pavel opened his eyes wide. "What?"

"Their urine can pierce stones, but then after that, the stones can be used as a talisman to drive the Mori away."

Spluttering, Pavel dropped the stone, rubbed his hands against his pants, and laid his head on his backpack. "I'll wash the other ones before I touch them again."

Zima laughed all the way to his sleeping spot.

Theo would have chuckled, too, but dealing with too many monsters had worn him out. They were one day away from rescuing his father. Theo was terrified. Who knew what Lamia and Zlo had done to the king of Dragon Village?

Chapter 20
Into the Earth's Bowels

JULY 3

THE NEXT MORNING, they discovered an entrance to a cave on the opposite side of the oak forest. But there were problems, as usual. The two guards posted on either side of the opening were the least of their worries. The dragon king's former warriors. Now, the Knights of Darkness. The heavily armored men wielded spears and wore shields, one depicting a golden three-headed dragon, Lamia, with the other portraying a Z with a snake slithering around it, which Theo thought must be for Zlo.

"It's unbearable to see men who once protected Zmey now holding him captive," Theo whispered.

"I'm not so sure they're doing this willingly," Diva whispered back. "They were hesitant to bring harm to Kosara when Zlo held her captive."

"Zlo must use magic to make them obey," Pavel added.

"We'll deal with them shortly," Zima said. "First, we have to figure out how we're going to pass through the cave entrance."

That was the major problem. Theo now understood why Zima had said the cliffs surrounding the forest were dangerous. Not only did the cliffs ahead of them have the appearance of a monster, they were moving entities, not alive so much, but able to sense presences. A valley ran between twin peaks, each with areas gouged out to represent eyes. Theo thought they probably had the ability to see, although that part of the monstrosity didn't move. The peaks sloped down to form a split nose. Below that, was what was most terrifying.

The entrance to what they hoped was Magura Cave lay between two enormous rock formations that looked like a horde of petrified guards. With pointed heads, glaring eyes, and jagged teeth, the stone men crowded together to prevent entrance. With horror, Theo and his friends observed the rocks for quite a while. Every time an animal crossed between them, the rocks slammed together, crushing their victim.

Theo unzipped his backpack and pulled out a silk drawstring bag. "I think I have something that will help us get past the rocks."

"What?" Pavel asked.

Theo removed the white silk scarf, the birthday gift from Diva's sisters.

"How's a woman's scarf going to help us?" Pavel laughed.

"Don't you remember? It's special." Theo wrapped it around his neck, and he disappeared. He removed it and reappeared.

Pavel slapped him on the back. "Ha ha. That's great. So much has happened since your birthday that I'd forgotten. I'm sure that'll work. I wonder how Baba Yaga didn't notice this when she dumped out your backpack."

"Invisible is good," Diva said, "but the knights have a keen sense of smell, like dogs."

Zima stepped closer. "Diva's right. We'll have to get rid of the guards."

"Save that plan for later. I have a less-violent solution." Diva took a vial from her seemingly endless supply in her pouch and sprayed a mist into the air around all of them. "This herb will mask our smells."

Pavel waved his hand in front of his face. "Yikes, I really, really don't like this. It smells like rotten meat or farts. I'd rather smell like me."

"Don't worry." Diva grinned. "It'll wear off in a little while."

Theo grimaced as well. "It's not Chanel No. 5, but we have to trust each other and do whatever we can to pass the guards and the live rocks."

"What's Chanel No. 5?" Diva asked.

"It's a perfume, a special scented water that human women use to attract men," Theo explained.

Diva frowned. "To hunt them?"

Pavel laughed. "In a way."

Theo elbowed Pavel. "No, to make men like and follow women."

"You have strange customs." Diva shook her head. "Anyway, them hearing us is going to be a bigger problem than them smelling us." Diva looked from Pavel to Theo. "I know Zima can keep quiet, but can you two?"

Zima cleared his throat. "I think it would be best if I remained here, ready to end the traitorous guards' miserable lives if necessary."

"So, we'll make two passes through the rocks," Theo said. "I'll take Diva and Pavel over first, then return for you."

Zima shook his head. "No, I think you may be able to do the trick once, but the guards will be more diligent if the rocks slam together for no reason. I'll eliminate them easily if they sense you, and then I'll return to be with Jega."

"You think they'll slam together even if we're invisible?" Pavel asked.

"From what I've read, they react quickly to visible objects, but they can also sense vibrations," Zima said. "Their reaction will be slower if they don't actually see you."

"We have to try." Theo's gut clenched. The rescue plan was beginning to unravel. "I can go alone."

"No," Pavel said. "We have to do this together."

"But if we can't pass the stones again, how will we get Zmey out after we find him?" Theo asked. "And how will we get out if we don't find my father?"

"Tunnels," Zima said. "Countless tunnels traverse Zmeykovo. I'm sure you'll find Zmey, and he'll know the best route." He turned to Diva. "After you make your way back out, have the birds send word to your sisters where you are. Jega and I will remain with them, then come to your assistance with the deer."

"Agreed." Diva turned her attention to Theo. "Let's figure out the best way to do this silently."

"I need to wrap the scarf around all of us." Theo spread it out. "It's not that long, so we'll have to walk close to each other."

"That's fine. I'll help Diva." Pavel squeezed up next to her.

"You're squashing me." She pushed him gently. "I'm sure we don't have to be like two wet leaves stuck together."

They lined up side by side. Theo held one end of the scarf near his neck and handed it to Diva, who passed it down to Pavel.

"Let's see if this works." Theo wrapped his end around his neck and disappeared. Diva and Pavel followed his example.

"Wow," Pavel said. "This is so cool. I'm invisible."

"Shh," came from Diva. "Let Theo finish."

"We'll take steps together. I'll count so we can keep the same pace. On one, move your right foot, on two, the left. When we get closer to the guards, I'll stop counting, but you keep counting in your mind. Agreed?"

Pavel and Diva both responded, "Agreed."

Theo took a deep breath. His heart was pounding, but he kept his voice calm. "Here we go … one … two … one … two …"

With slow rhythmic steps, the group approached the rocks. When everyone had the same beat, Theo stopped counting out loud, and they continued forward with a slow uniform pace. The nearer they got, the more Theo patterned his breathing to match his steps. The guards hadn't demonstrated any signs of sensing the three of them.

But Theo almost gave them away as they got closer. He tensed and barely held in a gasp when the guard closest to them sniffed and grimaced. The man turned his head in their direction.

Diva squeezed Theo's hand to the beat of their steps. "*He's not looking at us,*" she thought to him, "*but at the other guard. It's the smell.*"

Theo relaxed. "*Oh, he thinks his companion let a raunchy one rip.*" Now he had to hold in his laughter.

He, Diva, and Pavel passed the guards and inched their way through the opening between the jagged rocks. Moments after they passed through, the rocks clashed together. Theo jumped and Pavel gasped.

"Shh." Diva squeezed Theo's hand even tighter, and probably Pavel's as well.

Theo strained to hear angry words from the guards, but detected nothing.

The other side of the opening wasn't what Theo had expected. He thought they'd be entering a cave. This space was open, a valley surrounded by a forest, which itself was surrounded by a cliff. A prison worthy of Alcatraz, with limited means of escape.

When they walked farther, Theo removed the scarf, and pulled his friends behind a large bush. He motioned for everyone to remain silent. He wanted to be sure no one had followed them. Finally, the scraping of the jagged-mouth rocks as they opened reached them, followed by silence. No other feet had passed through the opening. Theo wasn't even sure there was a way for the guards to pass the rocks safely.

"We're okay for now." He crept out from behind the bush. "Let's follow this path. It's overgrown, but someone made it, so it must lead to something."

Theo felt guilty that they'd left Zima behind, but he was glad to be able to make decisions or at least discuss what to do with his friends. The Kuker always expected people to unconditionally follow his lead. *I guess that's what an experienced leader does.*

They followed the path to a dilapidated stone building, resembling a gutted beehive with an opening for a door. Several pigeons cooed and flew away as Theo entered. The sparse room held nothing more than a lopsided chair and tumbled table. Thick dust coated the floor, disturbed only by pigeon feet.

"Do you think this is the way?" Theo asked. "I completely imagined a cave, not a run-down hut."

Pavel called out from the back of the room. "There are stairs here. We should see where they lead."

They crept down the creaky steps. Theo hoped the boards weren't rotted.

At the bottom, they entered a small room much like the one Sitara had made to confine himself in when he changed into a Vurkolak. A dusty metal lid covered what looked like a deserted well. Metal brackets and the thickest padlock Theo had ever seen secured the lid in place.

Theo tugged on it. "How are we going to get this off?"

"The two of us can." Diva positioned herself on the opposite side. "Concentrate on your dragon strength. I've seen you use it before. Samodivi can call extra power when they need it, so you can, too. You've gotten good at controlling the spiritual and emotional sides of your power. Now is the time to master the physical aspects. Calling this power is the same as the others. You just have to name it and believe."

Pavel shuffled his feet in the dirt. "We don't know what's inside. It could be another monster."

Theo straightened his back. "If you're talking about my father, he's not a monster."

"No, not him." Pavel held his hands in front of his face. "Some other thing that will try to kill us."

"Okay, sorry." Theo wiped his sweaty hands on his shirt. "I'm so afraid of what we'll find. Zmey's been locked away for a year."

"It's okay," Pavel said. "If there's a monster in there, Diva will turn into a wolf and terrify it."

Theo positioned his hands over the metal bracket. He focused on his inner power and called on his dragon spirit to assist him. "Ready, on the count of three. One. Two. Three."

He and Diva pulled up the cover. With a snap, the brackets shattered, and the cover went flying to the ceiling, then dropped again. A musty odor fled the confinement of the opening and permeated the small room.

"Wow, that was awesome." Pavel held his phone out, capturing the action.

"You still have power in that?" Theo asked.

"Yah, I've saved it. Most things were too terrifying to record."

A gaping hole, surrounded by a circle of rocks lay before them. Moss crept down the sides for as far as they could see. Beyond that lay only darkness.

"It does look like an old well." Pavel stooped over the edge. "Hello." His greeting echoed down the opening. "I can't tell from the sound how deep it is. I have a better idea." He dropped a rock into the hole, and a moment later it clattered to the ground. "It doesn't seem to be too far to the bottom, maybe about twelve feet, but how will we get down? I don't think we can jump, and I don't have rope long enough."

"We could use some of our spare clothes," Theo said. "I know you always pack more than you use."

"Oh, man." Pavel scowled, but pulled out two T-shirts and pajamas, which he hugged to himself. "But these are my favorites."

"When we return home, I'll take you shopping at the mall and replace them, any style you want." Theo took the clothes and added them to his own, to make a colorful rope. He secured one end to the broken bracket and dropped the other side down the hole. It thumped when it hit the bottom.

"Sounds like it's long enough," Theo said. "Who's first?"

"I'll go." Diva scrambled down with the speed of a wild cat and tugged on the rope. "Made it. All's safe."

Pavel went next, and a *thump* announced his successful descent. "Ehooo, I'm in the underworld … wooorld … wooorld. Let anyone who dares, follow me." He laughed and shook the rope.

Theo wasn't sure whether to be annoyed or happy. Pavel should take this more seriously, but Theo was also glad his friend was back to normal and acting goofy.

"Right behind you."

Theo pulled the rusty metal lid closer, to cover the opening so it didn't attract any guards who might be around. But without Diva's help, it was more of a struggle. His insides gnawed at him, so he couldn't concentrate enough to get his dragon spirit's help. Finally, he managed to get a grip on it and the clothing rope at the same time, and he slid the lid on as he inched his way down, holding the rope steady with his knees. Once the cover was secure, he hurried the rest of the way down.

"Man, it's pitch dark down here now," Pavel said as Theo descended. "My flashlight battery is dying. It hardly lights up anything."

Theo hit the bottom and turned toward his friends.

"Wow. Maybe we can use your eyes to light the way," Pavel said. "They're glowing. You look like Diva does when she gets angry."

She poked Pavel's side. "That's because Theo has Samodiva blood."

The glow faded, and the room darkened once more. Theo looked around. They had entered a cave. "I can still see okay in the dark."

"I can, too," Diva added, "but that won't help Pavel from falling into any abyss we come across. He needs light for his safety. And I didn't find any torches."

"Maybe we can make our own," Theo said. "Pavel, you've made some before, haven't you?"

"Yes, with lime, sulfur, and an old piece of cloth." Pavel sniffed. "It smells like there's sulfur around, but I'm afraid to make one. Who knows if there's gas down here?"

"Oh, wait. I have something." Theo dug in a hidden pocket of his backpack and removed a box. He hesitated a moment. "The Firebird's feather. I want to keep everyone here safe, and I think this is the only way to do that right now. But Kosara said using it can be a blessing and a curse, and it will make our journey difficult and filled with loss. Are we all prepared for that?"

Pavel shuffled in the dirt. "Exactly what kind of loss did she mean? I don't mind losing anything I have with me, not that there's much left, but what if it means something more serious? Let's try without it first. You and Diva can guide me. It might be slower, but the saying goes that slow and steady wins the race."

Theo thought back to when Kosara had given him the feather. "Actually, I think she said just having it with us would be enough to trigger problems, so I think we're already too late to avoid any of its curses. What do you two think? Should we use it or not?"

"That's too much of a burden for me," Pavel said. "I can't make that decision."

"I think you're right about it already being too late," Diva added. "But, it's up to you, Theo, if you want to be more cautious."

Theo thought about it. They'd had so many difficulties and losses already. Could anything worse happen? *I have to take care of my friends. Pavel is as important, more important to me, than a lot of people. I have to make sure he stays safe.*

He took a deep breath and opened the box.

Chapter 21
Discovering Magura Cave

THE CAVE LIT UP as if brightened by the sun. Theo squeezed his eyes shut, but the dazzling glare penetrated his lids. He raised the golden feather over his head and waited until the spots dancing in front of him disappeared before he opened his eyes.

Diva smiled. "You're becoming a worthy replacement for your father, young heir. You have an idea for everything."

"This is great. One sec before we go." Pavel went over to the clothing rope, untied his pajamas, and stuffed them into his backpack.

Theo shook his head. "Really?"

"What? They're irreplaceable." Pavel walked a short distance away, looking down. "Darkness won't be our only challenge."

Theo came closer. A narrow rocky staircase circled around and around, deeper into the earth. Moss, dirt, and other debris fallen from the domed roof covered the steps, and water seeped out of the wall in rivulets onto the pathway. Far at the bottom, lay a body of water.

"Let's take one thing at a time," Theo said. "First we'll be cautious as we go down the steps. They're going to be slippery. We can worry about the lake when we get there. Everyone ready?"

Pavel and Diva nodded. Theo took the lead, carrying the feather above his head. The way down proved less of a problem than he had anticipated. He slipped a couple of times, but debris in front of him prevented him from sliding too far. From the sounds behind him, Pavel and Diva fared better.

They stopped to rest when they arrived at the bottom. Across from the lake, carved stone blocks encased a dark opening, and erect stones topped the structure like a turret. At either side of the base to the entrance stood a stone pillar. Each was constructed with the same stone blocks as the doorway, but the top stone had been formed into a menacing, alien-like head, with deep-set eyes, flaring nose, and grimacing mouth. Likely a warning not to enter. But another object commanded Theo otherwise. Above the archway, in an enclave, a skull stared into Theo's soul and beckoned him forward. Daring him.

Theo averted his eyes and peered into the still water. It reflected their images, but nothing disturbed the surface.

"Let's see what this does." Pavel tossed in a rock. The surface rippled a moment, but then returned to its mirror-like state. "It should be okay to cross. Nothing lunged out when it was disturbed, so I don't think there's a hidden trap."

"Try once more to be sure," Theo said.

"Okay." Pavel went to the wall and picked up a larger white rock.

Theo's gut clenched. "Ah, Pavel, that's not a rock."

Pavel looked at the object in his hands. The empty sockets of a skull stared back at him. Shivering, he replaced the skull where he found it.

"I think it's only water. Let me cross first." Diva walked to the edge. "If it's deep, I can shift into a bird and fly across." She stepped into the liquid with her leather sandals. It reached mid-thigh by the time she arrived in the middle. She continued across to the other side, wet but unharmed.

"You go next," Theo told Pavel. "I'll watch on this side to make sure nothing surprises us."

After Pavel sloshed across, Theo took his turn. The water seeped into his sneakers, but nothing else did. In a moment, he joined his friends and shook off as much of the liquid as he could.

Pavel wiped moisture from his glasses. "We're batting a thousand so far. Maybe there aren't any more traps down here."

Rocks crashed down, smashing onto the stairway.

Pavel jumped back. "I spoke too soon."

Diva held her bow ready to shoot, and Theo put his finger to his mouth. He listened and expanded his vision into the dark corners the feather's light didn't penetrate. No one was around. All was silent.

"Just rocks falling from the ceiling." Theo stepped closer to the archway. "This is the way. I feel it. Let's get going."

Their footsteps echoed as they trekked through the archway. At times, moss soften their steps. Farther and farther they descended, the heat becoming suffocating. After what felt like hours, the passage opened into a magnificent cavernous room. Water trickling down the walls sparkled like diamonds within the light of the Firebird's feather. The *drip, drip, drip* of each drop into a pool of stagnant water had an ominous feel, like the prelude to a horror movie. Monstrous rock formations jutting down from the ceiling like spears added to the terrifying scenario.

Theo had enjoyed it when his school class had visited a cave, but this cavern made his skin crawl. The stalactites and stalagmites had formed grotesque creatures like the demons that had swirled into existence during Zlo's resurrection ceremony. Ghastly creatures with fangs, talons, twisted limbs, and bloody eyes.

Pavel waved his hand in front of his nose. "Man, it smells worse in here than Diva's fart perfume."

Theo agreed. He'd become accustomed to the sulfur odor that had trailed them since they'd entered, but here, the stench of rotting flesh mixed with what smelled like vomit, decomposing garbage, mildew, and boys' locker room sweat, all combined into one obnoxious odor.

"Do you know where to go next?" Diva asked.

Tunnels led in all directions, but Theo nodded. He felt the pull of his father's presence. Zmey still lived, and they would rescue him. Theo led Diva and Pavel through countless tunnels, twisting and turning until he was certain they'd never find their way back. But, Zmey would know how to escape this dungeon.

At last, they arrived at a hideous stone face, shaped like a gargoyle. Its mouth formed a tunnel. Round stones circled the entrance like teeth. Although they weren't sharp like the ones that had once barred access to Devil's Throat, they still terrified Theo. Or perhaps it was what lay beyond the mouth that frightened him.

Three child-sized statues with huge carved heads of bearded men lined the stairs on each side, leading up to the demonic-looking formation. A black-and-yellow striped snake slithered out of one of the gaping holes that formed the eyes. The viper moved along the flattened, upturned nose, before it retreated through the other eye socket.

"Zmey's in there," Theo choked out the words.

Diva laid her ear against the stone wall. "I hear something, chains rattling."

"Yes. I know it's my father. I can feel it with every pore in my body." Theo stepped into the dark tunnel through the gaping gargoyle mouth.

The short passage led them into another cave. This one was less fearsome, and more fascinating, than the previous one. Ancient drawings covered the walls. This had to be Magura Cave.

Theo recognized some of the pictographs representing the seasons from his ancient history studies. He would have loved to examine them more if he hadn't come here to rescue his father.

Theo's skin tingled, and his heart raced. Zmey was nearby. At the far corner of the cave, metal bars blended in with the rocks. Theo ran toward them, crunching debris beneath his feet. A hunched figure lay in a corner of the prison cell. The man covered his eyes and lifted his head. Dark, stringy hair clung to his face, and emaciation had etched away the man's once strong features. A fragile man had replaced the powerful, loving, respected white dragon.

Zmey's faint voice came from the cell. "Theodore, is that you, my son?"

"I'm here."

"I knew you'd find me." Zmey struggled to move, to stand and come closer, but chains pulled him back to the soiled ground. He lifted his head again, a tiny glint in his eyes. "Zunitza told me you were on your way."

Zunitza had remained with Zmey. Theo was certain that was why he'd been unable to connect with his mother. She'd used all her energy to keep her presence with her beloved husband.

Sorrow and anger overwhelmed Theo. *What has Lamia reduced my father to? She'll pay.*

Theo passed the feather to Pavel, who had reached the cell along with Diva. "Please cover this so it doesn't blind my father."

Pavel took the feather and stuck it into his backpack, so only the tip remained exposed to give them some light.

Theo let his anger build. He called on his power and his dragon spirit. He didn't ask this time. He commanded. With a roar, he gripped the cell bars and ripped them apart.

"Whoa," Pavel said. "I wish I'd saved my phone recording for this."

Theo hurled the twisted metal aside and kneeled by Zmey. Summoning up dragon fire, Theo cast his eyes onto the chains that bound his father to the hateful cell. The restraints sizzled away. In moments, Zmey was freed, and Theo gently cradled his father. Determined to be strong for now, Theo held back the tears that begged to be released.

"I knew you'd come," Zmey repeated over and again with a weak, raspy voice. "I never gave up." Trembling with every movement, Zmey wrapped his arms around Theo.

Warmth flooded Theo, and calmness replaced the anger that had built up. He was home, at peace with his father.

This is how the love of a father should feel. He'd always had that love with his human mother, and again with his Samodiva mother. He'd even had a brief moment with Zmey before, but this felt so much more real, more lasting. Now the fuzzy, warm feeling of a caring parent's arms overwhelmed him. Everything Lamia had said was a lie. The man holding Theo was good. Theo could feel it in his soul. Zmey looked at his son. Light and purity flooded from the man's eyes, with the innocence of a child.

Zmey groaned, removing his arms from around Theo. The man rubbed his wrists where gashes dug into his skin from the heavy shackles.

Diva rushed in, bowed, and kneeled before Zmey. "My king, let me attend to your injuries before we leave this nightmarish place."

When Zmey nodded, she peeled aside the remains of his ragged shirt and discarded them onto the floor. She cleansed and bandaged the wounds on his wrists and ankles. Zmey grimaced, but held in his pain.

"Do you still remember the way out?" Theo asked his father.

"I do, but I'm too weak to tell you all the turns."

"Can Mother help?"

"No. Zunitza has used all her energy to be here with me."

Theo took a deep breath. He was glad his mother had stayed with Zmey, comforting him, her love keeping him sane and alive. Now, it was up to Theo. "Then I'll find a way."

The dragon king tried to stand, but he slumped back to the floor.

"You're too weak to walk, Father. Diva and I will assist you." Theo stood and showed Diva how people made a chair with their hands. "We can easily carry him out this way."

"What do you want me to do?" Pavel asked.

"Will you hold Zmey steady once I get him on his feet, so Diva and I can form a chair?"

Pavel bobbed his head. "Absolutely."

Theo placed his hands under his father's frail body and helped him stand. "Now lean against me."

Zmey grasped onto Theo's shoulder, and Pavel came closer to steady the man.

"Oh, you have Zunitza's bow," Zmey said to Pavel. "The snake can show you the way out."

Zmey whispered to the lifeless image of the snake on the bow. Its eyes lit up, and the bow twisted into a black cobra that slithered down Zmey's arm and slid to the ground.

"Thankfully, I had enough power left to do that." A thin smile crossed Zmey's pale face, and light shone from his blue eyes.

Pavel held Zmey while Theo and Diva joined hands, then Pavel lowered the dragon king onto the seat. "We've been through many hardships to get here, sir. Even if we encounter more dangers, we'll make sure you get back to your castle safe."

"Thank you." Zmey held out a weak hand. "You're a good friend to my son."

Pavel beamed.

"Will you lead the way with the Firebird's feather?" Theo asked Pavel.

"Yes, of course." Pavel removed the feather from his backpack and looked for the snake. When he found it, he saluted it and said, "Lead the way, kind sir or ma'am."

The cobra slipped down a rocky passage, and Pavel illuminated the rock formations with the feather's light. His commentary, as if he were giving a guided tour, lightened the journey. Theo was glad his friend felt—and was—useful.

Pavel pointed to bizarre-shaped rocks along the way. "What amazing rock formations. These look like stone mushrooms, and those two like people dancing or a wedding or a couple in love." He gestured toward murals as well. The sun here, a lion over there, and a dancing woman right up ahead. "I wonder how old all these are."

Once, when Pavel stopped and wiped moisture from his glasses, he said, "Oh, cool. These rocks look like a line of penguins from *Happy Feet*."

"They do, but please try not to lose track of where the snake goes," Theo said.

"I still see it. We're going up, and it's getting cooler. And … and … yes, I see daylight." Pavel ran ahead, and a colony of bats scattered in the light. "Let me clear the opening a little more, so you can get out without setting Zmey down."

Rocks clattered, and the light increased. Pavel slipped through the hole. "We made it."

Theo and Diva leaned over Zmey to protect him from being injured by the sharp rocks overhead. Once outside, they set the dragon king down by a boulder next to the opening.

Theo breathed in the fresh air and pine scent. "We made it, but where are we?"

"The top of Magura Hill," Zmey said.

Despite the smoke and fires raging around Dragon Village, Theo thought it was a magnificent view. The look of freedom.

Diva held out her hands and whistled. Once more, birds flocked to her. "Please tell my sisters we have rescued Zmey and are waiting here. Bring the Kukeri and the deer. Quickly now. Our king needs to be escorted home."

Birds darted in all directions.

Moments later, the sky filled with flying creatures.

"That didn't take long." Pavel cupped his hands to his face to look at the sky.

"That's not the deer." Theo grabbed his sword. "It's Lamia and her hoard."

Chapter 22
Losing a Friend

MAGURA HILL SHUDDERED, sending an avalanche of rocks, dust, and leaves tumbling down the slope as the three-headed Lamia thudded to the ground and drove her sharp claws into the soil. The dragon led an army of bloodthirsty Navi that descended upon Theo and the others like a raging swarm of hornets. The whistling of wings and the disgusting odor of rotting carcasses informed Theo that Harpies lurked nearby. All too soon, the fierce faces of the half-bird, half-woman demons appeared. Behind them, Youdi screeched as they swooped overhead in chariots drawn by savage wolves.

Pavel grabbed the black bow, which had changed back from a snake once they had left the underground. Theo and Diva, with their weapons at the ready, glued their backs together to guard Zmey and Pavel.

Lamia directed her glance toward Zmey. Her words rattled inside Theo's mind. *"So, we meet again, brother. I'd hoped you would rot and die in your prison, deprived of your family, but I see your weak son has managed to rescue you."*

Diva aimed an arrow at Lamia. "You're a fool if you think Theo's weak."

Theo tilted his head toward Diva. "You can hear her?"

Diva nodded and kept her bow steady.

"Ah, yes, secrets, secrets." Lamia snorted streams of fire. *"I'll deal with you shortly, Samodiva. For now, I must talk with my brother."* The dragon pawed the ground with her huge lizard legs, scattering stones and digging deep grooves into the soil. *"What am I to do with you, brother?"*

Zmey lifted his head slowly. Sadness, pain, and regret poured from his eyes. "I tried to help you for so many years. Protect you. But you let your selfish desires deceive you into thinking the world was against you. Together, we could have put things right. If not for …" Zmey's sunken face paled even more, as he choked out his next words with a whisper, "Your jealousy ruled you. Destroyed everything."

"Enough." Lamia roared. Her tail lashed, splitting a boulder and hurling more stones down the slope. *"No more lies. You know your wrongdoings, and you'll suffer for them. Zlo and I will destroy everyone you care about, all those who serve you. I can't kill you myself, but I see you have little time left. Your power is almost all mine—the way it should have been all along."*

Sorrowful eyes formed on Zmey's face. "What has happened to the sweet girl who was my sister? I can only hope there's still time to save you."

Pavel inched his way over, squeezed Theo's elbow, and whispered as he pointed to the sky.

Theo looked and took a step back, closer to Zmey. Another mass of creatures flew from their hiding place in the clouds. Mori. Like a tornado, they spun closer to the ground, threatening to destroy everything in their path.

At the same time, a steady beat of wings came from behind Lamia.

"Lamia's gathered an entire hoard from Hell." Pavel clung to Theo's side.

Theo shook his head and whispered back, "The ones behind Lamia are the deer. Sur's bringing his herd."

Pavel let out a long breath.

"Are you expecting help?" Lamia laughed and tossed her three heads. *"No one can protect you. My followers are gathering from all directions. Radan and his knights will soon be here. There's no one to save you."*

Theo grabbed his friend by the shoulders. "Pavel, I have to fight, but someone must protect Zmey. Please, will you do everything in your power to keep him safe?"

"Of course." Pavel stood taller. "I have your bow. I'll protect your father and king with my life."

"Your life?" Theo stepped back. Would Pavel die because Theo had the Firebird's feather? He wouldn't let that happen. "No, you must stay safe, too. This isn't your world, not your battle. Promise me you won't put yourself in danger."

Pavel slowly shook his head. "I can't make that promise. It may not be my world, but you're my friend, and so are Diva, Jega, and other people I've met here. If I have to fight to stop your aunt, I will."

Theo wrapped his arms around his friend. "Please, please, please, be careful."

A strong breeze and whistling wind disturbed the air as Sur and his herd appeared, carrying Zima, Jega, their other brothers, and many Samodivi.

Lamia roared. *"Kill them all except for the dragon boy."*

As the deer, Kukeri, and Samodivi rushed into the melee, Pavel dashed away toward Zmey, pulled the man to his feet, and dragged him back down the hole they had escaped from earlier.

Theo breathed a sigh of relief. Pavel would be safe with Zmey. But then Pavel returned and stood guard over the hole, holding Theo's bow ready to shoot anyone who came close.

The lives of Zmey, Diva, Pavel, and all their friends were in Theo's hands. He unsheathed his sword, holding it by the cold hilt. He spread his legs and stood his ground. The fear he expected to overtake him didn't. Instead, a feeling of ruthlessness overpowered him. His dragon spirit was ready to shed blood.

Screeches and screams of death surrounded Theo. The fireballs between the deer's antlers flashed purple in the fading light. Theo's friends held the enemy at bay from their king, but too many demons surrounded them.

"Mom," he thought, *"are you still here? Help me, please. How do I use the sword's power?"*

"I'm here, beloved son."

Her weak voice stirred his love for her, and he trembled at having been without her presence for so long. She and Zmey had suffered so much to protect Theo as an infant. Now, he needed her help to safeguard the man she had loved in both life and death.

Her words became softer. *"Use your dragon power to make the sword's magic surrender to you. It will obey your thoughts and desires. With it, you can control the elements."*

"I will. I won't fail you," he thought back, but she was already gone, back to the Forest of Souls to regain her strength. All her energy had been spent on caring for Zmey during his imprisonment.

The enemy pushed forward. Theo had no time to lose. *"Dragon spirit, let's drive these monsters back."* He and his warrior spirit became one.

The sword's silver blade turned blue, and a halo of light glowed around it. Quivering waves of energy spread from its tip to the hilt, creating a burning sensation in Theo's palm. He glanced toward Pavel to make sure his friend was still safe. Awe and admiration shone out of Pavel's eyes, and he gave Theo a thumbs-up. Pavel's support made Theo even more secure. He wanted to make sure Diva was safe, too. He found a falcon circling in the distance, and she dipped her wings. She was okay for the moment.

Now, to make sure they remain safe. Kill the head, and the body dies. Theo advanced toward Lamia.

"I told you to leave him for me." The three-headed dragon pushed aside demons who swooped toward Theo until she stood face-to-face with her nephew. *"You're stupid to oppose me. Because you disrespect me, your aunt, I'll burn you to ashes. Don't worry. You'll live but will be disfigured."*

Her chest swelled, and all three of her doglike heads spewed streams of fire and black smoke, which lunged toward Theo.

He swung his sword, the blue halo forming a shield that protected him from the tongues of fire.

Lamia's eyes turned fiery red. She roared and stomped closer to Theo and exhaled more fire.

He swung once more. The blue light from the sword froze the flames. Theo sliced through them, and they shattered into thousands of crystals.

Lamia's next roar shook the hill, and the army around her tumbled to the ground, but Theo stood fast. "*So, you want to play games, do you, dear nephew? Let's try a new tactic.*"

Her body shrank, scales giving way to flesh, until a woman with a snake's tail appeared. She held a trident. "Bring me my pets."

Two Youdi approached, each holding a three-headed black wolf that strained at its chain-link leashes. Bloody foam oozed from the creatures' massive maws, and their yellow eyes gleamed like coals. Their three heads snarled at Theo.

"How do you like my new pets?" Lamia stood between the two beasts and stroked each one's back. "The Youdi bred them for me."

Theo leaned forward, ready to defend himself. "You and your three-headed mutts don't scare me. Are you so afraid of fighting me yourself that you have to send mere animals to do your job?"

Scales bubbled on Lamia's face. She struck the animals with her trident. "Attack and maim."

The howling beasts rushed toward Theo.

Pavel shouted, "Theo, crouch down."

Theo did, and one wolf whimpered and tumbled to the ground, with two arrows stuck out of its throat. The other animal lunged toward Theo. His sword turned purple, and he sliced it upward, embedding it deep within the animal's guts. The beast dissolved into a mass of black smoke.

Pavel whooped from behind Theo. "You're a demon killer."

"Attack. Release the wolves," Lamia screeched. "Kill the others, but only disfigure my nephew. I need to keep him alive for now."

A Harpy soared toward Pavel. He screamed when its talons dug into his shoulder. Too far away to attack, Theo hurled his sword toward the half-bird, half-woman creature. The moment the blade touched it, the creature burst into a myriad of pieces, that dissipated into smoke. The childlike Navi buzzed around Theo like angry wasps as he stormed his way to retrieve his sword.

The thudding of marching feet made the ground shudder. Radan and his knights had arrived, covered in black armor. Metal grated against metal as the warriors drew their swords.

Diva had turned back into a girl and stood guard with Pavel by the cave entrance. She tossed Theo his sword. Slicing at any creature that got in his way, he rushed back toward his aunt.

Lamia pushed in front of her the two Youdi who had held the dogs. "Do it," she commanded.

Shaking, one Youda pulled out a cork from a purple bottle and sprayed the air. "Your sword can't withstand my strong magic."

"We'll see." Confidence soared in Theo.

He believed his mother when she said he controlled the elements with the sword. He swung it in circles, and fire sparked from its edges, burning up the purple mist. He pointed the weapon again, and tongues of fire scorched the two Youdi. They ran away, screaming.

"Your servants don't stick around long." Theo taunted his aunt and hurled his sword toward her.

Lamia pounded her trident on the ground three times, and one of Radan's soldiers leaped between her and Theo. The sword pierced his armor. The man dropped to the ground and lay still.

Lamia kicked the body aside. "You see, nephew, my true servants are willing to protect their mistress at the cost of their lives."

"Only because you've enchanted them." Theo willed his sword back to him. The wind picked up and forced it from the dead soldier's body, straight back into Theo's outstretched hand. "My friends at least are willing to die for a noble cause."

All around him, the Kukeri and Samodivi fought. Flocks and flocks of all kinds of birds Diva must have called had joined the fight, along with the deer.

"We'll see whose friends are stronger. I'll leave you in the good hands of Radan and his remaining fierce warriors." Lamia turned toward the army. "Kill them all. Capture Zmey and his son and bring them to me." With a sinister laugh, Lamia changed back into a three-headed monster and flew into the air, circling the battle.

Theo rushed toward the warriors. Radan shouted a command in a language Theo didn't understand. Spears hurtled through the air. One raced toward Pavel.

My friend's going to die because of me.

Theo opened his mouth to shout, "Pavel."

Before the warning left his lips, Zima sprang through the air and knocked the weapon aside. Theo let out a long breath. Then another spear followed right behind the first and struck Zima, piercing him from back to front.

"No." Theo's scream turned into a roar as he shifted into a dragon, larger and angrier than he'd ever been before.

He surged forward, spewing fire from his maw and nostrils at everyone in his way. The stink of burning flesh excited his dragon spirit. Theo let the warrior take control of their physical body, while he himself sank into the background to mourn his fallen friend.

It's all my fault. Theo moaned. *If I hadn't taken the Firebird's feather, none of this would have happened.*

His dragon warrior, kept at bay for so long, showed no mercy. He scorched and tore to pieces each fleeing foe. Harpies' talons barely scratched him. Navi and Mori could find no place to grab hold. The warrior tore through them all. When the initial bloodlust had been curbed, the Red Dragon swooped into the air, making a beeline toward the object of his wrath: Lamia.

The three-headed monster who had caused all this chaos turned in Theo's direction. Her golden scales shimmered and began to dissolve, and her body trembled.

Good, Theo thought, *she's so terrified she's turning back into a woman.*

Lamia's eyes darted from side to side, as if looking for assistance. Everyone on the ground had fled, and no one flew to the sky to rescue her. The beastly dragon expelled a fiery breath as if building up courage. Her scales returned, and she shot away from Theo.

His dragon spirit raced after her, but Theo said, *"No. We must be with our friends. Our strength is greater than hers. We'll defeat her another time."*

The warrior obeyed and retreated, returning control to Theo. He flew back, landed, and shifted into a boy. The dead lay everywhere. Charred meat, blood, and offal covered the ground. Birds by the dozens lay scattered among the dead Harpies and Navi. Sur stood by a fallen deer.

The Kukeri brothers and Samodivi had gathered in a circle. They parted to let Theo closer. Near Zima's prone body stood Diva with her arm around Zmey, keeping him steady on his feet, while Pavel and Jega both kneeled by the fatally injured Kuker.

"No," Pavel screeched. "You can't die because of me."

"It's my job to protect humans," Zima said with a ragged breath. He reached out a hand and placed it on Pavel's shoulder. "You did good, human ... Pavel, in protecting our king." He closed his eyes, and his breathing slowed.

Jega pounded the ground and wailed like a howling wolf.

White flakes drifted down from the sky.

Snow in July? Theo thought.

Zmey spoke as loudly as he could. "Zima's spirit has returned to the elements from which it came. We will never forget his sacrifice. In his honor, the season in which snow covers our land and becomes as white as the soul of our fallen friend will be called by the name of Zima. Every time snowflakes cover Dragon Village, Zima's soul will rise again."

Theo's legs felt leaden as he approached his father. He bowed his head and kneeled at Zmey's feet. Theo owed Zima something for his sacrifice. The request he was about to make was to his king, not to his father. "How can I honor Zima? He's been so brave and strong, and a good friend."

A hand touched Theo's shoulder, and he looked up into his father's eyes.

"It's difficult to lose friends and relatives, but it's the way of life," Zmey said. "You can do something I lack the energy to accomplish." The dragon king told Theo what would be the highest honor he could perform for Zima.

When Zmey finished speaking, Theo wiped tears from his eyes and went to Pavel's backpack. He removed the Firebird's feather, which stuck out of the top. As he grasped it, Theo shifted back into the majestic Red Dragon. He soared high into the sky and circled his friends. Golden sparks from the feather ignited the sky until the feather had completely crumbled. The dots of light mingled with the flakes of snow, neither eliminating the other. They glittered like fireflies and merged into a giant star, blinking brightly. The star rose higher and higher until it reached the heavens. Tonight, it would be the brightest light in the sky.

The miniature figures of his friends on the ground followed the star's journey. Theo gazed at the bright light a while longer. *When one thing dies, something new is born.* The power of friendship overwhelmed him. The land was wounded and ravished, but with the help of his friends and Zmey, Theo knew they could restore it once again.

Not wanting to return to the sorrow below quite yet, Theo circled the sky a while longer. When the ache in his heart lessened a little, he returned to the ground, shifting back to the boy from Selo. He withdrew his sword and kneeled beside Zima's body. The Kuker had given his life for Pavel, a human he so often seemed to despise. All Theo's fault. One life for another. Or had it been Zima's destiny all along to perish this way, a hero?

Pavel would be a wreck whatever the reason. Theo would have to be strong for his friend. He thought about Diva's words earlier in the day. He would not let tragedy consume him. He would make sure it strengthened him, becoming the hero and leader the Oristnizi had foretold he would be.

Chapter 23
Ouroboros

AT THE CASTLE, the hearty cheers of villagers dwindled into a sea of whispers as their king slumped into Theo's arms after sliding from the deer. Theo trembled with fear at how little his father weighed and how ghastly white his face had become. Zmey's blue lips opened and whispered an unheard greeting to his people. He lifted a weak hand and managed to wave to the crowd.

Everyone parted as Sava ran forward, followed by Ula. "Let us take him so we can heal him."

Theo didn't want to let go. He desired to remain with his father now that he had found him. But he didn't have healing powers. The Samodivi did. Reluctantly, he let Sava take Zmey.

The crowd's whispering increased, and someone shouted, "Look. The sky."

A stunning rainbow spread across the expanse of the sky and drenched the castle with its radiant light.

"Zmey, look." Sava touched his shoulder and pointed to the view.

The dragon king lifted his head, and a smile brightened his face. "Zunitza … Zunitza … my love." He sent her a kiss.

Sava let him look a while longer before she and Ula hastened up the marble steps covered with a red carpet.

All around them, whispers grew in the crowd again. "Zmey's son" and "Unborn Hero" reached Theo's ears. A cheer arose: "Hail the Dragon Prince."

Theo backed away as villagers pressed closer. Diva grabbed his arm and pulled him up the steps. The crowd cheered louder. At the top, Diva said, "Smile and wave. Then we can leave."

Theo shuffled his feet, waved, and pasted on as cheerful a smile as he could, but he was sure it looked more like a grimace. He didn't deserve this welcome. And how could he smile when his father was so ill?

"Can we go now?" he muttered to Diva.

She hooked her arm into his, grinned, and waved to the crowd. Their cheers intensified. She bowed, making Theo do the same, then she strode into the castle.

Pavel followed close behind. Once they entered, he said, "What a royal reception. Red carpet and all. They treated you like the prince of England or a Hollywood movie star."

Theo felt his face flush. "No kidding. I'm not sure I can get used to that. Let's find my father."

Farther in, they found Ula pacing a hallway. Theo approached her. "Where's Zmey? I want to be with my father."

Ula's eyes had lost their sparkle. "Not now. Our king needs immediate care. We'll come get you when he's past danger."

"If he's going to die, I want to be with him." Theo fisted his hands and held back the shout that brewed beneath the surface.

"He won't die, but he's too weak to have anyone there except his healer." Ula wrung her hands. "I couldn't even stay."

Theo's rage subsided. "Sava can heal him?"

"Not her. Magda's returned." A dark look passed Ula's eyes. "She's the strongest healer. Your father will recover with her care."

"Who's Magda?"

"Oh, not now, Theo." Ula rubbed her eyes. "I'm too weary for questions. I'll find you when you can see your father." She hurried down a corridor and disappeared around a corner.

"What a horrid day." Pavel sat on a dusty bench and held his head in his hands.

Theo sat next to his friend and slung his arm around Pavel's shoulder. Words wouldn't help his friend through his grief, nor would they ease Theo's troubled mind. He wanted Pavel to know he wasn't alone.

Matters still weren't resolved between him and Pavel. The more powerful Theo got, the more reserved his friend became. Theo hoped that the rift between them could be resolved soon. The longer and further they became estranged, the harder it would be to ever get back to the way their friendship had been before. If it ever could. Change was constant. Perhaps they'd form an even stronger bond by the time they defeated Lamia and Zlo.

They sat in silence for a while before Diva said, "Let's explore the castle, you two. Time will pass quicker if we do something."

Theo stood and sighed. Diva was right. Leaders did things. The son of Zmey shouldn't sit around moping. "Coming, Pavel?"

His friend nodded and got to his feet. Diva walked between them, her arms slung into theirs, leading them down a corridor.

"Where are you taking us?" Theo asked.

"On an adventure," she said with a mysterious smile. "I'm sure the castle has hidden secrets."

Secrets. There's that word that Lamia keeps repeating, Theo thought as he kicked aside a piece of a broken clay pitcher. *I'm not sure I want to learn any more secrets today.*

The Samodivi and villagers had restored and cleaned parts of the castle, but ash and broken stones remained in this passage. Although dusty, the magnificence of the murals on the walls shone through. Animals darting along landscapes replete with flowing springs were like scenes out of a *National Geographic* magazine.

Diva veered into another corridor. Countless marble squares covered the walls. Each depicted an animal or bird made of solid gold. Theo stopped counting after he reached two hundred. In the dim, torch-lit light, the animals' eyes sparkled.

Even Pavel came out of his solemn mood. "Look at this one. Its eyes are made of diamonds."

Others peered at them with ruby, topaz, and countless gems unknown to Theo.

A door lay cracked open at the end of the corridor. Theo pushed it in and stepped inside a ballroom, smaller than the one he'd seen the first time he'd been in the castle. Surprisingly, the room had escaped destruction. A crystal chandelier hung in the middle. A sun's rays decorated the high-domed ceiling. Vines, bursting with plump grapes, twisted along the tips of the rays and cascaded down the pink-marble walls.

Beneath the chandelier, a statue of two dragons kneeling on the back of a huge turtle dominated the room. The dragons cradled two eggs between them, one gold and the other white.

Theo approached and ran his fingers along the smooth, cool surfaces of the eggs. "Who are they?"

"Zmey and Lamia's parents, I think," Diva said.

Theo stepped back. "Are Zmey and Lamia twins?"

Diva nodded. "That's what I've been told."

Theo stared at the statue longer. The dragons gazed into each other's eyes as if they were in love. "I wonder if their mother knew the future of her children, like my mother did for me." Theo felt bad for her if she did. What a tragedy for her to endure, knowing the enmity that befell her children. Twins at that.

Aren't twins supposed to have a special bond?

Theo walked around the statue. Something had been etched into each egg. He wiped away dust. The symbol was similar to one he'd seen tattooed on Lamia, only this was a single dragon forming a circle and biting its tail. The dragons on each egg faced each other. They were smiling, and their eyes pierced one another with love.

What could have happened to break Lamia's and Zmey's love? It had to have been more than Lamia's jealousy over my mother.

Ula burst into the room. "Here you are."

Theo jumped. "My father, is he …?" Theo couldn't say the word.

Breathing heavily, Ula shook her head. "He's better. He wants to see you now."

THEO STOOD OUTSIDE a massive wooden door, embellished in gold, depicting two crowned dragons. Between them, the Tree of Life spread out its eternal branches. Taking a deep breath, he pulled open the door and entered a room dimly lit with flickering candles. Olive-green curtains had been drawn over the windows. In the center of the room, mahogany columns, engraved with vines, supported the dragon-sized bed, which lay in the shadows. On three sides of the bed, closed drapes blocked out even the faint candlelight. Hesitating to go closer, Theo examined the drapes' intricate weaving of entangled snakes holding up a crown with their mouths.

"Theodore?" Zmey's feeble voice drew Theo closer.

A woman sat by the bedside, holding Zmey's hand. Candlelight danced off her hair, highlighting red strands. As Theo crept closer, the woman stood and looked his way.

Theo's heart pounded. "Mom." He raced forward and wrapped his arms around her. He didn't care how she was here, whether it was permanently or only for a short time. She was here now. For him. For Zmey. Their family was together.

Something's wrong.

The woman stiffened in Theo's grasp and didn't return his hug. He pulled away and looked at her face. The woman before him made him shiver. Her hard stare quickly disappeared, and her lips curled upward in a forced smile.

Who is she? How could I think she was my mother?

The woman before him had the same delicate features as his mother, but they appeared harsher, sterner. She was taller than his mother, and her tousled hair wasn't Zunitza's fiery red. It was darker, auburn, tending toward black. She'd braided it into snakelike strands that flowed over her shoulders.

Her attire was all wrong, too, goth-like. Skinny bare feet peeked out from beneath her greenish-purple cotton dress. Golden snake bracelets with ruby eyes spiraled around her wrists. To

Theo, they seemed to undulate in the flickering light. Everything about the woman was dark, while brightness had surrounded his mother.

Zmey coughed and cleared his throat. "Theo, this is Magda, your mother's twin."

Her hard eyes softened as she tore them away from Theo and looked back at Zmey. She laid her hand on his. "Yes, I've returned just in time to take care of your father. Don't keep him long. He's weak and needs me to continue to heal him."

She strode away with long steps. At the door, she stopped and, without turning around, said, "I look forward to spending more time with you, Theodore." She closed the door softly behind her.

Theo shuddered, not certain he wanted to be around his aunt or learn more about her.

"Theodore." Zmey reached out a hand.

Emotions overcame Theo. He sat in the chair Magda had vacated and put his head on Zmey's shoulder. "I thought I'd lost you." Sobs wracked Theo's body. He didn't have to be strong and brave now. His father wouldn't demand it. Words of anguish poured out of Theo in spurts. "Zima's gone. Jabalaka's gone. I killed so many of Lamia's servants. Pavel's going to have nightmares for a long time. I ... I ..." He couldn't speak anymore. He let his tears flow, soaking Zmey's clean white nightshirt.

Zmey wrapped his arm around Theo and rubbed his son's back. "Everything will be okay. I promise."

When Theo had cried until no more tears would come, he sat up and wiped his eyes. A bit of color had returned to his father's face, but the man still looked deathly ill. Magda, or someone, had washed Zmey's hair, so it no longer hung in straggly strands.

Theo wanted to ask his father so much, but words escaped him.

As if knowing Theo's thoughts, Zmey said, "Let me start from when you left Zmeykovo."

Theo pulled the chair closer and waited.

"Zlo's soldiers captured me when I was heading out to tour the villages to determine the extent of their damage," Zmey began. "Someone set a field on fire and burned komuniga. The herb is toxic to dragons if the dose is high. For that reason, it's been banned in Zmeykovo for ages."

"Baba Yaga has all kinds of herbs," Theo said. "I'm sure she wouldn't obey any bans. She probably gave it to the Youdi."

"No, you're wrong about her, my son." Zmey coughed and took several deep breaths. "She has her faults, but she's loyal to me. People do all kinds of deceitful things when they're forced to. The Youdi, though, yes. I can imagine they had a part in the planning."

"If the herb's banned here, how did they get it?"

"They must have traveled to the human world. It's plentiful there. Only Samodivi know where to find it, so the Youdi must have followed them." Zmey took a sip from a rhyton at the side of the bed. "The herbs incapacitated me. When I woke, I found myself chained in the prison. I still had my belt at that time."

"Belt, what belt?"

The light in Zmey's eyes faded. "The Ouroboros."

"The Oreo … oribo … bo." Theo's tongue tripped over the word.

"Oh-ro-bor-os," Zmey repeated. "It provides Lamia and me our power. It's a symbol of a dragon swallowing its tail."

"Like the ones carved onto the dragon eggs on the dragons-in-love statue?" Theo asked.

Zmey rubbed his chin. "Dragons in love?"

"In the ballroom. Diva said she thought it was your parents."

"Yes, exactly like those." Zmey nodded. "The great goddess Bendis created the statue as a wedding gift for my parents."

Theo sighed. "They looked so happy, frozen in that moment."

"They were happy and in love, like your mother and me."

"Is there a statue of you and Mom?" Theo asked.

"No." A shadow crossed Zmey's face. "Our love was cut short too soon. We didn't have time to make it eternal in art."

Theo placed his hand over his father's frail fingers and gently squeezed.

Zmey took a deep breath and continued, "When Lamia and I were born, each of us received a dragon ouroboros belt from the gods. A white one for me and a golden one for Lamia. A gift for twins to show our unity."

Zmey closed his eyes and went silent, and Theo could only imagine his thoughts went to Lamia and how the two of them had drifted apart from loving siblings to hated enemies. One day, Theo would ask his father about that, but not now. Zmey was already showing signs of weariness. Theo would have to let his father rest.

"Maybe I should leave now." Theo started to rise.

"No, not yet." Zmey fluttered his eyes open. His voice was hoarse when he spoke. "I have to tell you about the belt."

"Here, take a sip." Theo handed Zmey the rhyton.

The dragon king drank then continued, his voice weak, "The belts give us power and protect us. When Lamia and I each had one, our strength was equal. It was a way for us to be connected. But Lamia took mine after Zlo resurrected her."

Something inside Theo clicked. Lamia always knew where he was, ever since Zlo had brought her back from the dead. "Would it give her a connection to me, too, since I'm your son?"

"I think so," Zmey said. "She's been slowly draining my power, so—"

"Is that why you're so ill?" Theo bent over his father and felt Zmey's feverish forehead. "Let me get Magda."

"No, please, not yet." Zmey's breathing grew ragged, and his voice faded. "I still love Lamia, despite everything she's done. Try to save her if you can."

As his father fell asleep, Theo nodded but didn't know if that was a promise he could make. Zmey was a broken man. Theo's hopes that his father would set everything right in Dragon Village were dashed. It was now up to Theo to accomplish that. First, he would find a way to get the Ouroboros back from Lamia, even if it meant killing her a second time.

About the Author

Ronesa Aveela is "the creative power of two." Two authors, that is. Nelly, the main force behind the work, the creative genius, was born in Bulgaria and moved to the U.S. in the 1990s. She grew up with stories of wild Samodivi, Kikimora, the dragons Zmey and Lamia, Baba Yaga, and much more. She's a freelance artist and writer. She likes writing mystery romance inspired by legends and tales. In her free time, she paints. Her artistic interests include the female figure, Greek and Thracian mythology, folklore tales, and the natural world interpreted through her eyes. She is married and has two children.

Rebecca, her writing partner was born and raised in the New England area. She has a background in writing and editing, as well as having a love of all things from different cultures. She's learned so much about Bulgarian culture, folklore, and rituals, and writes to share that knowledge with others.

Connect with us at www.ronesaaveela.com.

Be sure to follow us on Kickstarter for extra goodies when we launch new books: https://www.kickstarter.com/profile/ronesa-aveela/.

The Story Continues…

Discover what happens next in Theo's adventures in *Dragon Village Golden Apple*: https://books2read.com/DV4-GoldenApple.

Dragon Village Series

1) *The Unborn Hero of Dragon Village*
2) *Dragon Village Firebird*
3) *Dragon Village Ouroboros*
4) *Dragon Village Golden Apple*
5) *Dragon Village Colobar*

Special Offer

Would you like to learn more about folklore and mythology? Sign up for our newsletter and receive a FREE supplement to our "Spirits and Creatures" book series. To download the article about a malicious water spirit, Vodyanoy or Vodnik, use this link: https://BookHip.com/VFVPQJ or find the link on our website.

Further Reading

Discover more about the dragons and other creatures in this book in our nonfiction series called "Spirits and Creatures." Available in ebook, paperback, and hardcopy formats from your favorite retailer. You can also request your local library to carry a copy.

Household Spirits – https://books2read.com/household-spirits
Rusalki – Slavic Mermaids – https://books2read.com/rusalki
Dragons – https://books2read.com/dragons-aveela
Baba Yaga – https://books2read.com/babayaga
More to come…